Love and Glory

Melvyn Bragg

Love and Glory

Secker & Warburg
London

First published in England 1983 by
Martin Secker & Warburg Limited
54 Poland Street, London W1V 3DF

Copyright © Melvyn Bragg 1983

Lines from 'As Time Goes By' reproduced by
permission of Redwood Music Limited

British Library Cataloguing in Publication Data

Bragg, Melvyn
    Love and glory.
    I. Title
    823'.914[F]   PR6052.R263
    ISBN 0-436-06716-1

Printed and bound in Great Britain by
Collins, Glasgow

To Peter Copping

Chapter One

(1)

The man sang it all:

> "It's still the same old story
> A fight for love and glory,
> A case of do or die . . ."

The voice was tired yet convincing. His fingers travelled across the keys as if he were playing in his sleep and taking care not to wake himself. Occasionally he would look up and scan the bar, catching no one's glance, a worn performer's reflex long since drained of expectation, a little contemptuous of the noisy whites drinking past the midnight hour.

Beyond the thick glass windows, the Manhattan traffic slid by, silent as fish, yellow piranha cabs. Willie Armstrong was ready to be swallowed up by them. It was time to quit this seductive play-acting of irresponsibility. It was so easy to be someone else when you were abroad; and, Willie thought, quite a relief.

He finished his scotch rather quickly and felt the fumes swarm up into his nicely soaked brain. He wanted to say something to the piano-player, perhaps to redeem himself in front of this old black man whose music was so casually ignored. But he was too diffident, and it was time to get back to the hotel – his Heathrow flight left early in the morning. Besides, what could he say that would make a difference?

Even the slight effort of levering himself down from the bar stool made Willie sweat a little. His heavy spectacles steamed up. When he took out his handkerchief to wipe them, a five-dollar bill came along with it, as crumpled as a paper flower, a memento of a forgotten feast. Money would have to do, he thought. Edging his way awkwardly, his English accent muted

7

as he uttered apologies for his rather portly passage, he manoeuvred himself to the baby grand and dropped the still-crumpled note beside the mike. The man looked up, not right away, and nodded, just a little. "Thanks," Willie said, and went to the door. Big deal.

On the sidewalk, in the sauna summer heat of night New York, the scuffed buildings barred with black fire escapes looked a stage set for action he would never get to know. It was OK: a little alcohol, a little sentimentality, a little trip completed . . .

The garbage cleaners were working the streets; so was the woman. He shook his head and she moved on without breaking her stride. She knows a loser when she sees one, Willie thought, and suddenly felt cheerful at this secure self-description. As the cab halted to take him to the usual empty bed, the pianist's voice imprinted itself on the misty twilight of his slowly extinguishing thoughts – a memorandum, Willie, on what you have – or more strictly have not – done: a challenge to a barely-lived life:

> "The fundamental things apply
> As time goes by . . ."

(2)

For all the compromises a successful institutional career imposes, there are times when you pay for rejecting it, Willie thought (philosophically, he hoped) when he discovered, on his return to London, that he had been "transferred" to a smaller office on an inconvenient floor. "Make an appointment with Ruth as soon as you get back," the formal typescript – typed no doubt by Ruth herself – dictated. "We have things to talk through." Then the cavalier loop-the-loop signature – Eric – and underneath, in brackets, in case he was in doubt after all these years, more neat little type – ERIC CORDER, HEAD OF CURRENT AFFAIRS. Willie leaned on the desk for a moment to support himself; he felt dizzy, throat clutching dryly. He stood free and breathed in deeply. They always made their move when you were away.

He should have gone home and claimed jet-lag, let the weekend intervene between independent New York and hierarchic London. But his office was his real nest. Had been.

The new box he had been allocated looked dismally small, being bare. He started on it. He knew that his photographs and charts and plaques would open the place out. Despite his feeling of displacement he could already see how a clever arrangement of furniture could even make it appear comfortable. He would get a smaller desk, expel a couple of chairs, put his books on the sill. It would do. Most of the world worked in far less ease. Willie had never been able to become sufficiently sophisticated or ungrateful to eradicate such old-fashioned comparisons. He rang up Maintenance and requested a dozen picture hooks so that he could put his mark on the white-walled cell right away. Talking to the man flushed out the realisation that everyone would already know. He lit a cigarette, breaking his new rule not to smoke in the mornings, and inhaled deeply as he absorbed that unpleasant knowledge. Worse things happen at sea. "Yes," he said aloud, and exhaled through his nose, already braced for the embarrassed sympathy of his colleagues. He used the next few minutes to force out of himself what he considered a trivial access of false pride and self-pity.

When he phoned his secretary he was relieved to recognise Margaret's voice, and his energies were diverted into quiet and oblique reassurances to her that all was well, that he would survive, that his new office had certain advantages, that he was perfectly all right. Her imminent tearfulness moved him but it also allowed his poise to reassert itself. From now on he would share a typist with two others, she told him. "I'd like to meet her," Willie said. "If you're both free, perhaps you could bring her to the bar before lunch and we'll have a drink. Could you? I would enjoy that. Cheer up."

It was by his own choice, although it had followed his illness, that he had stepped off the career ladder; by his own choice that he had taken on the training programme as well as the administration and the obituaries, thus making himself one of

9

the most overworked men in the company although – or possibly consequently – one of the least regarded among the political. As in all big institutions, internal politics absorbed the keenest energies: by avoiding that game he had lost touch. And possibly his gentle "outsider" stance appeared to the rest as a criticism – something subversive, finally intolerable.

He rang Ruth. The appointment was made for the following Monday. Eric, he was assured, was *very much* looking forward to seeing him.

He had trained Eric.

(3)

Willie's flat in Camden Town looked as if it had been burgled by a nervous amateur, from which Willie concluded that Joanna must have suddenly remembered a date. She would be in no state to do anything – but drink, of course – when she came back and so before even taking off his coat he tidied up. There was comfort in it.

He turned on the central heating against the late summer chill and the radiators gargled loudly as if testing out the water for its taste. Out of habit he banged each one after he had turned it on. These Victorian mansion flats always needed a kick start – doors, taps, windows, even the original Burlington.

On the table in the tiny kitchen three half-empty tins stood almost in a row, their lids tilted as if saluting: beans, pineapple chunks and cat food. It was the cat which reminded Joanna to eat. Again, Willie cleaned up – including the greasy grill ribboned with bacon-rind on the grid. Easier just to do it and avoid the row. It was more than comfort, it gave him a sense of having some control.

Instant coffee, which he preferred to the real thing, a couple of Welsh rarebits, an unopened packet of cigarettes and the flat sufficiently unchilled for him to take off his coat. He sat down in front of the empty fireplace, his tray on his knee, and continued to find jobs to blot out what had happened.

Five days' accumulated letters ought to tell me something

10

about myself, he thought. Seven brown envelopes: bills for supplementary rates, telephone, water rates, the car respray, a mortgage readjustment, the newspaper account and the reminder from the wine merchant. He took out his cheque book, settled them all. An invitation to a Chatham House seminar on Political Biography and the Media had to be accepted: and it would fill up a Saturday. He was on the mailing list of several galleries; of them only one appealed to him, the Japanese exhibition. He wondered if David, his stepson, would be interested and, simultaneously, doubted whether he even ought to suggest it to him. He had missed a drinks party to celebrate the twenty-first birthday of the daughter of a friend: that was a loss. Willie had known the girl most of her life: he enjoyed turning up every now and then, enjoyed being surprised at the stops and starts of her growth, the fugitive mixture of sameness and change. One letter he did not open but slipped it into his pocket. He recognised the handwriting and guessed at the message: he was not ready to take it in just yet. There were two lots of tickets – one for a new play at the National, the other for *Louise* at the ENO. Joanna would probably come to the opera with him: she liked the chats in the intervals. Finally, there was a copy of a novel he had ordered.

Not a great deal to go on, he concluded, not unhappily. "Bloody boring," Joanna called their life; and him; and their friends, or whatever the cloud of her discontent settled upon. "And so bloody *care*ful!" It was when he smiled in partial agreement at her scorn that he encouraged her most venomous hostility.

He had been demoted. In institutions, once you start going up or down the process gathers momentum. He had failed, then, in his attempt to stand still. "Silly to try," he said aloud in the empty flat: he looked across at the cat as if to exonerate himself from the charge of talking to himself.

It was time for a drink but he let it pass. He had drunk very little all day. He wanted to be able to let the consequences work their way into his mind unassisted. But he wanted a drink. Later.

11

He finished his supper, washed up, saw the headlines on the nine o'clock news and, before his efficiency left him stranded in vulnerable solitude, he took refuge in his other staple: work. At one time the idea of sitting alone for the long slow span of an entire evening's reading and scribbling had been almost sensually attractive, like being in bed as a boy listening to a storm which could not reach him, hugging that deeply snug feeling of safety close to him as he imagined the wildness outside from the safety of his bed. Even though the voluptuousness had gone, that bank of habit was a godsend, unexpected credit for a middle age constantly threatening to overdraw his resources.

In New York he had collected footage on Reagan, Carter as well as some unexpected archive material on Fred Astaire and Bob Dylan. With no great pleasure he began assembling his notes on the two politicians. The possibility of finally presenting anything near the truth about the actions and personalities of the two men was too slight to bear the full weight of his interest but there was enough sorting out and arranging of material to occupy him steadily.

He would have liked to talk about the infighting, the deals, the image-making process and the apparent end to a time of independent minds in that highest secular office. He would have enjoyed discussing the frustrations of holding the Presidency without being able to use or even experience the heroic virtues which had traditionally accompanied leadership, the cipher and cynosure syndromes in a democratic land of the media which demanded its own reflection be distorted to a fantasy normality. In the USA it seemed to him that the tarty goddess of success now ruled absolutely and flattened all qualities not streamlined to her insistently suckled demands. The old glory had been marketed away.

Not that Willie particularly wanted to mount an attack on Carter and Reagan. Both were supremely contemporary nice guys: their nice-guyness, in fact, was essential to their emblematic authority, the nice guy was the monarch in the pageant of the modern republic. But how to discover what the men were

12

really like and whether their character mattered? When their obituaries were put together, the film would glide through the gate and ripple down the 625 lines of the screen telling little more about them than those brown envelopes and invitations had told about him. Still, even a small attempt to dent the charm and gloss of potted biography was worth making, he thought, and when Joanna eventually returned she found him sitting in a Sargasso sea of notes and books as if he were a small Neptune rising above the white waved papers.

"Damn," his wife said. "I hoped you'd be in bed."

(4)

"Sorry," Joanna added, "that wasn't very tactful, was it?"

But even as she was apologising, she was turning away, looking rather short-sightedly around the room.

"I was just going to pour myself a scotch," Willie offered. "Would you like one?"

"Just a drop," she said, studiedly, still not turning to him.

Putting a hand on a side table to steady herself, she tugged off her too-high-heeled black and silver shoes and planted her stockinged feet on the rug. "That's better."

She took the drink as if absentmindedly, settled herself in foetal contentment on the big sofa and finally looked at Willie. "Another corpse?"

"Not yet. Cheers." He drank: she nodded and sipped delicately.

"Does it never give you the creeps?"

"No. Perhaps it should."

"Waiting for them to drop off the perch." She sipped again. "You drowned it."

He made no move. With an irritated spasm of energy, she kicked out her legs and made for the drinks tray. She had good legs. The black stockings drew attention to them. Joanna's whole appearance was a signal for attention. Her thick shining grey hair was heaped in a late-forties Hollywood style which perfectly suited the heart-shaped sexy petulance of her face.

13

For her age – she was three years older than Willie – her figure, fully displayed in the tight black satin dress, was astonishingly well preserved. Preserved was the word; she did nothing to exercise it. It was as waywardly bestowed as everything else that had happened to her – the money, long since spent, the father of David, long since divorced, the cello, abandoned, the lovers, the booze, and the sudden fearful precipices of desperate fragility.

"Would *you* like some more?" Her voice never slurred; the words would be ejected carefully as if each one had been bitten off. He shook his head: she took this as a cue to help herself to yet another splash.

"I was thinking I would go and meet David off the train," he said.

"What for? It's only three bloody stops on the tube."

"People like to be met after a journey."

"He's only been to your mother's."

"Still . . . I think I'll do it."

"You suck up to him."

He needs someone, even to do that, Willie thought, and said nothing.

"You just want to get away from me."

Willie was long used to that one and he finished off his drink.

"You haven't bothered to ask where I went."

"Where did you go?" he asked.

"Oh – bugger off!"

He smiled, genuinely amused: she looked at him: it could go either way.

There were still times when the sadness of no longer being at all in love with her swept through him. Had they ever been in love? Yes. He knew that they had but he could remember only the history of it. Times since then had ground out all real taste and memory of it. He could still want it to happen again, want to feel warm towards her, to be quickened and embraced; but he saw no way to begin. He had known her at one time better than he had known anyone else on the planet and yet he did not now have any idea how he could reach her. It was as if two armies had met and joined a glorious battle, then fallen back stunned from the encounter determined never to meet again, to abandon all thought of arms rather than risk another test. But she could still catch him unawares, as now, when he knew the strange sorrow of looking at someone he had loved and finding them further removed than a stranger.

"You think you've got me all worked out, don't you?"

He shook his head. Oh no. Not at all. Carefully, she put her full glass down on the floor and then held out a hand to him. Willie quelled the fatigue which rose up like revulsion. She held his hand hard and looked him directly in the face. The intensity was fathomless. Although he could summarise her ways and chart her progress with and without him, he knew scarcely anything about the pain which seemed to him to charge such a demand. He had touched it once, for some time he had tried to share it and in the process been beaten down. Like many of those who have tried to help undertake the burden of an obscure shiftless disease of the mind, he had caught the symptoms himself without finally resolving or even understanding the cause. It required some effort, these days, even to meet that lusting search for recognition.

"I'll crick my neck," she said.

He knelt down. He was committed now to her rare whim, her monstrous pretence. Only that brief flash of regretted love led him on. She took his hand, pressed it strongly between her thighs, and let her head fall back onto the cushion, closing her eyes.

"What were the girls like in New York, Willie?"

She knew there would be no reply: knew there had been no girls. It would help her, Willie often thought, if there were.

"Something's bothering you."

He denied it. It was not the time to unloose one of her arias against the way he was exploited and overlooked at work: in such defences of him, he felt only further diminished.

"Come on, Willie," she urged, almost impatiently.

Although they occupied separate bedrooms, there were still some occasions when they made love, although that phrase to

15

both would have struck only the chords of irony. There was no pattern in her demand and no passion in her desire. He had vowed never to agree to it again: but, again, she had beaten him.

He slid her dress up over her thighs and tugged down the rather resistant knickers. She turned her head to one side as if averting her gaze, although her eyes were still closed. Willie reached behind her and slid down the zip, uncupped the breasts, and looked almost with remorse on the tartily dishevelled woman with whom he had once indeed made love. Although she moaned and then panted, cried out, assaulted him in turn violently, she said nothing: not his name, no endearment, not a word. And when, still kneeling, he penetrated her, and she flung around him, he felt that he was heartlessly servicing her. The thought seemed blasphemous: that all the variety of sex and love should be reduced to this. Unable, though, to resist his own desire, he shuddered into her uttering her name several times, as if telling a rosary.

They stayed, fixed in a coupled attitude, Willie merely waiting until courtesy ran its course, Joanna either lost or found, he would never know which.

Abruptly, she pulled back and grinned at him, knocking twenty years off her expression.

"That was good."

"Yes," he lied; his head felt dry with shame at the mechanical despoliation. No more. But he knew that whenever she caught his conscience with her sense or imitation of need, he would have to comply. Since her attempted self-destruction he had never denied her what she asked for: although time had worked the cruel trick of disabling him from offering her what she really wanted.

"You look funny with your trousers round your knees."

"I feel a bit stupid."

"You didn't even take your glasses off."

"All the better to . . ." He was relieved at the unaccustomed jokiness. Post coitum, usually, problems.

"You used to be so good-looking, Willie," she said,

smoothing down his hair, making no attempt to rearrange her dress while he almost surreptitiously was hitching up his trousers, reaching out for his jacket. "But you let yourself go," she said.

"Pity," she said and rolled away like a cat.

He gave her a cigarette, and returned to his chair.

They smoked in silence but the silence was unthreatening. Long ago he had read that "a cigarette after love-making can be sacramental." He had winced at the absurd pretentiousness while, privately, then, sympathising with the sentiment. Now, the cigarette was the most painless and convenient re-entry into their separate worlds.

"I *will* go and meet David," he said and stood up.

She made no protest and waved him away, glass in hand, still looking what he would once have thought tenderly sluttish. But now . . .?

"Drive carefully," she said. "The cops are out in force tonight."

(5)

He read the letter in the car under the courtesy light as the engine warmed up. He looked out for a phone as he drove along.

The distance from the Chalk Farm area in which they lived to Euston was so short that he soon decided to telephone from the station rather than risk a vandalised box. The booths were open in the station, as if privacy of no kind was to be encouraged on a modern journey, but at this time of night there was no crowd, the place was chiefly peopled by drifters.

"Dr Isaacs here."

"Hello. Mandy?"

"Willie." She hurried to seize the initiative. "I didn't mean to sound whingy in the letter, darling. I just wanted you to phone me soonest."

"I know. I ought to have phoned you this morning."

"I thought you might."

17

"Jet-lag. No. I didn't want to disturb you."

"You never disturb me." She leaned heavily on "disturb", mocking his explanation. "You sound a bit odd. Anything wrong?"

"No." It would seem so pathetic, he thought, on the telephone. Yet he could always plunge right into the most serious matters with Mandy. "Just . . ."

"How *is* Joanna?"

He saw her sprawled on the sofa, sexually fed, half-drunk, lost to him.

"She seems fine."

"She won't be fine until she's eaten you up."

Mandy had been Joanna's doctor: even before her connection with Willie she had been prone to impatience with her. "She's a vampire."

"Mandy, please."

"You're such a fool to stay with her."

"Maybe I am."

He was, he knew, when Mandy was there, Mandy so loving and attendant. Yet he refused to consummate this affair with her.

"You're frightened that she'll fall apart if you leave her," Mandy said, not only speaking his thoughts but answering them.

"Sometimes people have to be let fall apart," she added.

Against the sense of her argument he had no real defence. Mandy offered one of the most enduring of loves – a steady respect, the friendship of resolved minds. Her decisiveness was always impressive: she had disbanded her own marriage sadly but determinedly after a long realisation that she could no longer give anything but a hollow response to a husband she neither cared for nor admired. By her standards Willie judged himself a malingerer.

"You're hopeless," she confirmed, warmly.

"Are *you* well?"

"Oh, frustrated, sex-starved, pining for you, surrounded by psychosomatic bores, overworked, struck down with cystitis –

18

much the same as usual, really. A wreck on a sandbank already
– feh! Call yourself a life-belt?'

"Tuesday?"

"Where are you rushing off to?"

"I'm meeting David."

"That's all right. Tuesday. And darling: I do love you, you
know. That's not for nothing."

"I know."

"Don't sound so troubled. No. Sound troubled. It reminds
me of my father – gives me hope. Bye."

She only put on her Jewish-momma act when she was over-
wrought and determined to cheer him up: she had travelled as
far from her faith as he had from his. But what mighty forces
they had left behind them, he thought, as he walked through
the secular modernity of the station to reach the arrival
platform: what hubris, in a way, to leave such authorities and
traditions. And what risk?

He was alone at the barrier, not even a ticket-collector – the
tickets would have been collected on the last lap of the journey.
Down the ramps an occasional figure would stride towards a
sleeper. The cat-called songs of two drunks rang around the
concrete centre of congregation, defiantly cheerful.

When the train from the North came in, it disgorged so
many, fleeing up to the barrier for London, throwing their lives
into the city. Out of the crowd he picked up one wonderful, shy
smile, full of delight and almost wild anticipation: he wanted
to freeze it, to savour it; but the girl who gave him this
unexpected benediction walked on. He turned to watch her but
she did not turn back.

"Willie!" David shook his shoulder.

"Hello David."

"Good to see you!"

The young man was unable to articulate his thanks, but his
pleasure was enough for Willie to feel elated at David's own
elation.

"Good journey?"

"Great. Great!"

Willie had to step out to keep up with the fast lanky steps of his tall muscled stepson.

"I'm famished! They ran out of sandwiches on the train."

There was little to eat in the house.

"Listen," Willie said, "your mother will probably be asleep by now . . ."

"How is she?"

"Fine . . . but tired . . . we don't want to wake her, making a meal. Let's go to one of those Greek places in Camden Town. They're open all hours. I've eaten but I'll keep you company."

David hesitated.

"My treat," Willie said. "I insist."

"Mykonos," David replied decisively. "Lamb kebabs. And houmous with that glove bread. Great! *Thanks!*"

His vitality moved Willie and reassured him. This was a life being lived: please let him help it avoid the worst surrenders.

(6)

That night he broke awake again and again as the small craft of his controlled self threatened to capsize. In those kaleidoscopic moments of precipitous half-consciousness, fragments of the day returned like splinters spiking the flesh.

Why had he not cried out against that barren intercourse with Joanna? David had scarcely mentioned her, his mother, cut her out. "That's all right," Mandy had said, briskly surrendering her needs. "That'll be fine," he had replied to Ruth at Eric's decision to delay the meeting until after the weekend. Meek, side-stepping denials all. The controls and compromises suffocated him. Sleep had to be drugged and even so the claims of long-repressed fears and edited ambitions would run amok through the night like vandals let loose on the tidy streets of his ordered existence.

So privileged, his life: so comfortable, so accommodating. Perhaps his control was a paralysis, a way of lying doggo so as not to attract the jealousy of the gods at his good fortune in a world of persecution, neglect, tyranny, disease and poverty. Like so many others in the West, through no personal virtue, no private struggle, no solitary sacrifice, no superior qualities, Willie had been handed a royal flush. What did he do with the rest of the world's wounds and envy? Which were his own. Were they not? Or was that another vanity?

The most piercing feeling he experienced as he surfaced into half-thoughts was of his life tolling away, slithering through time, undirected, united in no adventure, embarked on no odyssey, corrupted by this unearned affluence which poured a silt over the will to mine himself and take the risk of discovering the least and the most of what he was.

The Valium began to numb his mind. He let go, let it sink into that deep relief, that unconscious third of life. The musky slow swirl of shapes seemed to draw him back in time, way before early morning; he always wanted to prolong this sensuous floating state of suspension, this grateful disembodiment, this inchoate return to a dream world . . . just before he fell asleep, from all the day's encounters and repressions, from instincts crushed and actions taken which he did not respect, there came the smile he had caught on the face at the station, that marvellous direct smile; and then the girl was gone.

Chapter Two

(1)

The smile strode out of the station and into the North London night. Penned in a train for five hours, unable to discharge its pleasure around the open compartment without creating a disturbance or being thought a dolt, the smile had restrained itself for most of those three hundred minutes and was now desperate for air. It shot through Willie like an X-ray and gunned across the Euston platform, actually waking up one or two comatose porters and causing a wistful alcoholic to pause at the bottleneck and temporarily dream of sobriety. It was not that the young woman was beautiful – her nose was certainly too big, her face a little too long, the whole set of her features more likely to command the evasive adjective "interesting" than anything more committed – but that smile came up with mysterious magnificence like the sun for the Greeks and radiated from her irresistibly. Perhaps it was the more irresistible because she was no great beauty and it could be seen as a gift possible for all to receive and enjoy. Perhaps a smile like that, surging from a secret, central and all-pervasive sense of power in being alive, that moment, that step, that breath, is the best there is: and when we see it we want to trap it, or be touched by it, share it.

In the street Caroline walked so buoyantly she promised to break into a run. She could have caught a tube or a cab at the station but there was some time in hand and she wanted to be alone in the city, to feel that sexily edgy solitariness of the night-time metropolis where strangers drift past forever alerting you to your own isolation. Echoes and evidence of others throb about you like the ceaseless traffic and yet so few

22

bodies touch, so few eyes meet. After the pressing crowd of the train, she wanted to escape but still, perhaps, perversely, enjoy the knowledge that others were nearby. Here on the pavements of the city, Caroline went as if towards a famous victory, the smile bringing a hum to her mind's ear, a pulse of thrust to her legs and arms, to her breasts and cheeks a fine tingling of memory and desire.

She was in love and, perhaps, she was loved. He had not yet *said* so but she could wait – for ever if need be: he was more loving to her than anyone she had ever known: the few days with him had annulled weeks and months with others. That she was in love there was no doubt at all, and the knowledge of it synchronised all the unsure forces and impulses of her twenty-two years, finally focusing them on this huge, unqualified and wonderful event for which her smile was a libation. She poured it out before the phosphorescent world, into its darkness and sudden glare, like one scattering seed.

For those minutes on that night she was one of the blessed.

(2)

In the flat she steadied herself by glaring at her image in the bedroom mirror, taking ten interminable deep breaths and repeating on each exhalation "Calm . . . down." This bedroom mirror had seen her audition for many parts – only a few of which she had got. She had practised her lines and expressions by the hour: if it could have spoken like the magic mirror on the wall the glass would certainly now have murmured "bravo" and added a wish that such vibrancy could be transferred into some of those roles.

She shared this top floor of a Victorian terraced house in Shepherds Bush with another actress who had been away on tour for two months. Caroline would have sub-let, but her friend (now, as it proved, mercifully) disliked anyone else squatting among her possessions and was prepared to pay for that privacy. Caroline could not conceal her rather disloyal relief at having the entire flat to herself.

23

There were two bedrooms (hers was the smaller), a kitchen you could eat in, a bathroom you could do your laundry in and a sitting-room big enough for most after-show parties. An oval dining-table stood at the end featuring the large window which overlooked the small park.

Ian had said he would telephone between midnight and one. It would take him about half an hour to reach her. He would not have had dinner so that they could eat together – "we'll eat and then go to bed and then it'll be time for breakfast and then bed and then brunch with booze and then – you aren't doing anything special on Saturday, are you?"

This was the last day of his filming: somehow – she dare not ask how – he had got Saturday free. They had never spent a whole night together, let alone a full day. Don't be greedy, she advised herself, sternly sorting out the fresh vegetables bought that morning in her home town in the Borders: you'll lose it if you snatch.

But he seemed to encourage her to snatch, to let go, to give herself up totally, to subject herself to him as he appeared to submit to her; in those few weeks she had been so deeply drawn into the way of his thinking and acting that it was already difficult to imagine life without or before him. But careful . . . she had no experience of such supreme good luck . . . careful . . . all common sense, all rumours, all of her life's pattern schooled her to resist this piratical takeover, this shazam of a sudden new life . . . He was contemptuous of carefulness, in their lovemaking, in his all but conclusive declarations, in his praise which jolted her who had spent most of her life receiving little more than a small appreciative word: above all in his own bold self-deployed and independent life.

"Calm . . . down". She had bought some thick-cut local ham to go with the ratatouille he liked and, luckily, she could make. There would just be time to chop up the vegetables. Tomato salad with a special dressing to start with; grapes, Brie and water biscuits to follow. Muscadet for the fridge in case he forgot to bring wine; the Wine Society's claret to follow – a gift from her father; and two splits of champagne to be tucked deep

24

away with the orange juice for a Buck's Fizz breakfast. Thank God her parents had paid her train fare back home for her aunt's funeral. No escaping that, and she had not wanted to avoid it – her aunt had meant a lot to her – but Caroline had longed for an excuse. Ian had been very understanding: the filming was fighting its deadline, things were not working out well at home, he had the new part too much on his mind, he would be OK . . . he made it easy for her.

Ian Grant. Just the sound of his name in her mind could bring her to a halt.

Roses from the Lowland garden brought three hundred and fifty miles south to provide welcoming bouquets: cushions plumped – pretty, hand-picked satin cushions which lightened the Victorian furniture. Shawls on the backs of sofas and chairs, prints and some of Olivia's sketches on the walls, fake art-deco sidelights, dark green candles ready to take over, a shower squeezed in while the ratatouille cooked aromatically, the Dior perfume he had bought her from Paris, duvet turned down? Or left alone? Left alone, shy still, red skirt and black blouse he said (last time but one) were "really lovely", a ribbon in her hair, out, in, too young? Finally, rather timidly, in, fruit bowl brought into the big room now looking set for a small string orchestra, the pseudo-coal fire threatening to over-egg the pudding, cork drawn on claret as instructed by father, wicked to see a married man, strike you dead they said, Mozart on low, no – Joan Armatrading, own whistling banned, lady downstairs enemy of pleasure, quick swish of bigger vase of roses on to dining-table – Oh God, what would the feminist sisters say? – all this forbidden "looking after your man" – sudden marvellous vertigo swoop of stomach, heart, senses and all intelligence as telephone rings: genuine moments of total panic having forgotten where telephone was, is, is . . . that? . . . Must be . . . "Hello . . ."

"It surprised most people that the great and glamorous Ian Grant would call me his best friend, (Willie wrote, some time after this, when he began to write about Ian in his notebooks. He had kept these notebooks on and off since schooldays, a habit that sometimes embarrassed, occasionally consoled him.) It took me a long time fully to understand that he was not playing one of his deep and devious roles; he was not employing false modesty, nor was he merely acting on the apparently universal impulse towards twinning opposites – the pretty girl with her plain friend, the clever guy with his dumb pal, the weed with the stud, the criminal with the saint. It was hard to believe but he liked, and admired me.

Of course, it would not escape his attention that to his brilliantly successful image, flashing across the screens like a sabre, I was a suitable shadow, one of these born to blush and do everything else unseen. Nor would I put it past his cunning to keep me as a thread of continuity merely, one who could always lead him out of his present labyrinth and back to a simpler past from which he could strike out again into his maze of adventures. We had known each other well at school, seen something of each other at University, where he had shone and I had rubbed along, and been thrown up against each other in those days at the BBC in Lime Grove when he was mounting his first assaults on success and I was already seeking out a secure and protected lair. People thought that it was I who was dependent on him – for glitter, for fun, for introductions. Sometimes I worried that might be the case and in those early days would often break away from him. He always followed; he always sought me out again. I was tempted to be complacent about that and sometimes I still am, but that petty pinnacle of triumph is soon pounded down by the overwhelming realisation, that in some way he loves me. Love is his greatest gift: to possess it and to spend it: a greater talent, in my reckoning, than his wonderful miming and impersonation and embodiment of character and all the skilful ambiguity and charlatanry of the trade or art of acting. I suppose the two talents could be twinned in the same egg.

Without that extraordinary love for life he could not imitate and re-invent it so well, perhaps; without that staunchless, naïf, almost defenceless giving of love which seeks out what is loving in the recipient and so often stirs up what has until then been drowsy or inert, there could, perhaps, be no giving of himself across the footlights, through the lens, at the microphone, with such generosity and nakedness that the audiences – and I have been part of many hundreds of his audiences – say, as they say to all great performers and artists, in recognition 'yes'.

To me Ian has been a friend, a case history, an extreme but somehow true representative of his (my) generation, a public icon swinging and bending in the wind but never quite breaking, and a private man almost unnaturally unprepared for what's to come. All this without talking of his outstanding roles, his Richard III, his Master Builder, his Hamlet and Coriolanus and Henry V in one season; his revived Jimmy Porter; his association with Pinter; the thinking girl's Burt Reynolds' role with the new Hollywood movie brats; the television series about sex and politics which made national headlines for months – banned, then shown and debated in Parliament; and his consistent instinct not to let himself get trapped. Not trapped by the subsidised classics; not trapped by coke and speed and what-you-want-we-got-baby Los Angeles; not trapped by established playwrights nor even by the notion of changing for change's sake, but seeking his own way, moving himself around, crashing now and then, a few incidents in bars, in a plane, at a first night, in restaurants – rarely, in truth, his fault, never his instigation, but always his name and his picture in the paper next day.

Inside that Polyfoto madness of identities adopted, identities discarded, identities retained, identities butchered, identities mistreated, identities distrusted, identities sublimated, even when he was bad, he was always full of that uncanny actual 'life' which stood and said 'Look – I am

27

here. Listen.' Inside that ever-receding album of poses and faces and characters I would scarcely know where to travel or even how to follow him.

I suppose I admire his willingness to show everything of himself: and, even more reckless, to show the darker side with such conviction that people like me – who know him or who are sensitive to the connection between his private self and the public mask – have to revise our desired impression and think of him not as a man stoked and fed by love but as someone driven by a hedonism and self-seeking ambition so strong that it would employ even the deepest resources of love and loyalty to get its ends.

One thing is certain: he is his own man. He is uncontainable. There is no pattern. Most people I know are somehow equalised or chastened or possibly guiltily content with what they have: their lives do not roar. They tend to look after their instincts, their health, their careers, their acceptability. It is all very careful and usually pleasant. Ian comes from a totally different stock. It is as if a character from Dostoievsky were to have been parachuted into the world of Jane Austen.

People are still surprised to learn that he is married and has a son. How Marion endures the flak of gossip I have no idea.

She has always been suspicious of me. I am sure she thinks that I indulged him too much. In one way I am glad: I do not want to make common cause with her against Ian.

Marion is: early thirties, 'county', an extremely successful literary agent, not at all part of the theatrical world in any of its manifestations – from the 'darlings' to the 'comrades' – handsome, distant; 'very cool', people say, meaning the term as a compliment or as a criticism, a saint, some say; nobody calls her a fool.

What does she think of him and he of her? Other people's private lives are impenetrable. They never seem less than calmly happy on their rare, confident appearances together in public: that, people say, shows you.

The boy is at boarding-school. Marion won that battle.

Their house is in those elegant peaceful acres around Holland Park. There is a 'cottage' near Maidenhead, scarcely ever used by the two of them.

For many people, a description of their work and their wife would give you the latitude and longitude of their character. Not with Ian. Depending on the day or his mood or, perhaps (although I have never found this reliable either), the part he is playing, he would strike you as single, married, uxorious, available, inaccessible, broke, flash, a man of substance, a gypsy. It is too easy to say he is always 'acting a role' – or doing so any more than we all do. All of us have different characters for different people and occasions: however slight those differences are, however we seek not to infringe our basic integrity. Perhaps I am saying that Ian had no basic integrity.

But I would deny that. I have known him act with wonderful magnanimity and then be as mean as a tick – but between these two acts is there the same man, a man 'of multitudes'? Yes, but even that does not satisfy me. We are all men and women of multitudes. With Ian they had a voice. Each one, it could seem. And each one stemmed from the sincere conviction that at the time – it was acting for the whole of him. His variety was uniformly sincere.

Caroline, in short, my darling Caroline, stood no chance."

(4)

Ian had met her in a noisy scruffy Edwardian pub in North Kensington where Jake, who ran the company, had his flat. It doubled as the headquarters and often trebled as the hotel. The company survived on a small Arts Council grant, very low wages and that sort of selfless devotion and dedication to work which would look quaintly Victorian in any other industry. After seven years of touring, haunting festival Fringes, playing in the upper rooms of pubs and halls around the provinces, The Connect Company had developed a taut, highly idiosyncratic style. Caroline had joined the company on one of its Scottish tours and now considered herself to be lucky to have got in

29

when its reputation was largely unmade. She judged, perhaps rightly, that the company's swift cohesion over the past two years, its apparent sudden leap from earnest competence to notable achievement, had now put it on a level of skill which would have excluded her had she not been in there already. Caroline was doggedly fair-minded and, as other young actresses came and auditioned, she would sit and watch, often subdued by what she saw as their superior talent even to the extent of offering Jake the chance to fire her.

"Don't be silly," he said reassuringly: but the phrase he used, she noted, glumly, was scarcely reassuring.

"You're good," he said, to convince her who could perhaps never be convinced. "All you need is to be more confident in yourself." That was true. But that was the whole difficulty for, after certain techniques and skills had been acquired, after experience had been banked up, what determined the difference was that fusion of talent and self-confidence. Caroline's confidence was a black hole into which she feared she could disappear at any time.

"Anyway, you're staying," Jake concluded, briskly. "And besides, who else would be cook 'n' bottle washer as well as all the rest?" The rest included doubling as ASM, being responsible for organising the journeys and the accommodation, keeping the accounts, sweeping the stage . . . there was genuine reassurance in that.

Besides, she told herself in one of her regular "pull yourself together" sessions, she had just started out as an actress: small parts were exactly what she needed and she was lucky to get them, lucky to be with such a good company, lucky to be doing what she wanted, lucky to be employed at all when so many were not, lucky . . . the talisman jangled around her mind and she told herself to stop being silly, earthing her anxieties in the pagan rituals which had reassured her since childhood.

When Ian came into the pub she, like the others, made quite successful-seeming efforts to be unimpressed. His low-key appearance was noted – jeans, dark blue sweater, the expensive leather boots a bit of a give-away, but on the whole he had taken

30

care to look the part. They were not so easily gulled: it could well be that he had taken too much care. When he came with Jake to the "gang's" table in the corner his nervousness was suspect: he could not be genuinely nervous of *them*, could he? There were other suspicions more basic: after all, Ian was the star of a theatre establishment they had set out to oppose, and, worse, he had Made Money In Films. Had he sold out? What had those boots cost? Was it true that he had paid £150,000 for his house in Holland Park? Was he not the worst sort – one of those who had Gone Over To The Other Side? And why had he sought out The Connect Company? Were they being used?

Caroline sensed all of this and shared much of it but soon her chilly suspicions dissolved in the warmth of her interest in him. So this was the great Ian Grant! He looked so very ordinary. His face much thinner than she would have thought, his presence shrouded, unobtrusive, not at all vibrant; his talk hesitant and rather formal; his genuine shyness endearing and mysterious. But so ordinary! It was only much, much later that she would understand how studied this appearance had been: and even then she would still cling to her instinct and memory of that first meeting – that here was the *real* Ian Grant, a decent, careful, modest man: with whom she fell in love.

"It's just that if you do have anything you think I could do, I'd like to think you might consider me," Ian said, making the request sound piercingly sincere. He could have had the pick – the RSC, the National, the Royal Exchange, any number of West End managements.

"Why us?" Jake asked, conducting himself in a slightly too blasé manner, Caroline thought.

"I admire your work," Ian said, simply. He sipped at his bitter and then went into considerable detail about their last three productions, all of which he had seen twice.

"I know you're a unit," he said, staring at the stained beermats, "and there can't be much chance of something coming up. I'd like you to keep me in mind, that's all." He paused and then smiled, a smile which relieved all of them, for

31

now, for the first time, they saw the public actor they knew and admired: the smile lit up their individual memories of his acting and, being so precisely well judged, drew them into his circle as friends and equals.

"Hell, Jake," he said, "you're bloody good: you're doing that marvellous new adaptation of *The Seagull*, I've always wanted to play Trigorin and I need a scotch. Anybody else?"

He went to buy the drinks and they laughed a little about him. The timing, they said – brilliant! And, no denying it, they liked him.

Back from the bar with a tray of drinks he appeared taller, more handsome, warmer, more vigorous, and their subdued corner of the pub began to pick up energy. People around the bar nudged each other: wasn't that the fella who was in . . .? Looked very like him. Like a testing taunt, his name was called out once or twice and he responded, finally, by turning and raising his glass. No false snootiness, doing the decent democratic thing, they all thought: no pretence.

As he swung back to look at them again, he caught Caroline's eye and nodded. She blushed. The others laughed. Jake slapped him on the shoulder. The deal was on the way.

"You've got to give it to him," Jake said, across the debris of empty glasses after Ian had left.

"He's got guts," Jake said. "Taking us on," glaring round the pub, "taking them on."

"Why . . . ?" Caroline began timidly.

"His instinct has always been very good," Jake said, reflectively. "*Very* good," he repeated, a little too knowingly, Caroline thought. "He sees this as a way to get back into what's really happening. Still, you've got to admire him for taking the risk."

"I'm still not convinced," said one of the founder actors, "that it's right for the company."

"Nor am I . . ." The earnest debate began.

Jake let the discussion run and gave every sign of being open and undecided, willing to be part of the communal decision-making, willing to go with the majority on this as on all the

32

other major decisions. But Caroline knew that he had made up his mind. Just as she knew that Ian would phone her soon.

And she remembered his look, nursing it through the rest of the day, the sole settled glance of the whole encounter, she thought. It was then that she had seen the power so often caught by the camera or seen on stage. He had seemed to draw her into him, the blue eyes promising a more charged life, the features, suddenly sprung to an undeniable handsomeness, promising fun and unexperienced revelations – of what she did not know but scarcely cared, it was the promise that mattered. Just as his sudden relaxation had charmed them all and lit up the drab pub with energy, so that certain look had charmed and ignited her. She tried to freeze that frame of him in her mind, wanting to file it like a beloved photograph. But he would not stay; only the feeling stayed.

(5)

It was the balance which was difficult. In the past few years, Caroline had persuaded herself of so much of the philosophy of the women's movement that in her work and in the few altogether unsuccessful liaisons she had so far had, it had become second nature. Not the obvious stuff like equal pay for equal work, or restructuring career opportunities to allow women an equal chance – that was totally taken for granted along with the crèches, the domestic job-sharing, the whole bit about the liberation of the woman from the social slave role. But she believed in the harder line, the reversal of the traditional masculine-feminine expectations and role-playing in what was always referred to as "a relationship": the revolution, in short, between the sexes.

But for Ian she wanted to paint herself like Cleopatra, vamp like Marlene Dietrich, smile the angelic submissive conspiracy of Marilyn Monroe, and cluck like her mother, thinking of warm slippers and "Daddy's tired, turn off the gramophone, ssshhhh."

Not that Ian demanded, or in any way encouraged, this

33

geisha role. To the contrary, he was conscientious to a degree in all that her women's group thought essential, particularly in "acknowledging her independent identity". It was as if he divined her wishes and took extra care to respect her opinion.

Love, as it had been talked over with her friends, had long since passed the stage of a weak and wilting excitement, she thought: that presupposed a dominance of the male with which she disagreed. Love, they said, was fundamentally a suppressive weapon, from courtly love to Romantic love to the desperate childishness of a contemporary pop-song: in those and a hundred other variations from the Kama Sutra to the casebooks of Freud, the idea of Love had been used by men as a cosmetic on the unaltering face of a dictatorship. The whole love cult had been developed and extended by men to enforce dependency because in all the love cultures, women were object, attendant, unrecognised for their individuality, there to be used by men for the Thousand and One Nights of their repressive or reinforcing purposes. Caroline had believed this.

But she wanted to spin a cocoon of affection around Ian; she was moved and secretly delighted when he confessed to insecurities or anxieties: for then she could help. In bed, his unforced consideration for her pleasures and satisfactions only drove her to want to please him and satisfy him more strongly. "Do what you want," she murmured and would have added, had she not been too shy, "All that I want is for you to be happy." That latter thought was treason!

She found that she wanted to be his, to let herself dissolve and merge into his life and regard. She was, she found, only just able to resist saying "I'm yours." All the clichés and banalities of pulp romance surged through her with a force she had never anticipated, a force which thrilled her. Yet *he* could stand apart and alone. She was proudly and regretfully aware of that. Even in their most tender coupling, when indeed they were one, his apartness was inviolable.

But what of the politics of sexuality which had burned so many filaments in the light bulbs of those late-night conclaves? Penis power equalled imperialism and led to oppression and

34

war, did it not? In that equation, if women lent themselves to the role of defenceless creatures they were serving that indisputable theorem. For men needed women to be defenceless in order to justify their own destructiveness: such women became the redemption of it all and those women who colluded in that were not only perpetuating a male-oriented world which found its only real goals in conquest but surrendering the chance to change things . . . was that not the case?

Yet she longed for his power to overwhelm her. Shamefully, she wanted to be conquered. In her honesty she had to admit to herself that she accepted what her friends scornfully referred to as the role of the victim. The fate of the world sank below the horizon of his presence.

In this turbulence she had lived some of the happiest weeks of her life. The major external terrors, that she was behaving wickedly with a married man (again a throwback to a world of fixed roles she had agreed was dead and gone) and that he might leave her (an inadmissible pre-feminist and feeble anxiety), were blocked out by the fact of her happiness. Oddly, the confusion she felt at the upending of her new ideas by her old daydreams only enriched her sense of intoxication.

By the time the telephone rang that night she had regressed, as her friends would have put it, to the quivering state of an adoring adolescent. Yet Caroline felt more vivid and more powerful than at any time in her life. Yes, powerful. Whatever else might happen, she had known this . . .

(6)

Even before he spoke, Caroline suspected that he might be about to tell her that he could not come to see her. Such moments of empathy were part of this unprecedented intimacy. In that second's pause, Ian caught her fear and changed his mind: he would not let her down after all; someone else would be betrayed tonight.

"It's just a bit difficult," he said.

35

"Oh . . . ?" Prepared to yield.

"How was your trip?"

"A bit of a rush. They were glad I went. My cousin had just seen *Deathsleep*: he said you were 'pretty good' in it. That's high praise from a Lowland Scot."

"Your mother better?"

"She cried a lot. They were very close all their lives. I haven't ever seen her cry as much."

"How's the party?" Caroline continued, covering the short silence.

"It's been good. We're all a bit drunk. You know what it's like when something really finishes – you feel you can go to pieces like a man."

"Yes."

"It sounds very quiet," she hurried on, still not sure.

"I'm phoning from the study."

"You sound tired."

"I am."

"Do you," she closed her eyes, "do you want to call it off for tonight?"

"I'll come. A bit later than I said, that's all. About two."

As he put down the phone, Ian was aware that he had spoilt it for her a little. It might even have been better had he followed his plan and called it off. Apart from anything else he was tired, tired in a way he had learned to respect, without any sense of energy at all: the filming had sucked it all out of him. His habit now would be to go into an indolent convalescence – it need not last long but it had to be blank, avoiding all decisions or actions, letting the next part coil itself into him. They were to start rehearsals for *The Seagull* on the Monday.

He sat down in the study and took out a cigar whose size and cost would have offended most of Jake's company. He had brought a large scotch in with him and he lit up and thought about Caroline. For the past few weeks he had loved her very much. Her slight physical ungainliness, her less than prettiness, the earnest way in which she stood for the ideals of the Company and the ideas of her friends – it all drew him into

36

yet another new world. By knowing her he was coming to know the way in which he would pitch the part: by knowing her he felt connected to a generation whose totems and taboos he wanted to know: and above that, Caroline was – unexpectedly – quite wonderful. That gave him problems.

He willed himself to imagine the night and the next day . . . he did not want to let her down . . .

(7)

" 'I think writers are very like actors,' Ian said, 'perhaps that's why they sometimes give actors a bad press: in a sense the actor is more like they want to be than they are themselves.' I gave him the necessary prompt (Willie wrote).

'I've read about why people write and the usual things come up: obsession, need, restoration, a sense of having to shape things – I'm sure there's truth in all of them. Just as there's truth in writing for money and success and to be that bit different. But in my opinion, they write for the same reason as we act. They want other lives. One is not enough.

'Remember when we were kids? Playing cricket or coming out of the pictures. We would want to *be* that person, Johnny Weissmuller or Errol Flynn or Denis Compton. Not be *like* – *be*. "I'll be *him*," we would say. We had no idea that we were just one person. For what it's worth, I think that writers and actors never let go of that. That's their real spur. They want to *be* hundreds of other people. Perhaps they can't see the point or put up with the boredom of just being one or two people. It's their way of trying to slow life down or get their own back for this merciless single deal you get. And there are readers and audiences who feel exactly the same but they don't have the trick of externalising it. So they read and watch. They want other lives as well.'

When he talked like this it was always in my flat, Willie wrote. I would be sitting in the armchair. The flat would become like a bachelor's lair. Ian would loll on the settee, as indifferently stretched out as Joanna: both of them, I suppose,

37

secure in a decision that it did not matter how they appeared to me. Perhaps that is why when I think of him and recall his face, it is there on the settee that I see him: the surprisingly slim features; the suggestion of a calf-lick on the hairline above a high forehead, the strong nose, thin lower lip. Light blue eyes flickering under the chestnut hair.

Another point he made – on several occasions: and again I noted it down – 'I've very rarely met a women I couldn't have spent some time with,' he said. 'Not go to bed with, not just that, often not that at all. But there are so many I've felt I would like to know better. They all seem so worth getting to know better. They think more about themselves, more deeply than we do, and I want to hear what they have to say about those battles with their bodies or their jobs or their men. And then there are the girls I could fall in love with.' He hesitated, but only to set me up with a smile meant to take the edge of seriousness off his next remark. 'And then there are the dozens I *have* fallen in love with. At the time I always thought not "it's the real thing" but "it's the only thing that matters at all." I've not only wanted nothing more, I've wanted nothing else but to be with that woman, to know her and I suppose to be known to her. Perhaps that's just as important, finding someone you can make yourself really known to. Can't understand why. I know how little there is to know about me.'

He meant that. It was not that he was unaware of his talents but he was not someone who had a great opinion of himself at all. This was often mistaken for false modesty.

For the world in a way expected him to be false. He played parts. He put on masks. He once told me how he loved lying because of the interest and ingenuity it came to command as the deceits snowballed down a particular slope. He once said that the people he most admired were those who were entirely faithful to each other because the strength of purpose necessary to resist the temptations and excitements of infidelity was inconceivable to him.

Lying, playing parts in his life, insisting on being open to love: on these pillars were raised those weeks of his affair with

38

Caroline. I suspect she knew about all of them: I suppose she thought that to admit this lack of substance would be to spoil the only reality he could give her."

(8)

In the morning they had Buck's Fizz in bed. They tried to drink it lying flat on their backs and the champagne-orange juice trickled stickily down onto the sheets. The drawn curtains let in a fond early autumn sunlight. The night had been good and in the time they were having there was nothing more on earth they wanted. Ian lit a cigarette.

"Let's," he said, "take a boat on the Serpentine . . . go to Kew Gardens . . . or the Zoo . . . or Greenwich . . . or Hampstead Heath . . . or the towpath to Richmond . . . and let's agree we feed any ducks."

"I'd like to do all those things." Caroline treasured their fleeting times together in London: with Ian, it became a tourist fantasy. He genuinely loved the obvious. It seemed to her that their happiness was somehow enhanced in public. It was as if they floated through the city, untouchably, the precarious privilege of their mutual absorption spinning a transparent glistening skin about them. Caroline felt extraordinary then and knew it was transitory: and wanted to taste it while she could.

"The good thing is that you know that so many other people have done those things – all those ghosts along the way."

"I'd like that as well," Caroline said and dug herself deeper between the sheets. "I like ghosts."

"It's where they send people when they want a larky lyrical interlude in a Young Love movie."

"Yes please," she said.

"Kew Gardens?"

"*And* the towpath!"

"Tea in Richmond?"

"*And* the boat back up the river!"

"I'll take the bread for the ducks," he said.

39

There were posters drawing-pinned to the wall, paperbacks neatly arranged on bookshelves made out of planks and bricks, a frilly mob-cap lampshade, and around the bed a trail of clothes, victims of the night's battle.

"I feel sore," said Caroline.

"I'm not really surprised. I thought we would kill each other at one stage."

"I had no idea . . ." she began and trailed off, turned to look at him. He winked and reached out for the split of champagne.

"We'd better stop if it hurts."

She reached down his body.

"There's nothing there anyway."

"All gone."

"Poor old thing."

"RIP. Booze?"

He poured it carefully while she gently tickled him, staring at her like a hypnotist, refusing to register.

"Aha!" she said. "Something moved."

"A death rattle. Drink your drink."

"How can it go on for so long?"

"Sheer grit," he said solemnly and failed to blow a smoke ring.

"Is it," she began, "like this . . .?" Then her boldness stalled.

"No." He clinked his glass against hers. "Cheers."

As so often, Caroline felt herself balanced on the middle of a see-saw. She wanted to guard for herself those times in bed, or wherever: Ian was reckless in his choice of location and in some of their night meanderings through London he had surprised her in the most risky side-street or alleyway, but at the same time –

"I've never been able to talk about it before," she said.

He did not reply.

"And not just that. I've never been able to be intimate before, not worrying about walking around undressed or," she smiled and he knew again that he was fathoms gone, "do things like – go to the lavatory, with anybody else, a man, in the flat, without being embarrassed. Or get dressed with somebody

40

watching. Or just lie like this without feeling 'should we get up?' or 'should I go?'"

"What next? I suppose you – "

"Ssshhh . . . Listen."

She raised her head an inch or two from the pillow. The faintest street sounds, the lowest murmurs of the radio downstairs, their own breath. He looked at her.

"This is us," he said.

He took her glass and put it down with his own, stubbed out the cigarette and came gently into her, just staying there, holding her closely, side by side.

"Let's have a snooze," he said and closed his eyes.

"I do love you," but he seemed asleep.

In Kew Gardens they fed the ducks and admired the swans. On the towpath they walked towards the copper cut-out sun. Caroline wanted to talk about the rehearsals which were to start after the weekend. She had her biggest role so far – Nina – and Jake's "thinking" was that the character ought to be played as a pre-Women's Lib figure, a woman trying to leap in one bound from feudalism to modernism, truly heroic in her attempt and in her apparent defeat, the only one of the characters who grows. Caroline's nervousness about her ability was compounded by her anxiety over playing scenes with Ian. So much buzz had now built up in the company about his stage-acting, his routines and manners and demands, that she was afraid she might dry completely. Nor did the uncomfortable parallel of her own relationship to him and that of Nina to Trigorin escape her. Sometimes she saw their weeks together as the real rehearsal and whenever she told him so he would not flatly deny it.

But nor, this day, would he discuss it. To have persisted would have been tiresome and she let it go.

"We've got all this," he said, looking around at the Gardens, the first autumn leaves, the sky empty but for that perfect sun. "It'll do for now, won't it?"

It was as if she were watching her life in slowest motion percolate through the afternoon, grain by grain of incident each

41

hesitating to fall, as clear and inexorable as the unclouded sinking sun, glittering into darkness. Yet at the same time the moments were as fragile as soap-bubbles. Nothing mattered but what was happening between the two of them: yet the more precious that became the more inevitable an outside disruption appeared to be. She was on a high wire and felt at once more alert and more relaxed than ever before.

On the promenade at Richmond where the Thames bends away down to Hampton Court and promises of pastoral England, scholarship, poetry and plenty, they stood hand in hand as if gazing out onto a promised land.

"You're very beautiful," he said.

She did not respond immediately and then, carefully, she said "Nobody's ever told me that."

He shrugged, almost imperceptibly.

She knew not only that he meant it but that in some way she did not understand, he had unearthed it. The shadows and apprehensions which had lain across her had been dismissed by the force of his possession of her. She could see the change in the mirror, and in the looks of others.

"Let's skip tea and go back for a drink."

"How long have you got?" she asked, wishing she had not.

"I said I'd be back for dinner."

She tightened her lips and nodded, following the rules. His rules? No, that was too simple. Theirs? In some way.

But what were the rules of their feelings, she thought, as they went back into town? They could not cut out or cut off. Owning up to them panicked her. Yet he felt as strongly: he must, she thought, or she could never be sure of anything else in her life again. There were no lies in what he did. He seemed so true. Yet the whole thing could be called a cheat.

She was prepared to repress that conclusion. She was prepared to take her chance, she thought. At that time she believed that the happiness and passion of a few weeks could be stored up against a winter of misery. She did not know how fleeting it was, how it served the present only and left for the future far more emptiness than remembered pleasure.

42

Ian had not taken his car and to get home from Caroline's flat he hired a cab from the firm he had an account with. Again, even in this small matter, his carelessness or brazenness impressed Caroline with the openness of his nature. If deceit could also be open, then his deception of Marion was just that.

The mini-cab driver belonged to that floating world of metropolitan men who are treading water: bust businessmen, failed graduates, the aspiring self-employed, men on the way to better things, men licking wounds, men stealing time against the worse which they know is before them. Quite deliberately, Ian always sat in front beside the driver and talked to him – or, more precisely, began by talking, as an Arab trader might begin by offering a cup of coffee – and then he asked questions.

In this case he found out that the young man, twenty-eight, was new to the game, had sold a photographic business ("I did schools, groups, the kids, I got bored with it"), sold his house and taken a job in South Africa. The only alternative had been Saudi Arabia ("and the wife didn't fancy that for the kids, they don't go to school yet, she thought they'd get burned"). He did not like "the way this country's going." He had talked to people from South Africa and they said "there was less trouble than we have here." Anyway he just had a three-year contract – he could always get out. He would not be drawn on politics ("I don't believe in any of them"). He would say little about the Asians and West Indians in London except "they bring problems, you can't deny that." Ian concealed his liberalism trying not so much to coax as to find out more about the man. He saw struggles he had never had, an ambition clear and simply aimed. In that fifteen-minute drive he worked out to his own satisfaction as careful a portrait of the man's background as he could, neither condemning nor, he trusted, sentimentalising.

As importantly, he noted the involuntary laugh – not giggle – a short soon-pricked bubble of laughter which ended each sentence that expressed an opinion. He noted the flick of the man's eyes to the target of his answers, half-angry, half-expectant, a lizard flick of a look. He noted the way the man, who was very big, not fat, strongly built ("used to do a bit of weightlifting"), rested his hands so very lightly on the steering wheel.

All this was consciously filed away, to be used some time, for someone, whole or in bits and pieces.

Not once in the trip did he think of Caroline, whom he had left, naked still in the bed, dumbly understanding, believing that both of them would be consumed for days in the fires they had gone through.

(10)

"I saw *The Seagull* towards the end of its limited run, (Willie wrote in his notebook). It had been the most tremendous success. The production was praised for its radical re-interpretation of Chekhov's classic and further praised for its good sense in not going so far as to spoil what three or four critics called 'the basic meaning of the play'. The cast was praised for its ensemble work, its vigour and commitment, its freshness. Jake was applauded for bringing out the play's social commitment 'in all its nakedness'. And Ian, save for one or two who qualified their notices, received a better press than he had enjoyed for years. If he had not been going to Broadway to take over the leading role in a new play which had already been a great success in London, he could have led the company into the West End for what would have been a substantial run. I learned later that Jake had revised his opinion of Ian over that point and led the company in denouncing him as an opportunist. Jake had wanted the West End run. But by then, of course, Ian had got what *he* wanted.

It was a remarkable performance, made deeply uncomfortable for me in retrospect by what he said in front of Jake, Caroline and two others in the cast when, at his prior insistence, I went backstage to see him afterwards. 'There's a lot of my old friend Willie in Trigorin,' he announced, lightly, his arm around my shoulder, welcoming, almost embracing. 'Look at him closely and you'll see some of it. But it's in there,' he pointed to my head in an absurd dumb show. 'If you could get in there you would really know how much I owe him.'

After that it is a little embarrassing to describe what I thought of his performance but I am determined to try to set down everything here, in this notebook.

He made Trigorin a man of all but ungovernable sexual passion, but someone who had succeeded in finding a method of locking it away. Though it could be repressed, however, it could never be dismissed and even its compulsive sublimation or employment in the obsessive collecting of materials for writing and the writing itself was not secure. This gave a sexual charge to everything, making his mistress seem not someone in control of him but a woman allowed to hold the leash, always aware that the animal could turn or walk away whenever it chose. Trigorin's manner was not that of the languorous aesthete but ravenous, prowling, looking for live meat or carcases to feed on. And Nina quite suddenly released all those subdued feelings: with her he saw again what he really wanted and went for it, breaking his rules, breaking her, naked again.

Caroline was praised for her portrayal of Nina, but not enough. When she was with Ian there was such a weight of pining, such an intense will to change and challenge all that she knew, such a fatal lust to leap into the chasm of what was totally new to her, that I wanted to cry out 'Don't do it!' like a child at a pantomime. In that performance alone she showed what she was capable of as an actress: but it was in that performance only. Without Ian there and without that personal connection of hope and desperation, she could not raise herself, as he apparently so easily could, onto that rare plane where the great actors make you totally believe in them and know, as you know, that they can touch and move you with every gesture.

When they took their bow, Ian was next in line to Caroline and as the cast clasped hands and she smiled, for him, that heart-turning smile, I watched their fingers interlock tightly. She knew he was going off to America for six months at least, most likely longer. She knew that already he had passed on, although that mysterious code of his insisted that he see it through with her until it became inevitable they part; that he would not humiliate her by being seen to break it off before the understandable excuse of his departure for New York. He had talked a little to me about her and, seeing her now, for as I thought the first time, I felt a sickening fear as palpable as if it had been part of my own life which was being torn away. For I had fallen in love with her. Instantly. And I knew that nothing would change that. The impact and the certainty overwhelmed me, simultaneously. And for Ian, whose monstrous faults and childish self-indulgences, whose corrupt exploitation of the permissiveness of a directionless society I had excused for so long, I felt a jealous hatred."

Chapter Three

"Come in, come in," said Eric, flourishing his pen like a baton, "Sit down, sit down. These bloody memos! Ruth! *Ruth!*"

Willie sat down, reaching for a cigarette as if that were his talisman. Ruth all but trotted in.

"'Explicate'," Eric announced, jabbing his thick forefinger at the word. "You've typed 'explain'."

"Sorry."

"And this one," he picked up another sheet neatly starched in type. "I think we should copy it to Griff and Gruff" – those were his private nicknames for his immediate superior and that superior's superior. "They ought to know what I'm up to; forewarned." Eric's embarrassment brought out a self-caricature.

"Do you mind," said Eric, launching an almost pleading glance at Willie, who was now rather preoccupied in spying out an ashtray in this non-smoker's office, "if I scribble a note to the lads. This bloody reorganisation has caught everybody on the hop." The implied apology made Willie smile: he shook his head and made as if to stand up and leave. "You needn't go. *Ruth!*" She was at the door: slammed on the brakes, turned. "Get Willie a coffee and an ashtray, would you, love? Black. And for me."

Willie settled down as Eric began to work on his note, literally grunting over it as if he were digging a ditch.

The office was spacious and attractively scruffy. Its size denoted Eric's position in the hierarchy of the institution, its scruffiness reassured you of his continuing links with his past: the school rugby photographs, lopsided on the wall, were reminders of his Welsh mining-valley background; the awards

47

and trophies stacked on a shelf were tokens from the recent days of his blunt and fiery heart-rending social documentaries which had led to action groups being formed all over the country and yet, as Eric was the first to say, "very little actually being done about anything: all the proof you need that television has a lot of impact but no real power."

Eric's decision to climb up the institutional ladder had surprised many of his friends and supporters – only some of whom had been convinced by his statement in the surprisingly long and flattering *Times* profile that he "saw it as his duty to create the best conditions for those who were serious about television." Willie was convinced, however: he believed that Eric had not used his conscience to further his career, even though, in the nervous, socially-conscious ambience of television, such an indignant conscience could be the enabling equivalent of great wealth or connections in previous centuries. Those who controlled this rampaging, barbarically energetic technology and strove to give it an institutional respectability and tack a defensible morality onto the one-eyed monster now sweeping the skies in satellites and snaking multitudinously under the earth in cables, reached out gladly to an Eric. It gave a purpose to it, a theology, an organisational *raison d'être*, especially in Britain, which wanted to avoid the parodic capitalism of American television and the imprisoned propaganda of Russian television and discover an element of service, public good and a link with imperialistic benevolence.

"Done!" Eric said, banging down the full stop as if he were scoring a try. "*Ruth!*"

In she came instantly: Willie wondered if she ever actually sat at her desk or just stayed outside Eric's door in her starting blocks.

"This is to go out to everyone. Soon as poss. Please."

"Now," he continued, sidling out from behind his desk to join Willie on an equal level in an equally low-slung equally uncomfortable leatherette armchair. "Sorry I couldn't see you when you got back, and" – Eric reached out and grasped Willie's arm, an action which threatened to upset the coffee –

48

"I'm sorry – really – about that office mix-up. I didn't know you'd been chucked out like that. It must have seemed like the classic dirty move, get the guy while he's out of the country."

"That's all right," Willie said, safely settling down his half-drunk cup and searching out another cigarette. "These things always tend to happen in a rush."

"Right!" Eric's relief was undisguised. There was no cover for deception on that open and burly face. Eric's size had always impressed Willie: he still kept his fourteen stones fit with ferocious games of squash and tennis. Eric had been easy to teach. Willie had simply given him the scent, the few basic instructions, and watched him pound over the terrain like a huge hound, tail up, ears cocked, straining for the prey.

"This next bit's difficult," Eric said, scowling a little as if an unfair penalty had been awarded against him. "The whole trouble with this job," he went on, as if making a profound observation on the philosophy of leadership and responsibility, "is that you keep having to do things you don't want to do."

He paused, waiting, Willie knew, to be helped out as he had so often been helped out in the past. But Willie said nothing. Eric was a new baron and needed to delineate his own domain unaided.

"There has to be a shake-up," Eric began, grimly placing his big hands on his big knees. "I had no idea what a bloody mess everything was in." Willie waited. Eric, visibly, took a deep breath. "The thing is," he went on, "that the challenge of the eighties is different. Television coming from every direction, control slipping away all over the place, more and more money in pap and more and more need for quality. If we don't hold the line and, more than that, make television grow up, we'll hand it on to the next lot as nothing much more than *Comic Cuts*. There are plenty of people who would like that. And it's even more important when you think of society as a whole." Eric's conviction shone with a choirboy's religious sincerity.

"And that's where you come in," Eric said, bounding to his

49

feet and starting on his usual lurching trudge around the office. In another age he would have been a farmer or a roving preacher, Willie thought, something outside the cages of the widening modern web of bureaucracy, a crusading knight, most appropriately, a man of clear faith, full of the urgent need to go and do something simple and effective about it. As it was, he now resembled one of those wired-in apes prowling about their cruel quadrangles in a city zoo.

"Yes?" Willie prompted, for, perhaps exhausted by his own eloquence, Eric was now pressing his nose against the window-pane, gazing over London as he hoisted himself up and down on his toes. He spun round.

"I want you to concentrate more on the Training. We need to build all that part of it up as fast as we can. We'll need more people and I think we should train more of them ourselves. There's nobody better than you for that."

"Are there firm plans then?" Willie asked. "A new budget? Any agreed establishment?"

"Not yet," Eric conceded, rather reluctantly. "I have to fight that one through."

"I don't quite understand."

"Why you were moved? Well . . ." now Eric stood facing Willie, legs planted apart, shifting his weight from one to the other as if testing them for reliability. "If – or to be more precise, when – we put you in charge of this bigger Training programme, we'll have to let you off all the other admin. stuff . . . And the obituaries." Eric's attempt at a careless throwaway failed through his lack of duplicity.

"I see."

So the decision had been made to take him off programme-making. Willie felt literally sick in his stomach. Although the obituaries were regarded by him as by others as rather a morbid and almost a joke assignment, they did allow him to put together painstaking and thorough profiles which had often been acknowledged to be well made. Above all, despite Willie's readiness to accept his fractured state, they had kept him in touch with the work which had drawn him into television in the first place. That was what he loved: making programmes.

"I'd rather hold on to the obituaries if I could," Willie said, in a voice whose briskness surprised him.

Eric stopped moving and looked at Willie with the slightest hint of annoyance. His plan was being challenged: therefore his authority was being challenged. But by someone he had once been grateful to learn from, someone he respected . . . It was unfair that it was so difficult, he thought.

"You see, I've got bound up in a lot of them," Willie continued, taking great care not to let any tone of pleading or reproval tincture his words, "and the whole business fascinates me. Profiles, not deaths. Seeing how far you can go."

"You've done very well," Eric replied, fair and generous. "The Mountbatten piece was a classic. I don't know how you managed to dig all the stuff up."

The digging-up, Willie reflected, had been no more than patience and commonsense detective work. It was the putting together that counted. But he let it pass: he usually did.

"I think I could manage to keep them going," Willie went on. "Provided they don't drop off the perch, as Joanna puts it, in too rapid a succession."

"How is Joanna?" Eric asked, clumsily concerned and, instinctively, playing for time.

"Fine," Willie replied and pressed on for the agreement he needed, "and so – especially as this new training project – which sounds excellent – "

"You yourself suggested it years ago," Eric reminded him, sternly.

"Yes . . . but as it's not quite worked out yet, I think I can carry on with the obits as usual. The other little jobs, by all means, they're all yours."

Eric nodded, heavily, and turned again to gaze out almost piningly at all the uncomplicated weather. If this move was Eric's idea, Willie thought, then I can block it. He knew how to steer his man. But – and this was the real cause of that sickening spasm which had not yet left him – if the order had come from On High, what then? In his programme-making

51

days, Eric had considered On High to be the enemy rather as those intelligent young officers in the First World War considered HQ to be their greatest adversary. But now Eric had joined HQ and the common power of institutional command had him in its service whether he enjoyed it or not. The matter was fragile, though. Willie had often found that the balance in such a conversation would be determined by the decisions made in the silences. It would perhaps be fanciful to describe these silences as moments in which vibrations and psychic forces were exchanged, weighed and countered: more likely that the pauses gave time for the whole reasoning, with all the inevitable alternatives, to be drawn on and considered. For Eric was considering – how he was appearing in front of his former teacher, how to cope with the awkward fact of now being his boss, whether to divulge that he had, in fact, been advised from On High that Willie's time was up?

He did not want to lose Willie's respect by seeming to be merely a messenger for orders with which he patently did not agree, and yet he feared to go back On High and begin to uncouple what had seemed, in Willie's absence, a sensible, humane, and yes, even helpful, plan. Willie recognised Eric's fear although Eric himself would have disavowed it indignantly. But Willie knew about the insidious bonds which institutions inevitably bind about both the weak and the ambitious: he knew of their power to enforce dependency, of their tendency to become the metaphorical mother and father, mammying with security until death, fathering with institutional importance and public participation in life. It was a pity that Eric, who could have been something of a free spirit, had surrendered.

"I don't know what to do," Eric declared finally, plaintively.

So they *did* want him out. Willie's resistance stiffened. Eric was on his own now. No more help.

"I expect it'll sort itself out," Willie said, standing up, bringing the interview to an end.

Eric turned to him, all but begging, "Isn't it too much work for you, Willie?"

"I enjoy it. And I've grown quite fond of all the old monsters we've laid up."

"We'll have to talk about it some other time," the younger man muttered, aggressively.

"Whenever you want. Anything I should be doing about this new Training scheme?"

Eric waved his hands in the air as if warding off a swarm of midges. "I'll let you know about that soon."

"Good," Willie said. "Nice to see you." He was already on his way to the door.

"Willie?"

"Yes."

"Think about it, will you?"

"I won't change my mind," Willie said, and all play was gone.

He left Eric glumly scratching his groin.

(2)

"They aren't trying to ease you out altogether, are they?" Mandy asked in her blunt manner.

Sometimes Willie wished her manner were not quite so blunt. It had a way of striking at the jugular of his unease which might have benefited, he thought, from the calming anaesthetic of being ignored.

"No," he replied, a little shortly. It was rather unbecoming to have to defend himself against the implied charge of being so dispensable. "I don't think they want that. They just think the old boy's a bit past it, let's have a change. It always makes people in authority feel dynamic if they can institute a change. It doesn't much matter what the change is. In a way the only method they have of expressing their authority is to enforce arbitrary changes. Mostly junking things."

"It makes *you* feel insecure," Mandy struck again, her large brown eyes growing even larger and threatening him with death by drowning in her bottomless understanding.

"That's the way new bosses reinforce their own sense of

security," he said, carefully rolling long ribbons of spaghetti around his inadequate small fork. "The funny thing about institutions is that for all their promise of stability, only a few people feel really secure. Perhaps you feel secure if you have tenure at a university; perhaps your unfireable civil servant or school teacher feels it. I doubt it, though. There's something about the way they're organised which demands that insecurity is built in. Maybe it's the psychological payment exacted for the pension."

"You're ducking the real question," Mandy said, and she laid down her knife and fork like a gauntlet.

They were in an unpretentious and unfashionable little Italian restaurant in Soho. The table cloths were red-and-white checked; the pasta was made on the premises; the wine was not unduly marked up. They were generally given a corner table which enabled them to talk quite intimately even when the place filled up. On this Monday evening, it was almost empty. Willie had rung up Mandy on spec. after discovering that Joanna intended to be out again. He needed someone to talk to about the implications and consequences of his meeting with Eric. But Mandy's clear-cut solutions – take these pills three times a day! – were already proving more unsettling than his interview with Eric.

For months now, he had known that this affair, this unconsummated affair, with Mandy was, for him – but only possibly for her – more a liaison of convenience than of affection. Once again a sense of another's dependency had developed; as with Joanna, as with his mother, as with Ian, as it would with David if he allowed it, but he would fight that. Willie's superficial vulnerability seemed to attract powerful comfort which came to help but stayed to be succoured. Mandy wanted companionship. He was more than willing to supply that but at this moment of real professional anxiety, the coddling nature of this companionship palled.

"The real question," she went on, bright eyes now on her remorseless mission to be protective, "is – "

"Have some more wine," he interrupted her, smiling

54

but deliberate, and he wished she had the style to laugh.

"No thank you," her hand slipped across the glass as if to protect herself. He filled his own glass, full.

"I didn't really want to analyse it," he said in his attempt to be honest with her.

"Then why did you bring it up?"

"Because I wanted to talk about it."

"Exactly. You want to talk but not too much." At last she smiled.

"Guilty as charged," he said.

"So," she went on. "What are you going to do?"

"Hold on," he said, kissing goodbye to the conversation, the self-indulgent but salving conversation he had hoped for. He drank some more Frascati and blessed the men who picked the grapes.

"'Hold on' is the story of your life," Mandy said.

"Of all our lives."

"Schmuck!" She took his hand: his drinking hand. "You're better than that. You're much better than that. You've gotta start believing in yourself. Even at your age. Especially at your age."

"Mandy," he glanced around: no one was taking the slightest notice of them. "Let's drop it."

"Let's not drop it."

He withdrew his hand, drank some more and looked at her carefully. What a nice, good-looking, self-contained, intelligent, decent woman she was. The sort of person who did good, worked late, complained legitimately, saw things through. A battler, a doer, a skewerer of pretence: what was she doing with him in a hideaway restaurant in Soho?

"You're off thinking about Joanna again," she said. "I can tell. The whites of your eyes take over the whole socket."

"You are funny."

"I am your friend, you stupid old bastard."

But even as she tried to brazen out her mood with affectionate insult, Willie knew that she too recognised that a tidal turn had been reached between them. It was so strange;

55

like the sea itself, at one mysterious but definable moment, the ebb would begin. A last longing look came to him from her: it has been a fine friendship; it could have been a good affair, even a true love. Now, though, in this funny little hideaway of theirs, the hands were parting, their lives were turning away from each other. In this look was the regret for all that could have been if only their lives had fallen out a little differently.

"I know you are," he replied, after the long pause, sealing the dis-union with a barely perceptible toast of his glass. "To you."

"So where's my wine?"

He poured her another glass.

They were good at smalltalking their way through difficult times: it was a talent each one had been obliged to develop. Now it served them well. The meal passed away pleasantly; there was not the suspicion of a scene; no tears, no reproaches, a stoical understanding of the greater loneliness ahead, an acceptance, now, that to depart was better than to remain.

At the door of her flat he kissed her on the mouth and they held each other closely, like shy lovers on a first date. As he walked away he knew she was watching but he did not turn back.

(3)

It was not late and he decided to walk back to his own flat. It was a mild evening, and once upon a fairly recent time, Willie would have quietly revelled in the homeward stroll. He had grown to love London and knew parts of it well. He had never lost that particular pleasure of straying through the streets which had been one of his only affordable luxuries on his arrival from the provinces over a quarter of a century ago. Especially at night. It was like tracking his way along dried-up river beds: the backs of houses, some lit, some dark, could be the camping ground and small night fires of mysterious forces landed in the metropolis, garnering their resources for the next day's assault. There would always be a few other strollers, like him, and they would avoid each other's gaze, each intent on the private dreams which could be spun so easily in the crowded emptiness of the city streets. The dogs came out with their conscientious owners, cars hurried their passengers from building to building, there would be an occasional burst of activity – a party of people suddenly surging out of a house, a flurry of late shoppers around the short stretch of a parade – but it was not difficult to think that you had the streets to yourself. Lately, though, Willie had begun to catch himself feeling uneasy at times on these walks.

Perhaps it was yet another aspect of this turning middle-age, but he sensed a readiness for violence which had not been there before. It was not that he encountered gangs of youths idly bent on rampage, although the scent of that was certainly in the air, but the city itself seemed to be losing the general benevolence he had felt so palpably before. The riots, the IRA bombs, the scare stories of muggings in the popular press – he was capable of digesting this to some extent, or at least of putting it in perspective, finding sound commonsense comfort in comparison with New York, L.A. . . . but that did not satisfy him. He felt that the city was losing those intangible qualities – niceness, cheerfulness – and that they were being replaced by a growing edge of watchful fear. Maybe it was no more than the correspondence of his own state of mind: cities, like the country, can reflect almost any mood or image you cast on them. But if he was right, he regretted it, regretted the passing away of the simple pleasure of walking through the evening streets feeling the common hum from the extraordinary complication of city life, regretted that a time of ordinary quiet pleasure might be passing. Sadly, he wended his cautious portly way, trying to digest the unhappiness.

He went over the meetings with Eric and Mandy – or rather they drifted through his mind in that salving, unravelling way which, he found, was prompted by such solitary strolling. Moments from both encounters recurred and he let them loll in his mind as if he were scrutinising them, looking for flaws even, before he allowed them to sink down into the accepted

57

past. He would miss Mandy a great deal, see her now and again of course, but miss that bond, even though it had been chafing. Perhaps, after a while, they could indeed be friends, without the pressure of unattainable possibilities . . .

David had brought some of his crowd back to the flat and Willie blinked at them as if he had unexpectedly stumbled into an exotic den. The stereo was on low but everything else was loud – the splayed untidiness of the young people, their swarming domination of his small domain, the violent hairstyles and dress.

It seemed to Willie that David's generation had made up its mind to fudge as many images as possible. They spoke cod cockney or pastiche posh; they dressed the men half young buck, half heavy metal, the women part pert tart, part careless art student; they came together on a philosophy of fierce equality, idealism and immovable cynicism about the established controlling world; they seemed to aim to shock and frighten and yet, Willie always found, they had reserves of gentleness and accommodation unknown to his generation, which had early begun to carve out a career with a scalpel. It was as if they wanted to muddy all the signals, to jam the Morse code which came from this generation, to blur class, talent, effort, ambition, intuition and will and skulk behind this bewildering barrage of negatives – in order to do what? Willie had no idea but he had got over his initial annoyance and dismay and now thought that theirs might indeed be a saving strategy for the times they lived in; their irresolute anarchy could be the fertile rummaging for a new way. Certainly they were not inheriting much wealth of purpose or achievement from the older ways.

There was a crate of beer on the floor in front of his chair, Kentucky Fried Chicken had been the meal, the sweet wreath of marijuana curled above their heads, CND badges speckled the jackets. David, who was lying on the floor, got up and came across.

"Willie! Good to see you !"

Willie almost shook hands with his stepson.

58

"You know most of them, don't you?"

"I think so. Hello."

His greeting was rather languidly returned – not unfriendly, but no one stirred or by any sign acknowledged that this was the man who owned the place they were in. Willie took an odd pleasure in that: by contrast, almost, remembering how correct and dutiful his generation would have been. And it was perfectly clear that just as they were not at all "fazed", would be their word, that he had come in, so they would not be put out if he stayed. His own lot would have sweated out the Adult/Parental Intrusion with a politeness which would have become hypocritical as time went on and they desperately wanted the intruder gone but did not know how to manipulate it.

"Have a beer," David said.

"Thanks."

"Jim?"

A black leather jacket topped with dyed blond curls put out its arm, plucked out a bottle and cheerfully chucked it across to David, who whipped an opener out of his pocket, knocked off the top and handed the foamy-topped beer to Willie. It was a little like a music-hall routine, he thought.

"Cheers," he said, and drank gratefully, thirsty after his walk.

"We seem to have finished the fried chicken," David said, apologetically. "There *might* be a bit left . . ."

"I've eaten. Thanks."

"Jim's asked me to join his community arts group," David continued, proudly. Jim was a rather wispy-looking man, goatee board, very pallid skin; he nodded.

"That's good," Willie said.

"He needs someone to do the heavy work, the carpentry and building. You know? I'll enjoy that."

"Good," Willie repeated and suppressed his urge to ask – will you get paid? Is there a future in it? What do they do, this group? Are they any good? Is community art any good? "That's very good."

"It is, isn't it?" David grinned – and the sun on his face

59

finally drove away the clouds of parental anxiety which had so patly scudded across Willie's mind.

"Mum's in her room," David said and grimaced slightly, avoiding disloyalty but signifying worry.

"I'd better go in and see her then."

"Yes. We'll keep the music low."

"That would be considerate."

"Another bottle?"

"This'll do, thanks. Well then." Willie's awkwardness asserted itself again. It appeared that he did not know how to leave. All the more ridiculous here where no one would pay his going the slightest attention. "Well then," he repeated as if mustering up his limbs. "I'll go and see her."

"Thanks, Dad."

David rarely used that word and Willie had never dared tell him how much it meant to him. He nodded at his stepson and went down the corridor to see Joanna.

By now he ought to have been an expert on the many grades and declensions of her drunkenness, but she could always take him by surprise. He used to think, for example, that a certain stage or – more baldly – a certain level of alcoholic input resulted in a predictable degree of irritability, somnolence, sentimentality or whatever. For a while he had tried to plot these correspondences but Joanna was altogether too cunning or wayward for him. Now he simply expected the worst and pitched his battleground there.

Her room was well served by the single dim *art-nouveau* lamp which was all the illumination. The disarray of clothes, shoes, cosmetics, handbags, paperbacks, cigarettes and bottles was mercifully masked and became, in this artificial twilight, almost bohemian, an effect heightened by the dark red Japanese-patterned Liberty's wallpaper and the few *objets trouvés* picked out by the treasured lamp. She was lying on her bed, still dressed, drink in one hand, cigarette in the other, spectacles on, indicating a clearly failed attempt to read. The book was face down on the floor: *Earthly Powers* by Anthony Burgess.

"Where've you been?" she asked, and as if in answer to her own question, she added, "Don't lie."

I don't lie, Willie wanted to say, but dug in firmly. "I thought you said you were going out. I had something to eat in town."

"I changed my mind." Or *he* did, Willie thought: or both; or God knows what. "You were with that bloody doctor, weren't you?"

"Yes."

"Well, don't stand there holding that disgusting beer bottle like some comic in a Northern pantomime. Come in and shut the door. I can't stand the racket those kids are making."

He did as he was bid and sat down on the rosewood Victorian armchair over which she had slung her coat. The chair creaked when he settled on it. One of its legs was going.

"They seem to be having a fairly quiet party to me," Willie said, reasonably: but as the words came out he wanted to catch them and put them back. Such a remark would certainly be decoded as provocation.

"You encourage him to annoy me," she said. "I want you to throw them out."

"I can't do that." To David, he meant.

"No," she finished her drink and reached out for the whisky bottle. "That's the problem."

He winced at the measure she poured and her recklessness now provoked him. He had helped her, pleaded, talked, advised, arranged for doctors, psychiatrists and been led to the realisation that he could not influence her. But it was wrong, he thought, to let it go without any comment, to watch her poison herself without a word.

"You ought to ease up," he said. He stood up and took a glass from her drinks table. "I'll take half of that."

She looked up at him standing over her, made huge by the light throwing his shadow large on the wall, and moved perhaps by a remembrance of love or a recognition of loyalty, she unexpectedly acquiesced and poured half of her whisky into his empty glass. Her hand, he noticed, was remarkably steady. Was she now so inured that it was not even getting to her?

61

"Water?" he asked.

"No thanks."

"Just a little," he said and filled up her glass and his own from the bottle of Malvern Water before retreating to his seat, which collapsed as he forgot to sit carefully. Joanna laughed as Willie slid onto the floor, a loud, pealing laugh, not at all malevolent. He stood up and sat at the foot of her bed.

"Didn't spill a drop," he said. "Cheers!"

"You're such a clot, Willie. How the hell I . . . " she sipped the whisky.

Yes, he thought. I have been a terrible disappointment to you. You wanted glamour and thought that my television career would bring it: it hasn't. You would have liked interesting friends, but your illness and then mine seems to have scared most of them off. You were never bothered about money, but that was because you always had enough: the wage that seems very generous to me seems peanuts to you – we can't even buy ourselves out of this flat. As for your own career, it's more of a wreck than that old Victorian chair, which was a bad buy in the first place. Sex – can't leave that out – I no longer seem to satisfy you, if I ever did. And you can't stand my caring but even more, or so I believe, you could not stand my not caring.

"We should have dinner parties again," Willie said.

"Don't be absurd."

"Why not? You were very good at them. Eight or ten people. We had some good times."

"The trouble with inviting people to dinner is that they invite you back."

"Let's try it."

"Who?"

"Oh –"

"Not that pious prick Eric. Scheming his way to that job with his creepy do-gooding. You should have had that job."

"Joanna –"

"All right. Dinner. But not the boy wonder. And not Dr Mandy either. What do you see in her?"

62

"I like her."

"Rubbish. She lets you cry on her shoulder and you think that makes her sympathetic. She's a piranha – just waiting to swallow you up." She remembered her spectacles and practically flung them off. "You've always been a sucker for that sort of wallow."

"She's helped us – both – a lot."

"That woman helps herself. Pretending to be a doctor gives her a good excuse, that's all. You're not serious about her, are you?"

"No," Willie replied, taking the short cut, too tired to explain.

"I was beginning to think you were." The sound of voices came from the other room: not loud, not really intrusive, but heard. "That's those little sods taking over my place," she said and began to cry. "I'm sorry, I'm sorry. But I just can't bear to think of them out there, sprawling over everything – taking over – it's silly I know, I'm sorry, but I can't *bear it!*" The last two words were shouted out, like a challenge or a threat to David and his friends.

Willie nodded and went through. He took David to one side.

"I think your mother's getting upset," he said. David, thank God, understood immediately.

"Shall I . . . ?" Willie asked, to make it easier for the boy. David nodded.

Willie cleared his throat and stood there for all the world like a councillor hauled in late to propose a vote of thanks.

"David's mother isn't very well," he said. "I'm awfully sorry and it's not your fault at all – there isn't too much noise or any-thing – but she'd rather be alone. I hope you don't mind. I hope you'll come again. I'm sorry."

There was no fuss, but as they reluctantly prepared to leave, somehow signalling that this was an act of connivance and not obedience, Willie once again felt that low murmur of potential violence he now picked up on the night streets. He spotted one or two pitying looks, and was sure they were not for the dilemma he and David found themselves in with Joanna: rather

63

they said "We're going this time, but we're doing you a favour. This is no precedent. Squatters' rights in everything." He chased the thought away – the fears of middle age again, young enough to want to be part of them, debarred by the fact of the age gap and not yet old enough to feel that it was no longer any of his concern. They went – eventually, without fuss: that was what mattered.

"You go with them," Willie urged David. "I'll tidy up."

"Will you?" David glanced around the thoroughly messed-up room. "It seems pretty tidy anyway."

"Yes. And take the beer."

David picked up the crate with one hand and followed his friends to another lair. Willie went back to Joanna's room and found her asleep or pretending to be asleep. He left her, quietly tidied up the flat and put on some coffee which he took through to her on a tray. She woke up as soon as he came in.

"That's nice of you," she said, warmly, drowsily.

"Where are your pills?"

"In my handbag. The red one."

He sought them out.

"Have they gone?"

"Yes," he said.

"Do you think I'm a monster, Willie?"

"No. Here are the pills."

"You won't leave me, Willie, promise?"

"Promise. Take one at a time."

She swallowed them with great difficulty.

"Help me undress, Willie, please?"

Docile now, she submitted meekly as he pulled off her clothes and put her into bed.

"I haven't taken off my make-up," she said dreamily, already half out of the world. "My daddy used to say that only tarts slept in their make-up. Goodnight, Willie. I'm sorry about it all . . ."

He watched her fall asleep. In sleep her face smoothed out, her skin in the half-light seemed fine, uncoarsened, her hair lay bountifully on the pillow like the tresses of a heroine in a fairy tale. Once upon a time, Willie would have been unable to resist kissing her cheek.

He left the light on. She was frightened to wake up in the dark. In his own bed that night, he yearned for another life.

(4)

In the three or four weeks that followed, Willie engaged in a holding action. At work, he continued as if the meeting with Eric had never taken place; at home he attended to Joanna; he was glad to see David's growing enthusiasm for his community arts centre; he telephoned Mandy three or four times to chat; in the evening he read widely to prepare an updating of his obituary on Begin; he stopped trying to give up smoking in the mornings. And in all that time his nights were disturbed by those surging clusters of faces and forms demanding satisfaction, gathering force like a current which cuts deeper, runs stronger, pulling the river towards rapids. He clutched out, looking for help.

He was delighted when Ian came around. Ian had rung a couple of times but cancelled at the last moment. Joanna had gone to the theatre with an old friend from her palmier days now the wife of a Euro-MP. Willie had never worked out quite why Ian took such care to avoid Joanna. He was the only friend of his she had a good word for.

Ian was growing his hair long for the part of Trigorin and as he stretched out on the sofa, Willie in his armchair as usual, he seemed to belong more to the crowd so politely ejected on the night of David's party than to Willie's thickening-waist generation. He had brought a bottle of scotch – a rare act of thoughtfulness, for Ian could be surprisingly mean or forgetful about such things and he had drunk Willie's whisky by the gallon over the years. Only very occasionally did Willie go to Ian's place and invariably Marion would be there, welcoming, hospitable, a barrier.

Ian was in the mood for reassurance. He so trusted Willie's discretion that he behaved towards him with the barefaced

65

defiance of an analysand to an analyst and the questing of a pupil to a trusted teacher. Yet it was all dressed up in a laconic condescension as if the conversation were equally poised and the discoveries equally necessary.

"I'm beginning to regret going in with this Company," he said. "They're perfectly OK and they know what they're doing. But the grimness of it all! God, I'd rather suffer the old queen panto circuit than put up with these discussions. Every time we break somebody gives us a sermon on the latest state of the workers and every time we talk about the play they all talk about it in terms of British Leyland or North Sea Oil. It was interesting for a day or two . . . but no fun."

"Perhaps," Willie said, seeing that he was being called on not to change the course but merely to trim the sails, "by taking it seriously they are having fun. In fact I would guess they were. They're probably anxious to feel plugged in to the trials and perils of contemporary society."

"I'm sure you're right," Ian replied, as always, absorbing rather than arguing. It often seemed to Willie that Ian considered arguing simply a waste of time. He took in opposing views and, like a beast with many stomachs, summoned them up and chewed them over at his later leisure.

"But it's no fun for *me*," he added, exaggerating his petulance, so that, for a moment, he was acting the spoilt younger son. "I came into the theatre for a bit of glitter, not to hear the history of the Tolpuddle Martyrs every time we take five."

"Ah. Your bit of glitter is their enemy."

"Oh God. Is it as bad as that?"

"They see the theatre as much more than entertainment."

"So do I."

"I know. But you like to think it's all about great art, you see: they see it as helping to educate society: even re-shaping society."

"If only any of them told jokes; or had a funny-peculiar mannerism; or farted; anything! I'm getting out as soon as I can," Ian said firmly.

"Have you told them yet?"

"Don't be daft. It's taken me a month to prove that if I'm pricked I bleed. This would be construed as deepest treachery – their very own Richard III caught in possession."

"Look," Willie said, rather reluctantly giving Ian the very blunt reassurance he so curiously but sorely wanted. "You've done the right thing. Your success in films has done you no good at all with the theatre critics. You haven't taken on a serious heavy role for some years – "

"I prefer comedy. I *love* comedy!" He mimicked Richardson perfectly.

"Never mind, you want to continue to be thought of for the big roles. This is a shrewd choice with a well-thought-of company full of integrity and worth and freshness – "

"All the things I lack." Ian collapsed, foppishly

"Exactly, all the things you lack. But some of it might rub off on you and it should see you through another year or so. You'll have to put in a real stint soon though. What are you doing next?"

"Broadway." Ian mentioned the play. "It's a good part," he continued defensively "and I shall enjoy it. I haven't had a real hit on Broadway."

"Depends what you call a real hit. It's a good part, but it won't *do* anything for you."

"What do you want it to do?" Again, the mood of the moment took over and Ian slid uncannily into the role of a fretful man past his youth, frustrated at his impotence. Sometimes Willie thought that he brought out the worst in Ian and that was why he came to see him: to exorcise that childish poison.

"It'll keep you in the public eye which you don't need and you'll be bankable which you don't need and you'll come out of it with exactly the same worries you have now."

"But richer."

"You're not going on about money again, are you?"

"It cost me thirteen hundred quid to get the car mended the other day. I could have bought a house for that when I started out."

"You're rich enough."

"You always say that! Everybody says that. But I pay tax up to my eyes, I have a wife who likes to make up for whatever she lacks by redecorating the house every ten minutes, a boy at school gobbling up fees, an agent, a lawyer, an accountant, a dentist for these bloody calcium-starved teeth, a face that demands over-tipping and a name that seems to announce that I'll pick up the bill."

"You've always worried about money and you've always had it."

"Because I've worried about it. Don't forget that between jobs I earn nothing."

"If you want to be rich," Willie said, following an old course, "go to Hollywood for three or four years and come back rich."

"I don't like Hollywood quite enough, dear boy, not quite . . . enough." Gielgud this time.

"You want to be a famous actor. That's what stops you."

"Does it matter?" Ian suddenly plummeted into gloom. Willie could have laughed but the despair was real enough. He filled up his friend's glass. "Who the hell cares, anyway? And who even recognises it? I've been praised for parts I've fumbled and criticised for parts I thought were – well, pretty good. It's always out there that the fame comes from. It's the audience and the critics who make those decisions. I have no centre."

"You can't change that."

"But if they're wrong? They have been, many a time. What if they're wrong about you being good or wrong about you being bad? Where does that leave you? At least in films there's some sort of perpetuity. Another lot can come and look; you can get another chance. But on stage, it's *then* that it happens – it can be just one or two nights when you know everything's absolutely right: and who's there? Who remembers? Even I can't properly remember, only the feeling. You want to shout out '*Look at me!* I've done it!' But you can't and you don't and it's gone. Like the whisky?"

68

"Yes."

"Duty-free. You may go on about my money, William, but I want you to tell me if it's really OK." He detailed his assets: the house, the pictures, the investments, the insurances – checking values with Willie at every point, marking these down like a reluctant buyer. "I'm still nowhere near being able to stop working."

"There's no reason why you should be," Willie said, tartly. "And you'd hate it if you were. No, you're OK. Comfortably off, not wealthy; probably never will be."

"But these sums I earn for films! It seems so much."

"It seems disgraceful to me," Willie agreed. "But, as you say, tax, and then what they call your life-style." Willie paused. "And those expensive and time-consuming affairs."

"Hm."

"Tell me how they're setting about the production."

Deftly, Ian outlined Jake's ideas, related them to other productions of the play and to other plays by Chekhov, and then, much more circumspectly, answered one or two questions about his own role.

"You know I don't like to talk about it."

Willie did not press him.

"What about you?" Ian asked, as if suddenly aware of his egocentricity.

Willie told him about the Begin project and now it was his turn to be helped because he had never met a better listener than Ian. Once again he seemed content to absorb, but the quality of his attention was such that Willie found himself articulating and clarifying ideas which would have lain buried for weeks and perhaps forever if Ian's concentration had not prised them into life. Ian was never afraid to assume total ignorance and ask the most obvious questions: who exactly formed the Irgun? Was Begin a literal believer in the biblical Kingdom of Israel? Was he a racist? Why did he emerge when he did on the political scene? Why not sooner? Would he never concede that there ever should be an independent Palestinian

69

state? Willie, whose reading had taken him into the Borgesian labyrinths of Middle East politics, found those and other simple questions to be grappling-hooks which hauled him back onto his main course.

When that was done and the whisky considerably lower, Ian, by a few almost unnoticeable touches, light as Japanese water-colour brush-strokes, discovered all he wanted to know about Willie and Joanna.

"Are you going over to New York again?" Ian asked.

"I've had my little outing, I'm afraid."

"We'll have to meet again before I go, then," Ian said, frowning as though to etch that thought onto his memory. "Though it's cheap enough to fly over for a weekend. I'd put you up."

"We'll see," Willie said, without much hope.

"Well. I'd like you to come. See the play. Tell me off."

Ian finished his drink, glanced at his watch and then flung out his arms in a long, unashamed, yawning stretch.

"I'll be off. We all clock in at 9.30 sharp. Donkey jackets *de rigueur*."

"You're loving it."

"Not so much *it*," Ian said, casually, keeping, Willie perceived, the last worry until the end.

• "Again?"

"Don't be like that, Willie," and Ian bounced up like a spry athlete, making Eric's sport-muscled movements seem dinosaural by comparison.

"And . . . ?"

"She *is* wonderful."

"And . . . ?"

"I'll tell you about her some day. It'll take a day."

"When she's gone."

"Maybe not; this time. Anyway," Ian was now impatient with the tease, "it isn't as if I swan around."

"It would be better for everyone if you did," Willie replied, earnestly.

Ian was made uncomfortable by this criticism of his morality.

There were certain things he disliked hearing, even from Willie.

"I'm not promiscuous, is that a crime?"

"You do fall in love."

"Is *that* a crime?"

"Sometimes I think it most certainly is," Willie said, emphatically.

Ian laughed. "You know the first girl I got, as we used to say, 'serious' about, you would remember her – you remember everybody – Jean Tomlinson, she was about fourteen, I was the older man: fifteen. Looking back it's like some terrible black Spanish sexual farce, one of those sickly chaste orgies Dali writes about in his nauseating memoir. We tortured each other. Both of us wanted to sleep with each other so desperately but – we didn't really know what to do, not with any feeling of certainty, and the one thing we did know was that we *should not do it at all*. We would cling to each other in the dark corners of the dance hall in the County Ballroom, Carlisle, practically soaked with the sweat and the tension and that wonderful honey turbulence that seemed to come from the devil to warn you off and egg you on at the same time. We had this elaborate scale of numbers – I can't quite remember, but kissing was number one, that was always OK; I think number two was touching tits through pullover or shirt and bra; number three touching tits through bra; number four touching tits full stop; number five holding hand between jammed-tight thighs – they *all* wore stockings then, now you're called a fetishist; number six was, if I recall correctly, one finger, generally index, not to move once in place, just lying there like a dead fish; number seven was when, I think, to the astonishment of both concerned, she moved in and rested her hand lightly on the flies above the old Adam now groaning and straining in the isolated darkness of its blessedly loose 'underpants'; number eight was her next move but I think I was allowed a little digital advance by then; number nine was a frantic breathless essay in frenzied mutual satisfaction without connection and number ten lay before us for two years, for twenty-four months, for a hundred

71

and four weeks, for seven hundred and whatever-it-is days before we finally, guiltily, terrifiedly, and so rapidly it was like a conjuring trick, became, as Barbara Cartland might say, one. See you."

He had heard the key in the lock, bowed to Joanna as she came in, made unimpeachable excuses and left.

"He hates me now," Joanna said, sadly, and waited to be offered a drink.

(5)

When Willie finally went to see Ian as Trigorin he was prepared for Ian but not for Caroline, whose smile which had given his miserable nights their only fleeting consolation.

After going backstage he walked the streets of London again like a newly arrived youth perturbed by both ambition and anxiety. He could scarcely believe that the pack of worries and preoccupations which had been on him for weeks and months had fallen away to such insignificance. It was as if he had become a vacuum and she the force sent to replenish it. He literally shivered at the thought that he might not have gone to see the play and might have missed her. As for Ian, such potentially murderous thoughts pounded into his brain – for Ian so clearly possessed her – such Sicilian revenges that he felt that he was turning into a different man, becoming his own Hyde on those same streets of London.

The alternation between the fragile but full and instant blossoming of a love and the savage onset of jealousy first exhilarated and finally began to exhaust him. It was as if two extremes of himself, only most scantily known and scarcely ever employed, had surged through the north and south gates of his long-fortressed self to sack and loot the city he had made of his cautious character. As if two hitherto repressed characters within him, one so light and loving that it shone with transcendental happiness, the other evil, sewer-dark and loathed, had been waiting all along to enter the stage of his life and now took their cue.

He did not know himself when, in the early hours of the morning, he arrived back at his flat. Partly to keep himself sane and partly to begin preparing and organising the long campaign to meet and know and perhaps he could dream, live with her, he went to his notebook.

Chapter Four

(1)

"I have poor eyes, he wrote, and without my spectacles I peer about like a mole in a mist. Huge sickly white half-moon circles hang blankly under the lower lids. My face is too fat and my chins indisputably plural. Hair: lustreless, in need of a seven-year course from one of those bouncy television shampoos. Eleven filled teeth, nicotine stains highly visible. Three teeth missing, thankfully at the sides. One duff kidney, long ago infected and diminished, now allowed to stay there only because I took the more sympathetic doctor's advice and ducked the not-quite-necessary operation. Blood pressure to be watched, however, as a result. A back which years of under-exercise has left exposed to sudden torturing wrenches and pulls. A belly; a pot belly; an established pot belly. Flat feet. Smoke. Drink. Eat convenience foods. No dress sense. Medium height, just."

That was about the external sum of it, he thought. The only possible optimistic conclusion could be that there was plenty to work on.

(2)

The crowd which had assembled for the Ban-The-Bomb march was estimated at a hundred and fifty thousand. Willie got there early: so did thousands of others. He had imagined there would be some sort of column he could carefully walk along until he found her. He was sure the Connect Company would be there. Ian had left for America three days before: he had left a couple of messages for Willie, who had not returned them.

74

Despite the fact that the crowd was made up of thousands of individuals of all ages and classes come from the four corners of the United Kingdom to walk a few miles through the middle of London, Willie felt that he needed an excuse to be there. His common sense told him that there must be many, like him, come for reasons other than the declared intention of the march. Yet he felt a parasite, selfishly set on a private course when all about him were devoting themselves to a public act of conscience. His excuse, if challenged (by whom? He recognised that it was crazy but still needed this insurance), was that he wanted to get a feeling of such a march so that he would be able to comment from first-hand experience should the peace movement prove influential enough to crop up in any discussion of the foreign policies of Reagan, Brezhnev, Schmidt and Thatcher, four of his current obit projects. It was not very convincing.

It was difficult enough to set about the task of finding a single body in this throng; much more difficult if you felt compelled not to seem to be looking. Willie could not overcome the shyness which oppressed him in crowds, however friendly – and this one was friendly to the point of heartiness. He did not like to stare in case he was caught staring. So he pecked his way down the jangling mass of anoraks, pushchairs, banners, punks, overcoats, sports jackets, fancy dress, sensible shoes, wellingtons, carrier bags, haversacks, trenchcoats, scarves, badges, placards and gravely polite policemen. He spotted David and turned away quickly, feeling guilty for the next twenty-four hours at that act of rejection, unabsolved until he met David the next day and learned that he had not been seen. Yet the small betrayal bothered him. He was losing himself.

Everything bothered him and yet nothing on earth would stop him searching for her. He only wanted to see her again. When Ian had introduced them after he had seen the play, he had been tongue-tied. He had longed to go back to the theatre for all the remaining performances but the tickets were sold out and he did not want to go through Ian, his only contact, to bypass the House Full notice. So he had stood in a doorway some distance from the Stage Door and waited, on those three remaining nights, for the sight of her coming out after the performance. Each time, she and Ian had come out last, each time slowly, arm in arm, in the contentment of two people who have just made love: and before Willie could focus properly, Ian's hired car had drawn up to take them away. He tried not to think how curious his behaviour was.

The need to see her was too strange to analyse. It was a need, though. He woke with it and slept with it, throughout his day he lived with it or sometimes it seemed in spite of it. He could imagine it to be in his bloodstream, in his nerves, in his infected brain – it saturated him and insisted on its dark presence every minute. He felt as if he were being withdrawn to this need, like an army to a redoubt, like antibodies to the source of a disease, like a trauma fingered to its cause. To manage it, to placate it, he allowed himself – he could not prevent it – the luxury of the most lurid dreams of possession and revenge. For the obsession was not only to love her but to have her love for Ian destroyed. He was ashamed of that. He was humiliated at the malevolence which roared through him like a fireball. He tried to quash it by calling it demeaning, useless, degrading, corrupt, immoral, by throwing the stones of his contempt at it – but it was like launching paper aeroplanes against a gale. And at other times he would feel prickled with the power of delight that he could engender such a force, feel himself almost literally exploding with a new delirious want to live, and everything about him, the furniture, the books, the streets, his colleagues, would themselves seem charged with an hallucinatory aura they had never possessed before. On those occasions he felt mythically strong: nothing, he knew then, and no one, could resist this torrential need – she would sense it, she would know it, she would understand that it was for her, for them; for ever, always – the Technicolor promises of idealised love clanged through his mind like the mad bells of Notre Dame roused to fury by Quasimodo: *forever, always, always, forever*. Caroline!

There she was.

Her windscreen-wiper wave threw him off balance. He stopped and gazed at her. He must have assumed his Mr Magoo expression because she waved again and directed him over to the gaggle around the white banner which carried the black message "NO BOMB – NO WAY – NO, NO, NO!"

"Marvellous, isn't it?" she cried, above the discordant sounds of a group which announced its views in a hastily-written song. "You saw most of this lot, didn't you, in the play?"

Willie nodded at the other actors and their friends who were huddled, he thought, in a rather too dramatic attitude, as if they were about to march on the Bastille. But, recognising Caroline's sincerity, he chided himself for being too critical. Perhaps, in a way, they were marching on the Bastille.

"I didn't expect to see you on one of these," Caroline said.

"I," Willie prepared to outline his elaborate excuse but it seemed so pompous that all he concluded was "thought I'd come along and see what it was all about."

"It's all about breaking the international suicide pact," Jake interrupted, grimly. "The people have to take the initiative now. Politicians have to be made to listen to the voice of the streets."

Caroline nodded and Willie was annoyed with himself for feeling embarrassed. Why could he not more easily accept this patently genuine and serious view?

"Who were you going to march with?" Caroline asked him.

"Well, I thought I'd just . . . tag along."

"You can join us," she said, helpfully. "It'll be a long morning."

A couple of young men dressed as skeletons cycled past shouting "Death to Cruise!" A mother snatched her small daughter from out of their path but her expression was not reproachful. Willie was beguiled by the multiplication of good feelings: it was as if everyone there was determined to

77

demonstrate not only against the bomb but for the belief that people could be benevolent towards each other.

"That's very kind," Willie answered. "Thank you."

She smiled at him and he let that undivided gift imprint itself on his memory. That was the last direct contact he had with her for some time. Like the others, he found himself looking around. The crowd seemed full of people wanting to know who was with them. Like the others he ticked off generations, classes, accents, backgrounds, building up his own portrait of this massive gathering. He had read about the spectacular revival of the CND movement over the past year: the unprecedented size of the meetings in centres such as Manchester and Newcastle, in suburbs, provincial towns and villages. He had followed the arguments in the papers, thought about E. P. Thompson's articles, but remained unconvinced by the unilateralist case. It was long past the time, he thought, when a gesture by the United Kingdom would matter at all to those other nations who were in the process of acquiring the bomb: and the influence on the USA and the USSR would be negligible – perhaps even dangerous, creating a small power vacuum which could result in another area of turbulence.

Yet as the crowd began its slow shuffle towards Hyde Park, he wished that he could have been a believer. It seemed so sane: clear the world of weapons, clear the world of bombs, seize the chance offered by these nuclear exterminating machines and work towards abolishing war. Perhaps this was the final test or joke of God: here is your earth, here are the means to desecrate it entirely – show me what you are. Who could not be on the side of these earnest, cheerful and determined people who were neither sandalled cranks nor flimsy bandwagoners but in the main a thoughtful army demonstrating for decency? Willie could approve the bringing of pressure to bear by such a show of strength: indeed, he too thought the politicians so petrified before mirror images of their own nightmare past and so suffocated by the commitments of their own complex-ridden present that it was conceivable that only the force of a simple street faith could introduce a fresh impulse or fresh thinking

78

into détente. It was the "I want it now" attitude of so many of the marchers which gave him pause: their impatience, though it could be justified by the evidence of the silos and submarines, the missile bases and the threatening talk of tactical nuclear warfare, seemed to him as dangerous as the impatience of the politicians with the arguments the disarmers proposed.

He had plenty of time to ruminate: the column was much longer than anticipated and the police control reduced the mass to a regulated flow which eventually took more than five hours to complete two or three miles. Caroline's attention, which dutifully included him, was generalised. She was constantly, almost nervously, chatting to her friends – but never for long, because her eyes would sweep away to scan the crowd, as if she wanted its size and temper to be indelibly registered, as if she were as much a witness as a participant, wanting to be able to say, "No, it was like *this*: I was *there*." Willie found relief in his lack of obligation to engage her in direct conversation. He thought of this as a lucky easing-in.

Only the slogans jarred. "Jobs Not Bombs," "Reagan – Out, Out, Out!" This not only reduced idealism to banality, it offended against his balancing soul. Willie was a comparative man. He would listen to a litany of complaints about the condition of the country but then find himself comparing it with two generations before, or with the conditions in other countries, or with the expectations you could reasonably demand given ordinary fallibility, and always discovered the situation to be far more happily qualified than any dogmatist or radical would admit. If anything, he considered the persistent fashion for complaint and the apparently perpetual licence to sneer not only self-indulgent and second-rate but, more importantly, usually untrue to any rounded view. Yet he had to confess that a rounded view could be a euphemism for passivity. And this placid snail of Britons could indeed be right, despite their slogans.

It was in the park that he felt the greatest cheat. While various leaders and politicians railed into the whistling microphones, while the television cameras turned and the

79

photographers snapped up the gestures, his sole concern was to stand just to one side of Caroline but slightly behind her so that he could look at her without staring. As the voices ebbed towards them across the surging crowd before them, she listened as intently as if she had been aware of being present at the Sermon on the Mount and needed no convincing by miracles added to the words. Willie caught, not her fervour, but a concern for the issue through her conviction. It was unthinkable that mere technology should be in a position to blast her into fire or cover her with the leprosies of fallout.

He had no feeling of the Apocalypse – nothing of the end in fire and flood which would surely come were these manufactured comets to come down like the judgement or contempt of a Creator. He listened to the speeches, speeches full of righteousness and statistics, but without the charge of peril he had felt so often from the pulpit when he was a boy. Surely if ever there was a time to translate brimstone into reality and to alarm the world with the threat of the Four Horsemen, it was now. Perhaps now that his own private emotions had been so deeply upset he could respond only to the most profound demands on his spirit, and these men did not make that demand. Where was the threat of the black pit and the end of all life and hope? Or was the End no longer a truly profound fear in an irreligious age? Surely no age ever became so detached from that most basic of faiths – staying alive? But because he could feel no revelation, Willie could merely nod thoughtfully now and then in agreement with this or that point. He could not be drawn in, not even by the piety on the face of Caroline and others he saw.

He wanted to leave. It was enough that he had been near her for so long. More than he had expected, more, he thought, than he deserved. He was not sufficiently internally organised to do anything but retreat, digest and imagine ways to secure further meetings. Nothing could come of this: there were too many people for any sort of privacy, and besides, it was not the right time. He found it difficult to know what to do. Had he been able to stalk her all the morning, then the possessive intimacy ot his feelings could have been sustained at a level of intensity which this mundane proximity denied. He wanted to protect his obsession.

Yet it was difficult to go.

In a break between two speakers, she turned to him, her excitement now refined into solemnity. She looked at him, as he thought, searching out the genuine basis of his commitment. He found himself unable to meet the look he so much longed to look on.

"Let's meet soon," she said.

Willie's heart seemed literally to leap up towards his throat. He nodded.

"That would be . . . shall I phone you?"

She gave him her number and then smiled, sweetly, conspiratorially, lovingly he could have thought. And with the seven numbers like a blessed code inscribed on his cigarette packet, he eased away, knowing that nothing better could possibly come from the day, cutting across the loyal pilgrimage of marchers still walking patiently towards speeches they would be too late to hear.

(4)

"It's very fashionable, isn't it?" Caroline said as he ushered her into the restaurant. Willie glanced rapidly around at the cool green panelled walls, the fresh flowers on all the tables, the young casually-expensively dressed clientèle, the costly lack of fuss: he had not been before.

"So they say," he replied as they were led to a corner table. He kept his gaze firmly forward not to seem to be seeking out celebrities.

They ordered drinks, Willie quickly decided what he would eat and waited for Caroline to choose. She read through the long menu as if it were a detective story – no line to be jumped for fear of missing a clue.

Like an alcoholic knowing the hopelessness of the gesture, he had forced himself to wait for a few days before ringing her up.

He was terrified of two things: of frightening her off and, equally, being too breezily friendly.

"I know this appears to be a contradiction," he wrote in his notebook, "but meeting her so easily in that march destroyed the plan I had. I would have been content just to watch her for a while. I did not want to get too close. God knows why, because I also wanted to be with her every minute. But I knew how difficult that would be and I had my own plan – to do it very gently, to test myself in some way, to observe her unobserved for longer and find out more so that when we *did* meet I would be more fully prepared. I had looked forward to that waiting. At that early stage I was alarmed by what I felt and I wanted to observe it – possibly even to give it a chance to die away. I had actually enjoyed the banal romantic waiting for her across the cold street opposite the Stage Door: it was a form of worship. So ridiculous, as if she were a Lady in a tower, but it made sense to me.

"That happy-go-lucky meeting at the CND march made no sense. It spoiled the pattern – it took me closer to her but in such a casual public way that my feelings, which meant so much to me, were forced down; there was no place for them. I remembered the writer Aschenbach in Thomas Mann's *Death in Venice* and how carefully he had stalked his – prey? love? – and from what a distance. I envied Aschenbach's peculiar, isolated pain. I wanted that loneliness. Love and fantasies could grow there and leave hope intact. The crowd killed all that.

"I forced myself to hold out for six days. In that time, IRA bombs blew up in London, the war went on in El Salvador, people all over the world suffered unjust lives and died violent deaths, the space shuttle stood by, the world of news I had fed on so attentively staggered through its dramas and most of my waking and unconscious life was directed towards Caroline. Sometimes I could not believe the strength of it and went to bed half wanting it to have disappeared when I woke up. But every morning it was there, again; and I welcomed it."

"We'll have two terrines, one Sole Meunière, one Monkfish, please. And a selection of vegetables."

82

"Thank you, sir."

Willie had not been prepared for her looking so beautiful or so elegant. As Nina in the play she had trembled with the strenuous emergence of her passion but the part had called up that vulnerable, outsider, failed-from the start part of her which was moving but not in any conventional way beautiful. On the CND march she had appeared more as one of a group than a distinctive individual. Tonight, though, her hair brushed finely back showing the high white front of her brow, her face lightly made up, eager with an unhidden sense of anticipated pleasure which made it a fit frame for that smile, her shoulders white as her brow, the thin straps of a fine black silk dress tracing the most slender lines of emphasis on the skin –

"Ian bought me this dress," she said, as she thought interpreting his look. "I could never have afforded it."

Willie pressed his feet onto the floor as the room swayed before him for an instant. With a hypocrisy of which he would have thought himself incapable, his face reacted unsuspiciously and produced the grimace of a smile.

"Silk," she said, rather proudly.

"Yes."

She wriggled, just perceptibly, remembering, he was sure, the giver.

"It's wonderful to wear silk."

"That's – " Willie reached out for his drink: his throat was dry. "That's what the actresses used to say in those old films."

"He's so generous," she said, shyly, prodding him on.

And now Willie knew why she had greeted him so kindly and agreed to see him so promptly! How could he have been such a fool as not to guess? He was unprepared – and unable, incapable of even thinking about Ian without a swirl of darkness mantling the jealousy which sat among his fears like an evil toad.

"Very," he agreed, emphatically.

"Has he always been like that?"

83

"Yes," Willie said, prompted by his sense of fairness to bend the evidence.

Caroline looked at him with a conspiratorial tenderness. If only the conspiracy had been about them. Now that Ian had given them a focus, he could see her again as he wanted to see her and he longed to reach out and lift the thick shining hair, to let his hand trail down the fine cheek, to stroke and hold her.

"Ah!" he said. "Food."

They ate between compliments on what they were eating but Willie found it difficult to swallow. This was only a respite. She would return to Ian the moment she could.

"He makes me feel so much more alive," she said. "He's got so much more life in him than anybody else I've ever met."

"Yes," Willie agreed, nervously wiping his mouth with his napkin – a rather spinsterish gesture, she thought.

"Was he always like that?"

"Oh, Ian hasn't changed much over the years."

"He isn't at all spoilt," she agreed. "You would never know . . . what was he like at school? He talks about you a lot," she added, perceptibly sensing Willie's reluctance and throwing him what she considered to be the flattery of inclusion.

Willie braced himself and, with all the patience he could assemble, he addressed himself to her questions. There was no end to them. The food and wine came and went, he smoked, ordered more wine, coffee, a liqueur. She drank more than he had expected – out of indifference, he thought, to everything but this new information. It was a torment. At times he almost panicked and wanted to cry out "He's a bastard! An unreliable, self-preoccupied bastard! Don't trust him or believe him and please don't love him because he will always let you down!" But, like a partial defence witness, he answered her as if he knew his evidence were crucial to the case.

He developed a severe headache and asked for a glass of water and an aspirin. Caroline looked concerned and a little crestfallen.

"You have a headache, haven't you?" Grateful as he was for the sympathy, he could only nod. "It'll be all right."

The band across his forehead tightened even more fiercely, being admitted.

"I've talked too much, haven't I? About Ian."

He waited, pretending to look for his water, wondering whether he had been caught out. It was imperative that she should know nothing of his feelings for her: to have them admitted now would give him no chance at all.

"I enjoy talking about him," he said, lying yet again. "I had a sore throat this morning – a cold – and too much drink has set off the alarm bells."

"Ian gets terrible headaches."

So she had simply meant that she had talked too much. The "about Ian" had been added for little other purpose than to hear herself say his name again. It had not occurred to her that it was the subject, not the act of talking, which had driven him into this painful psychosomatic reaction. There was some relief in that.

"Ian said you were a marvellous listener – and a marvellous friend," she rushed on.

He put the pill on his tongue and toasted her in mineral water.

"Ian only drank mineral water when we were rehearsing," she said. "After we'd opened he drank wine and everything, but not in rehearsals."

It was a nightmare. Willie coughed as the aspirin stuck and then had the humiliation of a waiter urgently pounding his back while Caroline looked alarmed at his fiery wheezing countenance. His glasses slipped down to the tip of his nose.

When he was settled, he asked for the bill.

"It's very expensive here, isn't it?" she asked.

Willie had no answer. It was. But what was there to be gained by agreeing?

"I made Ian start coming back to my place. I was costing him a fortune."

The bill came to thirty-six pounds. Willie rounded it up to forty for the tip. "That was lovely," she said as they came out into the street. "Is your headache any better?"

85

"It is a bit, yes."

"Aspirins are supposed to be very bad for you." Ian says? He waited. "I thought you were going to choke to death."

"Ah well."

"My treat next time," Caroline said, smiling at him. "It won't be as posh, but definitely my treat."

She kissed him on the cheek – such a brushed cliché of a kiss, he would rather not have had it, rather been thought of as better than what was described by this polite lip-service.

"Thanks again," she said. "I'd better belt for the tube. They stop around this time. Bye."

He watched her, as he knew he would, as she walked swiftly down the narrow street. She did not look back, as he knew she would not.

He felt an intolerable despair.

(5)

Willie rarely got really drunk. That night he got really drunk. If you were not rich enough to belong to a private club, the only place he knew where you could drink yourself insensible was in one of the mean basement bars he vaguely remembered. It was not difficult to pay your way in. The penalty was the music. He persuaded himself it was a blessing. No thought could exist in a head so full of alcohol and rock. That was good.

Joanna was waiting up, her green satin dressing-gown wide open revealing her too-young transparent pink nightdress.

"You've been with somebody else," she said harshly. "Don't lie."

The weight of exhaustion inside his head was such that he thought it might topple him over. He forced himself almost to attention and stared at her, stupidly.

"And by the look of you it was a disaster," she said.

"Do you want to be sick?" she said.

"If that's the way you want to go then you have to tell me, Willie. I can't throw stones but I've got to know."

"Who is she? Not that it matters. You are a silly old fart."

86

The room swung away before him like a sway-boat: it came into his head and seemed to scoop out his mind as it swung backwards and forwards, sucking out his brain. His forehead felt cold.

"Bathroom!" she said. She took his arm and hurried him there. Just in time.

On his knees in front of the lavatory, tears streaming down his face, his stomach retching up the night, the food, the wine, the coffee, the liqueurs, the whisky, the pain, his body ejecting the night in cramp-fierce convulsions. On his knees as if in prayer, clutching the rim of the bowl as if it were an altar rail, looking up to the cistern as to a cross, muttering "Oh God, Oh my God" in prayer and penance for the despair, shriven and shaken at last, shivering, stinking but emptied and cleansed of the poisons, he got up and saw his wretched image in the small oval mirror. His own image.

"I have to know," Joanna said. "You have to tell me the truth."

"Why did I refuse to? (Willie wrote a few days later). Why did I continue to refuse? It might have made her better: it could not have made her much worse. More importantly, I would have told the truth, as I was brought up to do, as I believe in doing, as I prided myself that I had always tried to do. But the truth would have admitted her to some inkling of Caroline and I could not bear that. I was not afraid – or only a little afraid – of Joanna's possible interference and nagging: what I most feared was sharing what I had. What little I imagined I had.

It had all gone wrong – not just that terrible evening which even now, so long past, in remembrance can make me stiffen with horror. Not too strong a word. The woman I worshipped used me to spend time by proxy with the man she loved. Her love for him was undisguised and so powerful that it slapped me across the face again and again like some primitive interrogation technique. I was ill for about three days afterwards – not just the booze, hardly that at all. I did not know whether I was mad or sane, whether I was a fool or finally wise

87

to a true and good instinct, whether I had any chance at all and if by some miracle I had, what I would make of it.

What puzzled me at the time was Caroline's buoyancy. I did not know then that he had written several notes to her, irresponsible in their commitment, and promised to hoist her over to New York when he had organised himself properly. I had expected her to be in the mood I had sensed when seeing her on the stage – strained with the effort of concealing her sense of imminent loss. His selfish, idle letters had reversed that. She believed them, she wanted so much to believe them that far less ardour on his part would still have had the same effect. Perhaps he found that he loved her still, even at a distance? To be fair.

What had gone wrong for me was the whole story I had constructed. I had thought it through so carefully. I knew that I needed to map out this unfamiliar ground in detail before setting foot on it. In my plan, I was to shadow her for days and even for weeks before encountering her. To ease myself in, to enjoy the pleasure – and it would have been that for me – of pursuing, imagining, dreaming, courting at a distance. We would have met, finally, tentatively. Met again, a little later, and gradually I would have become known to her, useful, reliable, perhaps even the role of confidant would have been given to me as she struggled through her misery at being so ruthlessly junked by Ian. But the CND march – that crowd, one-headed, like all marching crowds, each person wanting nothing more than to be at one with the next person and as alike as possible – that denial of her uniqueness followed by the dinner where her questions scraped across my mind like broken chalk over a blackboard. It should never have been like that.

Yet it destroyed nothing. When I began to put myself together again I found that her presence was just as powerful: and spiced now by an urgent physical desire. Lust says it better. In recollection I wanted to reach out and touch not only her face, but her breasts, her thighs, hold her as fiercely as I could and, I have to confess it, shameful though it is, even hurt her with the force of what I felt. It sickened me to think that, but there is no point in evasion or concealment now."

(6)

Willie learnt that his mother was ill but he did not want to leave London. He had been with Caroline only a few times since their dinner but he had managed to see her almost every day, spending his lunchtimes spying on her. The company was back in rehearsal for another play and it was comparatively easy for him to be certain of catching sight of her on the way from the rehearsal room to the pub.

In the days following the receipt of the letter describing her illness, he learnt to despise himself. He phoned his mother, of course, and wrote, advised, half-promised. He displayed all the appearance of filial concern but delivered none of the substance. He thought that he had never behaved as badly – and for what? A glimpse, another painful evening where he was treated more as a father than as the contemporary of the lover of the one he loved. A mind invaded by a disturbance was perhaps no more than the last attempt of a missed adolescence determined to assert itself before it was too late. For he could easily despise this new love, this apparently all-blighting crunch of feeling which was callously prepared to degrade so much else that he valued, so imperious in its demands on his energy that it drove out all those small contacts of care and concern which had worthily and pleasurably occupied his time. But yet it was glorious! He had never been so alive.

For he felt a power and zest of sensation he had barely imagined. Caroline, as the individual he was getting to know, as the woman he desired, as the undeniable object of so much that he had not known he wanted and longed for, gave him an energy which seemed to burn through the disappointed layers of his years and strip away the making-do, the patching up, the thrifty compromises of an undemanding life. Simply walking down a grim London street after seeing her on an unattractive

89

late November day could now be more exhilarating than anything he could remember. It had ignited him and he neither could nor would quench it. However dangerous it might be – no, because of the danger . . .

The neglect, though, of a clear duty unnerved him.

"Your mother phoned," Joanna said when he came in later than usual.

"What did she say?"

"Nothing." Joanna had long since given up the remotest pretence of being interested in her mother-in-law. "But she seemed to want to chatter on. So we chattered on."

"I'll ring her back."

"You phoned her last night. What's going on?"

"I think she's feeling a bit down at the moment."

"She sounded bright enough to me. David seems to have been a hit. She was fussing about him like an old hen."

"They get on very well. And," Willie regretted the next words the moment he uttered them, "he probably responds to a bit of mothering."

"Which I don't give him."

"Joanna," Willie said, uncharacteristically compelled to be direct. "You scarcely even like him."

"He's a drop-out. And he's a drip."

"He's not successful enough for you."

"I just want him to be good at something. He had all the talent when he was a boy, and all the chances."

"He wore himself out trying to please you."

"I don't want to talk about David."

"Why not? We should do."

"He's twenty. He has his own life. You don't choose your children."

"I think you've suffocated him."

"You want the whole world to pretend to be nice, Willie. I don't."

"Aren't you afraid sometimes what might happen to him? What he might do?"

"He has his own life. That's that. What am I supposed to do?

90

Stuff him with soft-boiled eggs and home-made jam? I can't do that."

"No. You can't, can you?"

"Stop casting me as the bitch-mother, Willie. He didn't want what I could give him and what he wants now doesn't interest me. And I don't want to talk about it. What's wrong with your mother?"

"I don't know."

"Why don't you go and see her? If one of your old boys kicks the bucket you can be back in a few hours on the train. Why don't you?"

"Perhaps I will."

"What's bothering you, Willie?"

"Nothing."

"You are such a lousy liar. Why are you losing weight and tarting yourself up?"

"Please, Joanna."

"It *has* to be another woman. Probably somebody young and pitiful. And I'd bet you haven't even screwed her."

Willie felt himself rock, slightly, as the image of Caroline suddenly reared up before him. An anger he did not know he possessed threatened to throw itself onto her.

"Well well," Joanna said, softly. "Bull's eye."

"I'll phone my mother."

"Willie." He looked at her squarely, without pretence. Her eyes panicked and then that flush of tears which had once been so ready came as if to disguise the fear or attempt to rescue it. But she continued. "You don't have to phone this minute. Why don't you tell me?"

He had no answer. As superstitiously or instinctively as some people are said to fear to have their photograph taken because they believe it takes away their virtue, Willie dumbly believed that to mention Caroline to Joanna would lead to the destruction of that image of her which now mattered so much to him.

"Worse than I thought," Joanna said, almost sympathetically, tapping, it seemed, the roots of his reluctance.

"I'll phone."

"I'll make some supper. Willie?"

"Yes."

"I could have had another life, you know, with somebody else. Not too long ago, either. Even now, maybe. But I thought we were together . . . after all that business." She hated to refer to her illness. "We are, aren't we?"

"Of course."

"I thought you needed me." She absorbed Willie's reaction quite steadily. "I know all your friends believe the opposite, it's good old Willie sacrificing himself to prop up that terrible boozy old wife of his, but I know it isn't like that. You're the one who has to be propped up. That's why I stayed with you. It was a way of saying 'Thanks'."

In the slight pause the true agony of the loss seemed to strike both of them. Joanna shivered. Willie saw that what they had was not without love or honour, that perhaps his acceptances had even provoked her serial of betrayals, that the cords and threads and thongs of a married lifetime could multiply as magically as they could seem to disappear. Joanna saw his going.

"I'd better phone," he said.

"Are you not going to answer me?"

He looked to her desperately for a lifeline. She hesitated and then she nodded and walked slowly towards the kitchen.

(7)

"It's just that I was thinking of going home to the Lakes for the weekend and it occurred to me you might like a lift. After all," Willie grimaced as he injected the distancing jocularity into his tone, "you told me you live over the Border. That's just up the road."

"When would you be going?"

"Oh, some time after lunch on Friday." He left the specific time carefully open: he had rehearsed.

"I could be free by about four. If I took my bag to the

92

rehearsal . . . maybe even before." Her part was not very big this time: Willie suspected subtle comradely punishment for her success with Ian. "It's a nice idea . . . Yes . . . Thank you."

Thank *you*: he prevented himself.

"Shall I pick you up? It would save time."

"That would be lovely."

"At the rehearsal room?"

"Yes. The address – "

"I know it. You told me," Willie added quickly, hoping he sounded chiding.

"Make it three," she said. "I'm sure that will be fine. What a *lovely* idea!"

Caroline put down the phone and glanced around the empty flat furtively as if she had been doing something wrong. Willie's invitation enabled her to solve, too neatly for comfort, a problem which had been taxing her. Ian had not been able to bring her over to New York in November as he had hoped to do but he was flying back to London for Christmas – a time, until now, spent by Caroline in a dutiful family circle. Nothing would have taken her away from London when the possibility of seeing Ian was there, but she owed her parents a seasonal visit. A weekend at the beginning of December would be much less than they wanted but at least it would be something. She could just about claim work throughout most of the holiday period; it *was* almost true that she could not really get away that far at the time. For Ian she was bending the truth.

Willie had been such a help, she reflected, as she went back to lie on her bed and sort through Ian's letters, telling her so much that she did not know about Ian. The table beside the bed was like a display cabinet for Ian. She had snaffled several of the production photographs and winkled some publicity stills out of him. They were arranged like a flush of saints about a peasant's cross. On the bed were his letters. Now and then he phoned from New York – at barmy times; she loved those calls. But the letters were her real treasure.

93

"Darling darling Caroline,

Are you real and truly mine? In my eyes you always shine; draughts of you like richest wine, pour into this Valentine – end of rhyme. Hello sweetheart. You have a wonderful name for my worse than verse; Amo Caro's lovely line. It's 2.33 a.m. by my digital tell-all and cold New York is thirteen (lucky for some!) storeys and five degrees below. Yes. But just wine. Californian. Good stuff. Believe the ads.

Well, they're still coming in and laughing where they should be and standing at the end to clap us on and off and we clap back as if we were party officials at a Soviet conference. Hard to keep the ego down to football size. It's a good place for the poor old thing to go on the rampage. Like taking a housebound Afghan onto a heath and watching it do what it's wanted to do for months – just race away. Everybody's seen the play or seeing the play or knows somebody who . . . and they know the takings, the reviews, the gossip – being in New York's like being in a musical anyway. Being in a successful play here is double cream on icing. So the domesticated British ego stuffed under the table or down the trousers for so long finds itself not only allowed but encouraged to behave like the ham it's always ached to be. I keep an eye on it, though, as it snowballs through Central Park and clambers up the Empire State like King Kong – look what happened to him! And snowballs melt.

It is entirely ridiculous that I sit here in this New World luxury with New Worlds below (cut the crap – Ed.) Sorry. It is odd (*odd*? What's *odd* about it – get to the point – Ed.) OK. Sitting here, in this luxury apartment with its walking telephones and twenty channel television, spaceship kitchen, pile so deep you can lose your slippers in it, rude-boy sauna and ruder jacuzzi. (That is nothing less than a straight show-off.) Who cares about the furnishings?

I miss you. I had no idea I would miss you like this. I miss your smile, your breasts, your sparkle at everything. I miss you undressing or being undressed and being there underneath, above, me in you until I think that I will reach up to

94

your heart itself. All I want to say is that I want you now and I think I will want you forever, to walk with, talk to, hold, sometimes feel a terrible tender savagery towards and love all of you all the time. I'll be with you soon. Remember what we've already had. There's more, more, and more.

Love,
Ian"

(8)

After the phone call, Willie went doggedly into the bathroom for what had become a nightly exercise. He locked the door.

The new contact lenses were hidden behind several unused bottles of aftershave – presents from secretaries whom he had not the heart to tell that he was allergic to aftershave. He opened the stiff plastic lids, took off his glasses and looked at the tiny lenses with trepidation. They hurt.

As if preparing a drug, he measured out minute quantities of cleansing and lubricant to prepare them thoroughly. The plug was in the plughole to avoid the most obvious danger. A dark green towel was on the floor as a safety net.

Forcing open his reluctant eyelids with two reluctant fingers he made a gentle stab at finding the pupil. A clumsy shot resulted in quite frantic pain and a messy search around the eye for the slithering off-target missile. Willie had always been squeamish. This time he popped on both at the first attempt and for the first few minutes enjoyed the relief of renewed sight.

He looked at himself. His eyes looked strange, foreign to the rest of his face, like those very thin, very white legs which appear on the beach when unfit middle-aged men roll up their trousers to risk a paddle. The skin around them needed to be weathered; it looked sickly, even on that unruddy face. He patted it to toughen it up. The eyes themselves stared back at him, apparently transfixed in a startled stare. It would never do. But the optician had said it would take time. Today's schedule was one hour and twenty minutes continuous. It was a long time to spend in the bathroom.

He ran a bath and slid into and out of it quickly, his hands cupped under his chin at all times, ready for any pop-out lens. When he dried himself he shut his eyes, despite the beginnings of soreness, in case the movement jolted the lens out or, what was worse, off into a remote corner of his eyeball from which all the squinting and prodding appeared ineffective until he would panic into a fantasy of bulbous lids and operating tables and the scalpel going in to recapture the escaped lens. Then he put down the seat on the lavatory, sat on it, reached out for his cigarettes and tried to work. It was essential, the optician said, to try to proceed as normal.

Willie gave himself some easy but necessary work. With the towel flopped about his shoulders and the cigarettes ready to devour, he took up his papers and checked through the roughout of the Begin profile.

1. Film. Begin SOF. "The settlement of the Jews in Eretz Israel . . . right of every Jew."
   Applause cutaway.
   Begin at mike for another twenty seconds, for the opening commentary.
2. Stills. Begin as a young man
   – Jabotinsky
   – Begin and wife
   – British Wanted lists: pan to Begin as Rabbi in disguise.
3. Nazi persecution of Jews: fifty-five seconds of people being herded, concentration camps.
4. British refuse immigrants. (Movietone News Film)
   Crowded ships, British troops brutally taking people to other ships. 45 secs.
5. British arrest Palestinians, armoured cars. (Pathé) 30 secs.
6. Haganah men in training. (Pathé) 30 secs.
7. Movietone story on King David Hotel – 1'30"
   Street scenes Jerusalem
   People at the Wailing Wall
   The new city
   King David Hotel

96

Explosion
Wreckage. Stretchers etc.
8. Begin SOF from Interview A. "All our operations were planned . . . as everybody knows in history."
9. British leave. Pathé film of farewell parade. Troops onto ships. Flag down. 40 secs.
10. Independence. Pathé material – Ben Gurion declares Independence Parade and celebrations. 45 secs.
11. Pathé Material. Border kibbutz. Shells. Jewish soldiers. 30 secs.
12. Jewish soldiers attack village. (BBC film) 30 secs.
13. Begin at mike Tel Aviv '49.
    Begin votes Jan. '49.
    Begin wife and child.
    Begin with grandchildren. '77.
14. Six Day War. (UPITN film. 12.6.67.) 30 secs.

As his itching weakening eyes worked on, Willie was conscious of missing what had always been the treat for him at such times, the wallowing which automatic pedestrian work enabled you to do. The feeling that you were firmly attached to facts but at liberty to drift about in the vague but pleasurable atmosphere of private speculations. There were still occasional flickers. He could not read through the script without being drawn yet again into the passionate history of this extraordinary people. Its roots and traditions were so powerfully transfused into the roots and traditions of his own so different culture. The faces of generations of rabbis and scholars merged into the photographs of the modern Israelis, the echoes of Gideon resounded about the modern wars; pogrom and holocaust were constantly present as their unimaginable shadow spread over all the twists and turns of contemporary attitudes; theories on life and work and sex were cross-hatched on the backcloth of this fierce story which switched so bewilderingly from the most ancient to the most present of days and dangers. Yet the vain discomfort of his eyes tugged away his attention. Another loss.

The gain, though, was there, he thought, and it was that

97

which preoccupied him as the minimum of attention was paid to the careful script. He had taken an initiative. Caroline would be with him in the car about seven hours there and the same number of hours coming back. The expectation from those hours was something he massaged through his mind with deliberate slowness. He did not want to plan everything at once, repelling the rush of things he would say and strategies he would employ; to be so close to her for such a time was enough for now. At last, he thought, it had a chance to start.

For the final quarter of an hour of his stretch, he was forced to put aside his papers. His eyes were streaming. He made himself go through with it, cold now on the lavatory seat, choosing to ignore the observation his former self would have made on this weeping, shivering figure; altered and sustained by a love he did not want to understand but had yielded to, for better or worse, wholly.

Chapter Five

"I never realised, (Willie wrote) how enjoyable – enjoyable! My restraint seems to be coming back fast, but I can't write 'wonderful' without putting inverted commas around it, somehow making light of it, back to the fear and the mockery of anything but subdued feelings, the grey zones of timidity and compromise – I never did realise, though, that being in a car with someone you love, driving a long distance, music playing, scenery changing, the pleasant fug of heat, the steadying remarks, the intimate moving through space together, could be so happy. I remembered those American films which seemed to consist of nothing else but couples in cars streaming across the central plains, rock on the cassette, vast landscapes and vaster skies swallowing up the midget missile. Those passages often had an exhilaration way beyond the merit of the film and I used to think it was to do with speed and music and the wide open spaces of the mighty USA, seemingly so gigantic and still such a wilderness. After that seven-hour journey with Caroline I changed my mind.

The real attraction was of being together in what was virtually a house and yet roving with the mobility of nomads. The satisfaction, of contented cohabitation are hard to show and rare to see. In the car, though, we were together, dependent on each other for security and company, living and working to one end during those hours; home. Perhaps that sense of being home is the most fundamental attraction of those acres of film in cars: all those Americans are actually responding to the best home they've got. Yet it satisfies that other extreme, as powerful as the feeling of rootedness, the urge to roam, to pick over the planet, to gypsy life away. These two states, the fortress home and the nomad world, the ego and the id, Cain and Abel, the man of property and the wanderer, are well met in a long car journey. It was our home for that while.

I often re-run that journey. We settled down in the front seats like the oldest of friends. She had brought a thermos of tea and some chocolate in case the motorway's cafés were too crowded or too repellent. I had cleaned out the car. Even settling into the safety-belts felt as if we were taking care of each other. I had taken the car in for a service.

It's like having a private film and a private projection room to be able to recall that journey, luxuriating in the search for finer details, 'seeing' her face, 'hearing' her comments on what we passed and what we saw, feeling such empathy when we agreed not to stop for tea but swing off the main road to search out a little pub for a drink and a toasted sandwich. The Oak Tree it was called, just past Birmingham. There was a coal fire, we were the only people in a bar which glittered with horse brasses and smelt of beer and wax polish. It was during that trip that she must have understood what I felt for her, I think: but she did not make any show of acknowledging it."

(2)

Although Willie did not get to his mother's house until after midnight, she was waiting up for him. It made him feel like a schoolboy again.

"I thought you'd be hungry," she said, "after the drive."

"You should be in bed."

"I have a nap in the afternoons now. Just like an old woman." She smiled to hide her vexation at this admission of weakness.

"I'm sorry I'm so late."

"It's a long way," she reassured him. "The weather report said that there was some fog."

In the South Midlands. Comforting fog, he had found it,

100

even further islanding Caroline and himself, slowing them down, splicing their commitment closer –

"Only a patch," he said. "How are you?"

"Fine," she replied. "I thought a cold supper would be best."

It was elegantly laid out on the dining-table: locally cured ham, thin slices of rare beef, a coleslaw salad, fresh Cheddar cheese, Carr's water biscuits "and there's some of my chutney," she said. "You say you like that."

He was touched by the perfect service. It came out of a world he had left so long ago, not only the world of a well-organised and attended-upon childhood but a world in which intelligent independent-minded women of character quietly accepted the task of looking after the man of the house, taking on the tradition which all his present acquaintances had broken with. It was as if the slow-motion film of a breaking egg were being run backwards before his eyes and things were instantly once more what they had always so perfectly been.

"Would you like a drink?" he asked her.

"Not at this time of night. What would you like?"

"I'll help myself."

The level in the whisky bottle was exactly as he had left it months ago.

His mother sat discreetly in profile while he ate.

The tranquillity of the house disturbed him. His own thoughts were strained and scattered – towards Joanna, Ian, the work he had to do, plans for driving Caroline back and perhaps teasing her into a day in the Lakes with him (he had subtly prepared her for that): this homely peace was foreign. He ate as if he were whispering in a church.

Heaving up the sense of obligation which had once come so effortlessly, he said something about his work, lied about Joanna, asked about his old friends in the town, painted a falsely optimistic portrait of David.

"I was worried about him, you know," his mother said. "He should never have been doing that farm work in the first place. He was forcing himself. There was something about him that worried me."

101

"He's had a difficult time."

His mother made no reply: few people – except those who were glaringly disadvantaged – were allowed to have had a "difficult" time compared with the privations of her own generation. Willie felt her censure but did not challenge it. He was beginning to be aware of the tension in that clear, almost baby-skinned face on which the severe lines lay uncomfortably like intruders which would soon be wiped away. The hair had been grey for a long time and it was still as neat as it had ever been; the hands were brown-stained – she disliked that, her hands had once been admired. Her dress was formal enough for her to have gone straight to one of her gentle coffee mornings. In her eyes, though, there was a watchfulness he now caught. She was trying to disguise something.

"I have great hopes for David," he said, wilfully riding over his own doubts.

"He is a likeable young man," she replied. "We got on very well. But he bothered me, William, and I can't put my finger on it. It was as if nothing would do."

"He seems quite easily pleased to me."

"Yes. He isn't a whiner." She paused and concentrated: and then shook her head. "He lost me, somehow, I couldn't follow him."

Her puzzled words activated the area of alarm he had been trying to ignore. He was neglecting David, he thought. The boy had had a wretched life – even though it would be impossible to convince his mother of that – and Willie had always seen his duty as doubly binding. But he let the matter drop and tried to re-enter the universe of this woman to whom he had been so close for so long. It was always the same problem. What to talk about which would engender that ease and mother–son complicity which was surely due. He could scarcely discuss the obituaries of Reagan or Begin! The small change of television politics was too deep in persons and practices unknown to her for him to be able to haul it to the surface. Her views on Joanna, though somewhat shared by him, would, if encouraged, upset them both. The conversational convenience of his own "future" or "career" had long since atrophied as the career itself had become stationary.

"Did they pull down the old stables over from the church?"

"Tore them down is more like it. It looks a terrible mess. They've just ruined that town."

It grieved her, this destruction of the small market town in the name of car parks and mistaken notions of planning. She had loved the place and passed on that affection to her son. In his early life he had often wandered around it with the awareness of her affection making him, too, aware of the many-layered accretions and curiosities which, over centuries, had melded into the charm of a well-worked, well-loved work of art. Yet in less than a generation, councillors with the funds and powers of mini-emperors and the vigour of vandals had ignorantly wrecked the patient accumulation of years. The result was a loss which had turned charm to melancholy and imperceptibly but profoundly depressed those, like his mother, who had cherished the continuity of the place.

"Are they still going to build old people's bungalows there?"

"So they say. But now I hear they've run out of funds. It'll be just another untidy hole."

"What about Henry? Has he won his fight?"

Henry Rudd owned one of the quaintest and most successful shops in the town. It stood almost on the road-edge on a corner near the Anglican church. The Rudds had kept the shop for five generations and their bread and pies, hams, teacakes, scones and sausages were still baked in the stable yard in a bakehouse which had stood for more than two hundred years. Henry still had the original long-handled irons and the old barrow which he trundled backwards and forwards every morning. People in the town were almost unconsciously proud of this working reminder from the past. There was scarcely enough of a nouveau middle class to make the place chic, but many of the older families in the town had always shopped there, as well as a lot of the working people who had bought from him and often been helped out in their hunger over bad years. Now, giving as their reason that the shop constituted a traffic hazard,

103

although there had not been a single accident recorded at that corner, the council had decided to order it to be pulled down and, as if determined to compound this arbitrary ruling with spite, they had put a compulsory purchase order on the bakehouse, saying that if it were not removed it would hinder possible future developments of the old people's bungalows.

"I just can't understand it," she said, in some distress. "Apart from anything else it's such a lovely little place. It just sets off that bit of road by the church so that when you turn the corner you have the whole of the High Street there – well, it used to be like something on a stage, all the shops with their displays and their bottle-glass windows. You never saw it at its best. Now they'll knock it down and all the character will be gone."

His heart went out to her. Through her work in the church and in the Women's Guild, in choirs in her youth and carnivals she had helped with, his mother had built up a friendship with the town which was deep and complex and was now being hacked to pieces before her eyes. Of course life could not stand still to please the sentiment of an old woman, but she was right, he thought, in her description of what was being forever sacrificed. It was shocking in its way that so much care and slow growth could be so recklessly and ignorantly abandoned for an ideology of newness which already looked shoddy. With a wry insight he saw his own case stand in the same order.

"Nothing can stay the same," he said.

"I don't see why not, if it's nice. Niceness seems to be the first thing to go."

"I thought that Henry had a QC."

"He seems pretty hopeless. Ada says he's given up before he started."

"How is she?" Ada, Henry's wife.

"Almost beside herself, poor woman." His mother glared in indignation. "She's never enjoyed good health and this business has put the hat on it. They haven't even accepted that there should be any reasonable compensation. Just because it

104

isn't to be used for other building purposes. I think twelve thousand pounds was the sum mentioned, which is perfectly ridiculous when you think that much worse shops are making twice as much, and that includes the bakehouse. It's a scandal." She relaxed or rather, he noticed, almost slumped back. "There's nothing they'll be able to do about it. These councils can get away with what they like nowadays. You have no say."

He wanted to give her world back to her – that nicer, kinder world, full of inequities, he knew, and material miseries now, though perhaps only temporarily, put behind, but a world which she had found pleasant and rich in common things.

"Lovely chutney," he said.

"I tried a new recipe. Some of those young women at the WI have marvellous new ideas."

Willie began to clear the table. She was on her feet.

"I'll do that."

"Please. There's no work."

"I'd rather." It was a plea.

"We'll do it together."

She was tired, and acceded. In the economic and efficient captain's cabin kitchen he ran the hot tap.

"You go and have another drink," she said.

"You dry. I'll wash."

"I don't like it," she said, simply, "and I never think they're properly clean when anybody else does it."

"There's one plate, Mother, one knife, one fork and perhaps another plate if we shove the ham with the beef. I'll take the greatest care."

It took a moment and then, re-appropriating her role, his mother put on the kettle.

"Tea?"

"If you are."

"You can go and smoke a cigarette," she said.

When she brought in the tray, daintily covered with a white embroidered cloth, Willie had steeled himself. He let her pour out the tea.

"So how are you?"

105

"As well as can be expected," she replied, her eyes fixed to the rim of the cup as she took a small sip. "It's these cold winds," she went on. "They seem to catch my chest. I've even been in two minds about my walk sometimes."

"Have you missed it?"

"Once," she said, scrupulously, with that impeccable honesty he loved and which now seemed as distant as the rest of his childhood. "A week last Tuesday."

"Are you sure you're all right?"

"Dr Thomas wants me in an early grave." She smiled, glad to be mischievous and blame the doctor for the disease. "He's such a fussy young man. I miss old Dr Dolan."

"He never found anything wrong with you."

"He had a good manner. That's half of it."

"What *does* Dr Thomas say?"

Willie's concern had become more latent, his questions more insistent; his determination got through to her.

"He says I need treatment."

"For what?"

"These pains."

"Does he say what they are?"

She took up the cup and saucer once again, as a shield, it seemed.

"Cancer."

He simply stared at her. She sipped very quietly and quietly replaced both saucer and cup on the table. Only then did she look at him and then calmly.

"They can cure it, you know," she said.

He could not digest it. His mother, who had watched over him, washed, brushed, held, nursed, helped, protected, fed, clothed, loved him – now before him being eaten by cancer.

"Yes," he agreed, the single syllable almost choking in the dry thickness of his throat.

"They use beams and things. Dr Thomas explained it well, I'll give him that."

He wanted to get up and take her in his arms, to rock her

106

in his embrace, to comfort her and lend strength to ward off this malign invader. He could not move.

"I have to go in for the first treatment next week," she said. "He's given me pills to help the pain. They're very good, but they seem to keep me awake at nights."

"Cancer."

"A lot of people recover fom it these days."

"Why didn't you tell me?"

"I knew you'd come without all the drama of that," she said, happily, confidently. And he was ashamed.

"You must see a specialist."

"They have one in Carlisle. I'm sure I'll be well looked after. The infirmary has a good name. You're not to worry."

"Cancer."

"I've been very lucky with my health so far."

Her resolution awed him. How many volts of energy had gone into creating this unflinching attitude which was not a façade?

"Next week?"

"Thursday," she said. "They keep you in for six days."

"I'll come up."

"No such thing. Annie will be there to help me when I get out. If I need more, I'm sure Dr Thomas will be able to arrange it. You have your work to do."

"I must come up," he repeated.

Her reply was to shake her head and rise to take away the tea tray. Had he said "I must come up" meaning it or merely in order to pretend to a willingness he did not have in the safe knowledge that she had given him a firm excuse? Alone in the room while she washed and dried the dishes he was shocked both at her revelation and at the speed with which his reaction had been tempered by selfishness. What was he becoming?

"You must be tired after the drive," she said, standing in the doorway. "I'll let you sleep on in the morning. Goodnight."

"Goodnight, Mother."

She left him in the ordered hush. He heard the noises from the bathroom and then a deeper silence. She would have said

107

her prayers and undoubtedly she would have included a prayer for him.

In his old room there would be the schoolbooks and the evidence of a Christian upbringing. She still hoped he would come back to the Church – although the Church, too, for her, like the town, had modernised itself out of most of its former powers and charms. In that room, on previous visits, he had quite easily been able to imagine himself slotting back into this small town life of piety and honest effort. Now it would seem as impossible to fit himself into as his first school blazer.

Yet, with a rush of longing, he wished he could accommodate to this: there was a life here, where he could look after both his mother and Joanna, where David could put down some roots, where he could look for a job and mark out his days in decent routine.

Cancer.

He would go and see Dr Thomas in the morning.

Cancer.

There was clearly that transparency about her skin: his own chest clenched as if in sympathy.

Cancer.

He would phone Caroline in the afternoon.

(3)

"Darling,

I've never written 'darling' to anyone except you. I never thought I would be able to. Even though in parts of the business they use it so often – to write it down is different. But – darling, darling Ian. I do love you so much. I can't believe or understand why you love me. I love (use that word too often!) to hear you say it and see you write it but I still can't believe it somehow. I know you say I'm – beautiful and all that but I'm not really. Not *really*. Not at all, I thought, until you started saying so. I still just think I'm lucky – that's all – and all I want is to stay lucky. The trouble is that since I met you everything has changed so much that I can't

108

imagine what it would be like without you. In fact – I suppose I ought not to tell you this – I get frightened thinking what life might be like if you went away. I just can't think about it. You are my life now – I never thought I'd say things like that but it's true, like all the rest – you *are*, and without you I would – well, I suppose I would go on. It would be silly to pretend I wouldn't. But it would be so meaningless.

I do understand about New York. I'll see you here at Christmas, that's all that matters – to see you. It looks as if I won't be doing very much! I got back to London to discover that our Arts Council grant is to be cut down. Jake is frantic and he's already talking about having to 'adopt a new strategy vis-à-vis the company and its intentions'. That means me, I'm afraid. So it looks as if I'll be on the dole!

I went home last week – Willie offered me a lift. He's been very kind to me. I'm afraid that all I do is ask him about you. He's such a good friend of yours. It's like talking to your brother. We went into the Lake District on our way back. Willie was very subdued when he picked me up – his mother isn't well, she has to go into hospital – and when he suggested that I might like a detour I leapt at it. He wanted to show the place off, I suppose. I wanted to see all the places you talk about. I made a rule not to talk about you that day, though. Do you mind, darling? (There it is again!) Somehow I didn't want to disclose all that you'd said to me, I didn't want to keep bringing up your words – they were private. And Willie was so drawn into himself that I hadn't the heart to go on and on and on about you, as I usually do. So we just motored around.

I've forgotten half the names already but Willie pointed them out like a registered tourist guide. This mountain – sorry, *fell* – and that lake – this town where Wordsworth was born and the village he went to school in and Dove Cottage of course – I think I enjoyed that the most. I could just see them all snugly sitting there. I would like a cottage like that with you – except you wouldn't sit for long. We walked for a little way behind Rydal Water – an easy walk – and came to some massive caves. I wish I could write like Dorothy Wordsworth. Willie bought me her journals. She would have made that walk sound marvellous and ordinary at the same time. All I did was moon about you and wish you had been showing me around. Do you think you'll be able to some day?

I'm so nervous about asking you anything to do with the future. You understand that, don't you? I read your letters every night and although you talk about me I still can't believe it's me you're talking to. What an anxious bore I must seem!

Nobody has made love to me like you do, Ian. Nobody has made me feel like this. Nor could they – nor would I ever want them to. I'm glad I saw the Lakes. That was another part of you. I want to know all the parts of you – not those! I know those, a little, already –

Remember that night you took me to Boulestin's and after that we wandered around Covent Garden looking for a back alley and after that – which you made seem wonderful even though it could have been so squalid – we went on and found a club where the old lady told our fortunes? 'You have the same patterns. You will travel along the same road,' she said. I hope so. To tell the truth, I pray for it. Am I playing too easy to get? Well– I am – for you.

All my love,
Caroline   XXXX"

(4)

Willie sat in the car for a few minutes before going up to the flat. He was completely exhausted. The doctor had told him that his mother was much worse than she had intimated. She herself had refused to discuss the subject after their first conversation. The treatment would be painful.

For a few moments the thought of his mother's wasting little body being shot through with rays drove out every other consideration. In those few moments, like an alcoholic who occasionally feels a grip of sobriety and understands the alternatives, Willie saw the life not without honour he could lead. A life, moreover, he was well fitted to lead and one which would be worth something for others. He could help not only her but the others who needed help, even including Caroline, whose severe avoidance of the subject of Ian that day had only confirmed Willie's deepest fears about Ian's terrible hold on her. In the concentrated focus of the news of his mother, he saw with clarity the danger of his obsession with a young girl who had scarcely noticed his existence although he had shown her, in those few hours in the Lakes, parts of himself which he had revealed to no one before. Ian, of course, whose knowledge of the place was laughably scanty and whose affection for it was the worst kind of exiled colonial sentimentality, would have drenched her in the excessive romanticism which beggared any reality. Yet it was Ian's version she had read in his scrupulous lines. It was hopeless, hopeless in a way which mocked the true hopelessness of his mother.

But the moment of clarity passed by. He had no choice. Wearily he got out of the car and walked towards the flat. The lights were out. He would phone Mandy: just to talk, revealing nothing, just to talk.

Chapter Six

"This," said David, fiercely, "is where it's at."

"I see," Willie nodded significantly.

It was indeed there to be seen. The Community Arts Centre was in a side street off the main shopping centre of an inner South London suburb. Most of the shops appeared to be in a terminal state of SALES, MUST GO, FINAL REDUCTIONS, MASSIVE CLEARANCES. These mottoes, Willie thought, spoke for the whole area. The grim slush remaining after an unexpected December snowfall seemed altogether too appropriate a dressing for the barren roads. It was an area often featured in the weeklies and the Sundays for its rate of youth unemployment, its apparently inflammable racial composition, its struggle to find the resources to meet the local welfare needs. There were those who ventured a contradictory opinion – that, despite the deprivations, here was a place full of life, of new-old London street cries in the markets, of throbbing Saturday nights in the discos and still the tributaries of city sub-cultures flowing through the pubs and clubs – but that was a minority, the serious said, grasping at the fleeting straws of cheerfulness which were only the lightest covering on a helplessly confused debris. The place was in irreversible decline and a fearsome indicator of the shape of things to come across the nation's cities. The Christmas season accentuated the sadness.

The Arts Centre itself both shared and defined the conditions in which it found itself. It was housed in what had once been a large and flourishing hardware store, one of those Victorian emporia which had breathed imperial competence and hard-headedness in one exhalation of confidence. There were still scores of brass-fronted drawers where different sizes of nails had been carefully packaged, where all make and manner of screws and hinges had been harboured, where chisels made of best steel in best Midland factories had been graded and polished before being laid in their precise location, where hammers and strings, pliers and screwdrivers, lamps, wax, lengths of wire and copper, rods, planes, axes, shovels, spades and all the armament of hardware life had been labelled and slotted away. Now those drawers which were not broken were garishly labelled 'KIDS' or 'CARNIVAL' or 'MAGS'; and the uniform image was paper, ill-printed, cheap, urgent, over-whelming. It was as if paper had replaced every useful thing in the hardware department, as if it were the cause-all, cure-all, answer-all, make-all of the new life of JACKSON, FRASER AND JONES, whose names, still gilded, had been allowed to stay above the front of the community centre as an example of the disappearing craft of sign-making.

There were about a dozen people working in the place and although some attempt had been made to change the rangy shop into a space more relevant for their different needs, the effect was still that of squatters, battening onto the old structure rather than having the energy to create anything new. Willie chided himself for that thought. He was already cowed into admiration for the attempt being made here even though he suspected he might disagree strongly with the ways, the means and the objectives. The purpose, though, was to help: that he respected.

The people dressed young and uniformly, even though most of them were not so young and would have hated anything as hierarchic and authoritarian as a uniform. All acted with a belligerent casualness, in an almost aggressive low-key, low-voiced way – but again Willie choked the criticism which sprang into his mind so readily. He had already designated them as trendies, as do-gooders coated with a lick of fashionable leftism, as out of touch with the real needs of the "community" they now seemed so possessive and certain about. All this was prejudice. He knew nothing about them.

"I'm building a stage through the warehouse at the back,"

David said. He went through, nodding very slightly to a girl in a denim jumpsuit. This half-nod seemed to be the statutory salute.

Indeed the place had been stripped down until it did have a barracks air; and the enemies were on the walls. 'FIGHT THATCHER' 'FIGHT RACISM' 'FIGHT JOB CUTS' 'FIGHT EDUCATION CUTS' 'FIGHT HOSPITAL CUTS' 'FIGHT THE PIGS: F--K THE POLICE.' As a complement to that was another battery of large printed posters advertising help, for people unclear as to their rights, for those needing to be helped through the maze of the social security system, for unmarried mothers, unemployed youngsters, the old and lonely, the militant, the radical and the revolutionary. And scattered throughout was the resurgent CND symbol, the most urgent of all the writings on the wall. Willie felt the chill of all outsiders suddenly propelled into a closed system. In a forest of causes he was a man without the thread of a mission.

The stage was impressively large. The empty warehouse was being painted white by two young men who were obviously amateur but doggedly energetic. An old man in a waistcoat and old-fashioned brown trilby was sawing lengths of wood.

"Alf," David announced, rather proudly. "Skilled craftsman, can't get work anywhere. He helps us out."

Alf took no notice of them. Indeed, the strongest of Willie's clustering first impressions was the grimness of the dedication of all those involved.

"We want the people to have a place to put on their own plays," David said. "Plays that matter to them."

"How are you finding them?"

"Dick has all that organised: come and meet him."

Again David marched ahead at a surprisingly brisk pace, rapping out explanations as he went through the network of rooms. "Art Gallery. All local work. The kids can use this at weekends for their own drawing." "We're trying to get an extra grant for developing rooms in there, and silk-screen printing. It's our biggest class so far." "This is where we used to have performances; we're setting up our own local theatre co-op.

114

When we've got the big stage ready, this will be used for the magazine – Dick's in a hole in the wall at the moment."

Not even in Dick's hole in the wall was there any evidence of that puckish and self-indulgent good humour – the name-same clippings from newspapers, the joke postcards and funnily captioned photographs – which covered the offices and walls of the television studios like a genial distemper. Perhaps, these people could argue, such "puckish and self-indulgent good humour" could only be afforded when you had safe privileged jobs. Here, the walls declared there was real work to be done.

"Dick," said David. "Willie."

Willie recognised what could have been his younger self. Dick was in his late twenties, open shirt collared but a suit, shabby but a suit, glasses, pale skin, earnest but not, Willie thought, grindingly earnest; above all, and it was here that Willie envied him, content in his vocation and believing it to be no less than that. Later, David was to confide that Dick was a bit too easy-going for the rest of them, not as committed to the ideology as the rest of them but a hard worker, got amazing results, difficult to understand really as he was the son of a county solicitor, had been to Oxford and then done a thesis on some poet or other at Berkeley.

Dick's office walls bore one or two of the posters which papered the rest of the building but its main, indeed its over-whelming, feature was the number of handwritten manuscripts and magazines. These were stacked in neat towers, some of which were as tall as Willie. There were books, too, and Willie gulped down the sight of them with gratitude: he felt illogically reassured.

"I have to see Alf," David said, still in the pseudo-military mode which he seemed to have swallowed whole. "You two can talk."

Dick smiled gently, waved a hand which both offered Willie the other chair and acknowledged David's exit. He rocked back on his seat, began to roll a cigarette.

"Would you care for one?"

115

"Have one of mine."

The young man nodded but first he finished the careful preparation of his handmade fag. Willie felt himself cast as an intruder: it seemed the only way to enter into any conversation with Dick, who was amiably counting this as a break.

"Tea?" Dick asked, cutting across Willie's run-up to a question.

"Thank you."

"Kettle's behind you. Just bung in the plug, would you, I filled it up last time."

Willie did as he was asked.

"You work in the telly, don't you?"

"Yes." The caution in his voice was involuntary. He could imagine the thoughts of this group on "the telly".

"I love it!" Dick said.

Coming from you, Willie smiled to himself, that invariably means that you "love" the feature films and game shows and by that "love" put down the sort of television I am concerned with.

"Especially the documentaries," Dick went on, puffing thriftily. "I just wish there were more of them."

By the time the water boiled and the tea was brewed in an old pot which resembled a fat galleon, Dick had turned Willie's notions about himself upside down several times and both men were enjoying themselves.

"I suppose you think we ought to make more documentaries about this sort of thing," Willie offered.

"I don't really see much point," said Dick, taking a tin of condensed milk out of a drawer. "We would just come over as a bunch of Lefty scruffs, rather strident and out of touch. More likely to do us harm than good. The documentaries I like have a much more precise focus."

"What brought you here?"

"It seemed one of the few things worth doing," Dick said, rather abashed, as if he were being caught out for doing a good deed.

"What *is* it exactly . . . ?"

116

"We are doing? Sometimes I wonder. But we all do that, don't we?"

That was it! Willie understood now. A hundred years ago Dick would have been a missionary in some far-flung colony – the sort of Christian hero whose life and work had so often dazzled and inspired him in his boyhood reading. He almost applauded that the "type" was still extant.

"It's simply a case of involving people and giving them a chance and a place to air their talents and see a bit more in life – if they choose to – than what's offered them in pretty average schooling and a fairly limited range of options since then."

"What about the political aspect?"

"'Thatcher Out!' 'Tear Down Parliament' 'End Capitalism Tomorrow'?" Dick produced the phrases with laconic mockery. "I accept some of them, not others. I wouldn't subscribe to tearing down Parliament, for example, but," and the mockery and lightness stopped, "there is the most appalling inequality of real opportunity, don't you think? You can't stand by and watch people waste away for want of a helping hand. There are times, in fact, when I feel even more extreme than the others here. Anarchy deserves its day, in my opinion; what do you think?"

"Only if you believe in the goodness of man."

"Don't you?"

Willie shook his head.

"It's probably the only faith one can hold," Dick said, briskly. He picked up a bundle of magazines. "We run a local co-op mag, did David tell you? No reason he should have done. The idea is to let people have the chance to see their own work in print. We have classes and discussions – quite a few professional writers have come along to help. They were surprised at the level of the work. As I was, at first. Some of it really is very good indeed: I was glad that the professionals agreed. Here, take these. You might enjoy them."

Willie accepted the magazines and flicked through the top copy.

"'Agony Column'?"

"Bit infra-dig?" Dick smiled. "Everyone thinks that. I tell the chaps it's meant to be ironic and that just about covers my tracks. But there's nothing at all ironic about it. It's a straightforward agony column."

"What sort of letters do you get?"

"Extraordinary range, actually. Basically people just want to write and to know that what they write is going to be replied to. Being read is, in this case, secondary."

"Do you have a co-operative committee for the replies?"

"As a matter of fact we do. If there isn't time, I do it myself and then tell the others. It's important to get the reply back as soon as possible and meetings can go on rather a long time."

"Meetings of anarchists would last for ever."

"So it would keep a lot of busybodies out of trouble," Dick smiled, sweetly; "that's always a good thing."

"What are the letters about?"

"Oh, the sort of things that you and your friends would probably regard as the results of stupidity. A great number of young people still don't know the sexual facts of life – it's almost criminal that the schools won't teach them properly. A lot of people are worried about their marriages. There's a regular clump of complaints about the housing and the vandalism, as you would expect. Some racist stuff, some Utopian suggestions, the long letters of autobiography and the long letters analysing the whole state of society. More and more letters from people on the dole – just waking up wishing the day was over so that they could go to bed again: that's what most of them say. Did David tell you about our job-hunting schemes?"

Very politely, Dick was indicating that he wanted to get back to work. Willie took the point, took his magazines and said he had better re-join David.

"Tea?" David asked.

"Thank you."

David led him off to what had been the shop-manager's

118

office. It was now rather like the common-room of a blitzed university. Tea was brewed.

"I like Dick," Willie said. "I hadn't expected to meet anyone quite like him here."

"He doesn't really fit in," David agreed. "But he makes a good job of that magazine."

"I thought he was rather impressive."

"People tend to like him," David conceded; and Willie gave up.

"He works very hard," David concluded, being fair.

"You seem to work rather hard yourself. We scarcely ever see you."

"It's easier to crash down around the corner."

"I understand."

"Why don't you do something on television about this sort of thing?" David, unrelentingly fierce, swept his right arm in a gesture which embraced the omnipresent posters.

Willie peered at the material.

"You mother would like to see you," Willie said, the thought escaping before he had time to consider it.

"She hates me."

"David!"

"Dislikes. OK. It doesn't matter. It isn't important to me any more."

"Maybe you should see her for her sake."

"There's no point in being nice if you don't mean it, Willie. At least she knows that much."

"*I* would like to see you."

"Come down whenever you want." David's invitation sounded like a rebuff but Willie took it at its face value.

"I will."

As they walked out onto the darkening streets, Dick overtook them, a college scarf slung about his neck, a pile of magazines under his arm.

"Thought I'd get some fresh air and deliver the latest creation," he said, cheerfully, skilfully manoeuvring past them on the narrow pavement and drawing ahead. "Very nice to meet you! Enjoy Christmas."

David insisted on waiting with Willie at the bus stop. About a dozen people were there, all of them, it seemed to Willie, tired and anxious. The street lights and shop lights gave the thoroughfare an electric tinsel. Shoppers moved along the displays, gloomily gazing at the boldly declared bargains. There was the strain of just holding on, Willie thought, the stress of barely managing, even with this apparent plenty beckoning behind thin glass. David caught his glance.

"You can understand why they smash the windows, can't you?" he said.

(2)

"Let me get this straight," Eric repeated, twisting uncomfortably on the bar stool which provided for only a portion of his rugby buttocks. "You're willing to leave obits, but in exchange you want to do at least one documentary a year."

"Two was what I said."

"I'm not sure I should be taking part in this horse-trading." Eric tried and failed to laugh. "I mean, isn't it a sort of – "

"Exchange. Your round."

Obediently Eric turned to the barman and waited to claim his attention. Willie felt good. If he was falling then the only course to take was to find ways to compensate by rising. He had played possum too long in this industry. In his days he had done considerable work; he wanted to be back there, not stuck with the dead. He wanted to return to doing something that he could admire himself for – more importantly, something that Caroline could admire him for.

"It isn't too difficult for you to do." Willie explained how Eric could re-organise a little here, shuffle a little there, "and you'll come out looking as if you've cracked three problems in one with the added bonus that you've given the old man – yours truly – a chance. People will like you for that."

Eric concentrated. People were not liking him enough these

days. He suspected that he was being talked about behind his back and the injustice of those imagined conversations hurt him. He was, after all, doing the very best he could for everyone. His instinctive reaction was to become even more severe and take his revenge on these uncomprehending renegades, but a certain canniness made him see the sense in offering some token.

"Why did you say that?" Eric asked, as he thought, most ingenuously.

"What?"

"About people liking me."

Willie was patient. He had seen Caroline for lunch. There was even less need to make for home these days.

"It's just the job. As a boss you become the focus for frustrations, that's all. You can live with that."

"Of course. So you'll give up the obits. Won't you miss them?"

"I will in a way." Willie, in truth, was much relieved by his decision. There had always been something predatory in the work.

"You won't be an easy act to follow," Eric said, employing a useful new managerial phrase with offhand confidence.

"I suggest – " Willie had worked it out. He gave Eric the plan.

"What I'd like you to do is to run it down slowly," Eric said, now much more at ease, off the pin-headed bar stool, thoughtfully scratching his buttocks back into life. "Say until about Easter, and that'll give us time to think about the documentary."

This was part of what Willie had suggested. "That's perfect, Eric," he said, "and thanks."

"Oh," Eric fumbled at the compliment as if it were a greasy rugby ball. "Well. Least I can do. Helps me a lot, really. They were getting very shirty about this re-organisation business." He began doing some knees-bends, clear proof that this crisis was past. Half way down a rather more ambitious bend, he froze, amazement rending his amiable face agape.

121

"Specs," he said. "Sorry – glasses. Yours. Gone."

"I'm trying out these contact lenses."

Eric pushed his face so close that Willie swung away.

"You don't notice them!" Eric declared, pulling back just as Willie thought he was about to topple. "Do they hurt like hell?"

"A bit."

Eric shook his large healthy head. "Couldn't stand it. In your eyes. Bits of plastic." He finished his drink and glanced at his chunky watch which seemed as full of information as a railway timetable. "Well . . ." he paused, some final gesture had to be made to clinch this unexpected success with a pleasant bouquet. "Have you thought of what to do yet?"

"A couple of ideas."

"You made some classics." Willie felt a swift shadow pass over him as he took in Eric's rather pitying gaze. "You've lost weight too," Eric observed. "Suits you."

He stood fairly still now, awkwardly unable to leave the small saloon bar – one of the few Willie had found within walking distance of the studios which had the four virtues of no muzak, no juke box, no space invaders and no fruit machines. Willie remembered that gauche stance later. He thought at the time it was just Eric's way, and had eased his departure with a grateful smile.

(3)

He went back to his office. It was always more agreeable, he found, to work there when everyone had gone home. The studios were still in operation, actors in costume wandering the corridors, the Tannoy calling in the crews, the editing machines spinning the tape through – but that was all in the bowels of the building. Up on his high floor, Willie could savour the sense of being voluntarily marooned.

The loss of weight and the growing success with the lenses had given him a greater feeling of well-being than he had enjoyed for years. He felt light on his feet, more eager to face

122

the world, keen to change. It was as if he had shrugged off an old skin, a skin coated with the crust of disappointments and failures: a skin inside which he had huddled to keep out the world. The sense of well-being stood in counterpoint to the more powerful sense of losing respect for himself and yet at times like this it could gain an ascendance. He could ride over his fears and think that he was setting out on the life he had finally discovered he wanted.

The office was very cosy, more of a den now. Its comparative smallness had been an asset. Books, pictures, an imitation Quom rug, a single armchair with a sidelight, a cane side table filled it amply. He phoned Mandy and enjoyed her affectionate aggression for a while. He phoned his mother in the hospital, as arranged, at eight o'clock precisely. The treatment had been successful, she repeated: the doctors seemed pleased. Willie confirmed that he would go up to be there when she came out. He was entering another phase with Caroline, he thought, preparing now to go onto the attack. She had not gone to New York, she would not see Ian for months. Morever, her threatened position in the subsidy-starved company gave him a chance to be of positive help to her. Over the years he had met many people now in positions to be of use. He would not go at it blatantly, but a nudge here, a word there: he looked forward to it. Yes. As he sat in the chair, cigarette, small scotch well watered, Crankshaw's Russian books to plunder for his piece on Brezhnev, Willie felt dangerously liberated from what he could regard as an over-protective past. Life was for the living.

Joanna phoned. "What time will you be back?"

"In an hour or so, I thought."

"I'm making some fish pie."

Willie hesitated. "That's very nice."

"Shall I have it ready for nine?"

Her briskness! That's what it was. Sober.

"Fine. Thank you."

"Willie?" She paused only for a moment and then went on with what had clearly been well prepared. "I thought we ought

123

to take a little holiday. I've booked us into a hotel in Bath for a couple of nights." He felt himself suddenly alert. She was not only sober but urgent. "I thought you could get off after lunch tomorrow and we could travel down then," she pressed on. "It's supposed to be a very good hotel." Her tone, which just stopped short of pleading, touched him.

"Two days?"

"My treat."

Caroline used that expression. The echo jolted Willie: he had arranged to go for a walk with Caroline on Hampstead Heath on the Sunday afternoon.

"Please." Joanna spoke quietly and in the quietness of his own office that uncharacteristically soft voice seemed to bring her presence vividly before him.

She would be in their sitting-room – drink beside her? – unaware of the untidiness, and the request spoke of loneliness.

"I have something to do on Sunday afternoon," he said. "We'd have to be back by lunchtime."

"Oh, that's fine." Her voice was instantly gay, avoiding the risk of pressing home the victory. "Nine o'clock, then," she said.

"Yes."

When she put the phone down he held it for a little while as if expecting an answer to another question. He found it difficult to re-absorb himself in the reading and took care to leave with enough time to get back promptly.

(4)

The Royal Crescent Hotel was near the middle of a magnificent Georgian shallow arc of houses which stood on one of Bath's hills in its splendid columned curve, overlooking parkland and the low landscaped hills beyond. The proprietor had made considerable efforts to gather together a collection of prints and paintings of the town in its heyday and to complement that with period furniture. The hotel comprised two of the houses. The

124

bedrooms were both stylish and luxurious – a canopied double bed, with tassels, heavy matching curtains, furniture discreetly chosen and placed to amplify it into a sitting room, the bathroom sporting large brass fittings and deep-piled towels, tent-sized. There was a typed note from the manager to Mr and Mrs William Armstrong, welcoming them, directing them and urging them to complain immediately should the slightest inconvenience strike them. Willie noticed that the cost was £75 a night.

"Is this all in?" he asked.

"No," said Joanna, happily unpacking her case. "I said it was a treat."

He looked at her but she yielded as little as she had done the previous evening or on their journey down in the train. She had sipped at a glass of wine at supper and had had nothing to drink all day. The surplus energy released itself in unremitting cheerfulness. Willie would have been amused had he not been puzzled.

The weather was cold, blue-skied, brilliant. Bath seemed designed to exemplify the show of Christmas. Its pedestrian precincts swung with creepers of glittering garlands; heavy tinsel draped the fronts of the well-furbished shops, small side streets were positively stuffed with decoration, fake Victorian lamps, twinkly Christmas trees; Father Christmas on his sleigh rode outside the Pump Room.

With Willie's compliance, Joanna acted the tourist. She took his arm firmly as they came out of the hotel and they walked down to Milsom Street making for the Baths. She seemed transfixed at the hot gush of spring water which surged over the lower reddened lip of stone: it was as if she were bathing her face in the steam, infusing herself with the healing powers of this ancient source. A young thickset bearded guide who spoke very slowly and very loudly – clearly resigned to addressing foreigners – took in hand this small party, all of whom were English but too shy to pipe up and say so. He described the measurements of everything, throwing in estimates of weight when addressing them on the lead covering on the floor of

125

the Great Bath, steaming furiously under the frigid December sky, and throughout the tour expressed a missionary love for the Romans and adopted a terrible line in sarcasm for all later settlers in Bath. His case was reinforced by the classical statues around the open roof of the Great Bath, which were inscrutably wrapped up in heavy plastic bags, like modern sculptures. Willie rediscovered a long-buried pleasure in trying to avoid Joanna's eye as the Romanophile marched them through the hypocaust and pointed to the infinite superiority of this system over any known before or since. Joanna handed him a tenpenny piece and he followed her lead and threw it into the circular bath already littered with small silver offerings and drowned wishes.

The spring and the guided tour were not enough. She insisted they go into the museum and they wandered around in docile contentment, reaching out to touch the simply carved lion's face, gazing at the jewellery – as usual, she said, so modern – standing on the ramp looking at the large broken slabs of stone which had once been the altar. Her mood was so determinedly interested that Willie soon found himself as absorbed as she was, his puzzlement and the growing question dissolved in what had once been a regular mutual pleasure, visiting, looking, reading up, talking about the past.

That evening they ate in the hotel. Willie selected a Châteauneuf du Pape but Joanna drank only one glass. In bed they made love, briefly but not perfunctorily.

It was the same pattern on the Saturday, following the diary of many a thousand tourists. They took coffee in the Pump Room and applauded the young trio so sedulously consecrated to the correct playing of pleasant light classical airs. Joanna wanted lunch in a pub – something they had not done together for years – and they found the Saracen's Head, which was full but not crowded, an amiable concourse of students and larger groups of older people whom Willie easily guessed were visiting rugger supporters laying down a foundation for a day's sporting debauch. Joanna drank a half of shandy.

After the Assembly Rooms, they walked along the gravel way

126

to the Botanic Gardens, flowering only in the gilt lettering which displayed the vast bouquets of recent awards. Joanna took his hand as they stepped carefully along the narrow paths where some of the uncleared snow had turned icy. Strolling back across Victoria Park they enjoyed the first decline of the huge isolated gouache-yellow sun.

"It would be pleasant to live here, don't you think?" she said as they turned uphill towards the crescent. "You can imagine a life that was calm and no fuss. All those lovely shops; beautiful houses everywhere you go . . ."

"Insulated."

"Yes," she agreed. "Lovely. Perhaps we *could* live here. It's only an hour on the train to London."

Willie smiled to deflect what he hoped was a holiday question. Joanna squeezed his hand and did not persist.

They had tea in front of the log fire. The immaculate furniture and the almost unearthly neatness amused both of them.

"I'd like a nap," she said. "You can read your book. You've been desperate to do that since lunch, haven't you?"

He confirmed that she was right, which seemed to please her enormously. She brought him his book from the bedroom. He opened it, read no more than two pages and dozed off.

When he woke up she was standing in front of him, dressed for outdoors, holding his coat.

"Let's walk through the town again before dinner," she said.

Again Willie made no protest.

The moon was up, stars out, trees crisp as the frost intensified, and the town was even more of a delight for being almost empty. The Christmas lights and fake Dickensian lamps, the alleyways of decorated trees and the undisturbed order of the pedestrian centre of Bath gave it the air of being at once a ghost town and a sanctuary.

As they walked, Joanna drew on the last day or two and they spun a little history of their visit as they had once done on all their holidays. They guessed at the life of the American family they had seen in the Pump Room, the four of them reverently regarding the trio as if in the Palm Court music lay the key to

127

the understanding of the whole of the Regency. Joanna talked about the man dressed up as Father Christmas in his booth outside the Abbey: his plummy accent had been somehow at odds with the pantomime scarlet cloak and rouged cheeks: what sort of life was it which allowed and enabled people to lead such leisure-filled public service lives? And there were the dog walkers in the Botanic Gardens . . . the company in the pub . . . skilfully she drew him into a conspiracy of small shared pleasures, holding his arm closely, walking at a brisk but easy pace, aware that he was aware of what she was doing and gaining an extra layer of enjoyment from their self-consciousness. She steered him to the Abbey where there was a carol service.

Willie did not want to go into the body of the Abbey and so they sat in the porch, listening to the carols which Willie had once sung so passionately. "In Dulce Jubilo" soared up to the famous fan vaulting and slow blurred images of his childhood paved the air from the flattened records of memory. He sat attentive, back straight, hands on his knees, as if trying to tune himself into the old meanings, his antennae straining to catch and resurrect the perished faith. A small humpbacked man came out of the church, stared at them in an unfriendly way and then left, perhaps as disappointed with them as with the performance of the choirs. Willie nudged Joanna and she giggled. He took her arm and they strolled back to the hotel, more amiably contented with one another than Willie could remember. Joanna stopped outside a shop which sold old lace and she pointed out a pin-cushion similar to the one she had bought during the afternoon while he was snoozing. "As a memento," she said, "and for luck."

"Do you want a divorce?" she said, smiling.

The candles had burned about an inch of fat white wax in the cloistered, hushed, well-appointed dining room. The soup was eaten, the wine begun, the fish on its way. Willie was in a gear of neutral contentment, all the more agreeable because the time before he would next see Caroline was shrinking rapidly. Joanna had kept her voice low even though the waiter had given

128

them a corner table further isolated by two empty tables in front of it: and the other diners had arrived much earlier, were into intimacies of their own and would soon leave, donating the freedom of the room to himself and Joanna.

"No," he said, automatically.

"Good," Joanna replied, sipping at her iced water. "Neither do I." She smiled again: alcoholic abstinence had done her looks a favour. "I've had one. I don't really think I could survive another."

"Why do you ask?" Willie knew it was a foolish question but felt impelled to say something.

"Willie!" Her tone was playfully reproachful.

The fish came. Lobster. They sat back while it was laid before them and waited until the vegetables had been tastefully laid out on side plates. Joanna ate with unaccustomed relish. Willie pulled at the tense flesh with no appetite. He poured himself another drink, glad to evade the attentions of the hovering wine waiter. Joanna shook her head and took a drink from her first glass, still almost full. Sancerre: "Hemingway's favourite white," Willie had said, as always, "But none the worse for that."

"Even though it's so easy nowadays," she said, as if the conversation had taken no pause, "it still throws up so much nastiness. Look at John and Elaine: their children had left home, both of them had good jobs, it seemed the simplest arrangement in the world. And they haven't stopped fighting about money and possessions since."

"I wouldn't be interested in possessions."

"So you *have* been thinking about it !" This time her good humour was contagious and Willie found himself returning her smile without at all being able to fathom what was going on. "You'd be surprised," she said, "the pictures, the books of course, this and that . . . people often invest things with all the affection that appears to have been drained away from their life together." She paused. "I wish I'd seen more of Elaine," she said. "Not just because of the divorce. We've drifted away from our friends over the last few years. Just as we've drifted

129

away from each other. We haven't put in enough work at it. I've hardly been the supportive wife."

Oddly, Willie found himself relaxing into the conversation. In fact there was a feeling of relief that the subject was now being aired.

"It hasn't been a very good marriage, has it?" she said, carefully laying down her knife and fork.

"Oh, I don't know."

"I've behaved badly," Joanna persisted, calmly, "and you've reacted by retreating so far that you've removed yourself from the battlefield."

"Battlefield?" Following her example, he, too, gave up the struggle with the rich food.

"I sometimes think that the basic attraction of marriage is that it is the best place for behaving at your worst. And we all need that. Maybe it's the only place."

"You seem to have thought about it a lot."

"I have, over the past couple of months. And I've thought about us a lot. You were worn out by it quite early on – not only by looking after me, but by being looked after. That seemed to weaken you: you wanted to get through that depression by yourself. You've always wanted to do things on your own terms and I should have admired that more. You weren't openly assertive about it, though. I suppose I would have understood it more if you'd made a thing of it. I blamed you for not getting on, for not making this or that impression when all the time you've been quietly doing one of the hardest things of all – simply getting on with what you wanted to do on your terms and without making a fuss of it."

"Why did you want to come here?"

"To Bath?"

He had to wait for his answer while the waiter performed the table clearance. Both of them waived dessert and cheese and agreed to take coffee later in the lounge.

"I was reading Jane Austen," Joanna said, simply. "It isn't that she makes life simple – not a bit – but there's something so reassuring about her exact assessment of what are the staying properties of a marriage." She laughed. "It made me want to marry you all over again. To sit down and work it out and decide that we had enough in common to complement each other: to wipe the slate clean."

"But you can't."

"No." Joanna looked apprehensive. "I suppose not. Do you think that once it has broken down there's no way to put it together again? I've wondered about that. We've been so awful to each other – I have to you, anyway – and you have too, you know, in a way: you seemed so tolerant that I thought it was indifference. I'm sure it was. But, Willie, there is enough, isn't there, for us to see each other through, to help each other down the hill? Isn't there?"

He was silent.

She sipped the wine and took out a cigarette.

"You've always been an idealist and a romantic," she said, "that's what frightens me now. Perhaps you'll think that with someone else it would all be wonderful and unblemished. And I never really gave you what you'd hoped for – that way, in bed . . . the illness, all that – you missed that. I'm frightened that you'll go away from me to try to find – I don't know – the adolescence or early twenties you never really had."

Willie was aware of a growing sense of withdrawal. The playful relief of their conversation and the elation he had gained from it vanished. He was being threatened and his guard was up.

"The trouble is there's nothing much I can promise you that you'll want or believe in," Joanna went on. "I think we could be good friends, but there's no reason why you should bank on it. I've thought that we could start having people round, I've been looking out for a part-time job. There's a chance I might get something with a music publisher – I've even thought I could help you with some of the research for those obituaries."

"I'm going to stop doing those." He was glad of the chance to switch the subject.

"Why? You like it. You're good at it."

131

"I want to get back into documentaries. Eric agreed. It's all fixed."

"Oh." She took it as a blow.

"It was always a holding operation," he said, eager to pursue it. "When I took it on I needed to freewheel for a while. I want to get out and do something more," he said, "alive."

"Another change." She nodded, carefully, and he knew that she took his news as yet further proof of his journey away from her. She was deflated.

"Shall we go upstairs for coffee?"

"Not yet." She lit another cigarette, regrouping her arguments. "You won't tell me who she is . . ."

"Joanna . . ."

"I do love you, Willie. I'm sorry that it's taken this . . . threat to make me realise it but I know now what I should have told you long ago and often. I love you very much. I don't want to live without you." She hesitated. "But I've got absolutely no way of holding on to you, if you want to go, have I?"

At that moment he saw the alternatives: an honourable attempt to restore their marriage. An attempt which would at least have some dignity and, who knew? perhaps the possibility of finally building those deep foundations of mutual respect and trust which saw happier couples through the final laps of their lives. He saw the chance to help someone he had always wanted to help and to be aided by someone whose character he had once loved so greatly. There was a good fight to be fought and the promise of succour. Against that was the giddy abyss of his undeclared obsession with Caroline who was, he could see in this moment, so far from loving him that his only hope would lie in the dangerous possibility that he could be ready to catch her if she fell. He could be left with nothing but the ageing addiction of a voyeur, the pathetic dedication of the silent acolyte, and the final fear that his unreturned passion had been no more than a barren illusion. For all good sensible decent reasons he wanted to reach out and comfort Joanna, moved, as he was, by the care and gallantry with which she had assessed their position and tried to air and resolve it.

132

At that moment the love he had for her rekindled and he took her hand in his most tenderly: but only to say, "I think we should go upstairs for our coffee."

(5)

"Willie took me for a walk on Hampstead Heath this afternoon. He did not talk as much as he usually does. I thought – if you want to know! – that he was getting rather keen on me and I was worried because I don't want to hurt him. He's such a nice man, isn't he? But his mother is very ill – he's going up to see her again for Christmas – he did not offer me a lift this time but he assumed I'd be going to Scotland. I didn't want to tell him about your coming over. I don't know why. I want it to be private, somehow. We met David his – stepson? – Joanna's son, anyway. He's not at all as I'd imagined – more of a Trot than Jake, I think. He wants Willie to make a film about what they are doing in his community arts centre. Willie listened but he did not seem terribly keen.

Isn't it awful when you are so happy and other people – especially people you like – are sad? You feel as if you're cheating the world, I think. You have to be so careful (or I do) to keep it to yourself because if you let it out and let them all know what you were really feeling, they would feel even worse. Or would they feel better? Anyway.

I am now officially unemployed. That's Jake's Christmas present. He had no alternative and he was very nice about it but the fact is that I feel that I want to get out and just prove I can act now without having to prove I can be part of a political movement at the same time. Any jobs in New York? London seems so very depressing – unemployment, everybody tense: and there's Poland and more and more bombs. Two hours in bed with you would blast all that away.

Sorry for the dreary letter. I calculate that this is the last chance I'll get to write to you before you fly back to England.

I'm dull because I haven't seen you for so long and without you I feel so much less than myself – which is an appalling confession for an anti-macho and anti-male oriented person but truth will out, as my mother says. I love you more and more; it never seems to stop or falter. Love, love,

Your Caroline   XXX"

Chapter Seven

"It was as if all of us hid Marion away, (Willie wrote). Caroline, as she was to tell me later, blocked her out, afraid to think of Ian's wife, preferring to take her version from the well-edited snippets fed to her by Ian himself. She said – by way of an excuse which she knew to be feeble – that she could simply not imagine Ian with anything as solid and restraining as a marriage: he seemed so free. That's as may be. Ian, of course, found it convenient to refer to his wife as little as possible. Like many selfish and successful men he had his cake and ate it. He accepted the security and the residual respectability of married life while behaving like a bachelor. And that was the least of it.

I myself never considered Marion at all. A foolish mistake. But my scheme of things was already bulging with Caroline, Joanna, my mother – and, trailing behind them, David, Eric, the job. Yet Marion proved to be the iceberg, as in that poem by Thomas Hardy where the *Titanic* sets sail, all splendid, all powerful, full of life, and meanwhile, miles away, deep under icy waters, the iceberg which will sink it is growing relentlessly as if aware of its fate. So, while I was hovering about Caroline, happy to wait, perhaps aware already in those first months of expectation that in the waiting would be the greatest part of the pleasure, and while Caroline and Ian (as I discovered) were behaving, one genuinely, the other affectedly, as if the notion of young romantic love had just dawned – Marion's wrath grew.

I remembered their marriage very well. I had disapproved of it. Poor but brilliant young actor and wealthy heiress, a friend of those titled and cash-stacked names which straggle through the gossip columns like recruits called up for what they know is a phony war. For a short while, I believe, Ian had quite enjoyed what, *mutatis mutandis*, could be referred to as the nouveau aristo embrace – but only for a short while. One of the striking things about Ian was the speed with which boredom set in; another was the powerful attraction his own work had for him. This meant that his engagement with the outside world was generally conducted in a series of flurries, lightning raids just sufficiently long to scan the territory and pick up any useful treasure and provisions. He quit Marion's Society within a few months, quietly but finally. He simply did not care enough for it – or more likely he had looked at it, taken what he wanted and moved on, like an asset-stripper.

From then on the little of a shared social world they had together revolved around his life, which usually meant the actors, directors and writers he was working with or his longest-lasting friends. I have to say that one of the reasons why Marion was so cool towards me for so many years – until these events – was primarily because Ian made no apologies for the fact that in certain important ways he could have more interesting and useful conversations with me than he could with her. He had been known to ring me from, say, New York, talk at length and then ask me to call Marion to tell her he was OK! And after the first months of their marriage, Ian began to foster that sometimes mock, sometimes real, preoccupation with money, masking it at first by protesting that he wanted to be able to 'support' Marion.

Given Marion's wealth, it was ridiculous. Given the burgeoning feminism of the sixties and seventies, it was wilfully reactionary. Given her brain, it was irrelevant. She was one of the best agents with one of the most powerful literary agencies in town. It suited Ian, though, to put on his cloth cap from time to time. He told me he even refused to have a joint account but solemnly 'gave' her housekeeping money by bankers' order every first Monday of the month.

God alone knows what really happens in other people's marriages. The marriage campaign seems generally the history of losses and retreats.

In that long march back from the flames of the dream of Moscow, though, many people find ways to survive and sometimes seem to flourish. Marion and Ian were like that. His failings and her disappointments were both 'known' and passed over: people who lived far further from the edge of scandal and disruption found their ankles nipped by the columnists and saw their names dragged through embarrassing paragraphs of cheap print. Marion and Ian – largely through her management, not to say influence: agents handle journalists as well – had succeeded in skating over the cracks. At times it was difficult to know whether Ian cared at all what people thought or what would happen to his marriage: at other times it was difficult to believe that anyone could be at once so publicly reckless and so thin-skinned about what people thought or said about Marion and himself.

When I came back to London from visiting my mother there was a note from Marion asking me to call her. I did and she invited me round for a drink that evening. I had already telephoned Caroline but she was not in. I went to see Marion ignorant of Ian's visit. I had caught a heavy head cold while in the north and throughout the encounter with Marion I dipped into a box of tissues as greedily as a child raids a box of chocolates.

Ian and Marion lived in one of those splendid houses in Holland Park, stationed around spacious private gardens the size of a small municipal park. White, cliff-tall, built at a time of Victorian domestic amplitude and low wages, they have a serene style and comfort which makes their proximity to the centre of London seem miraculous. At today's market value, the Grants' home would probably command £250,000. They bought it for considerably less than that sum a few years ago.

Virginia Woolf, writing about 'Great Men's Houses', says that 'it is no frivolous curiosity that sends us to Dickens' house and Johnson's house and Carlyle's house and Keats' house. We know them from their houses . . . Take the Carlyles, for instance. One hour spent in 5 Cheyne Row will tell us more

137

about them and their lives than we can learn from all the biographies.'

The Grants' house was far too discreet to stink of money, but the refurbishment had been expensively done. Damaged mouldings had been replaced; wallpapers and wall colours chosen to give an overall effect of accidental muted elegance; little 'new' furniture – what had been recently bought was in older styles and patterns and the new was intermixed with the antique and the slightly broken-down and cosy. There were a lot of books, mostly contemporary publications, little sign of the studied sets of classics anywhere but in Ian's study. The walls were crowded, almost littered with paintings and prints: Adrian Stokes, Rosie Lee, Patrick Caulfield, two drawings of Kitaj, Sydney Smith's paintings, watercolours of Norfolk (where Marion's people came from), dark, unframed oils of cattle, still lives, unknown faces, a big Sidney Nolan, a pair of Mike Browne's witty screen prints, some of Marion's family portraits, well-framed sketches of the costumes and designs from some of Ian's productions. And fresh flowers – several vases – an unashamed compulsion of Marion's. In one way you could quite easily disentangle the two of them, their tastes and backgrounds, and approvingly reassemble the house as an harmonious coalition. The disguise, though, was just this appearance of harmony, this appearance of homeliness. Neither quality was part of their life together. The house was almost a poster, advertising what they would like to have both themselves and others believe about them. Perhaps its preternatural neatness was the giveaway: only an image could be as neat as that. As for many people, the house represented not what they were but what they thought they should be.

I went there in the snow; the end of the day, street lights further whitening the snow-crested houses, an urban enclave, enviably safe, quiet, invisibly protected by the unseen bonds of class and order, a different civilisation from that which David butted against just a few miles south, across the river.

Marion gave me a scotch – for my cold, that's how she put it. She disapproved of illness. Or perhaps she merely disapproved of me and my cold was just another proof of my general unsuitability. I had always felt her high standards – of dress, achievement and savoir-faire – press down on me like the censure of a strict schoolteacher. But I was wrong: she was nervous – as an old hand at that I soon recognised a condition which can cause you to behave totally against your interests and intentions. So I relaxed. It was uncharacteristic for me to feel secure in front of Marion. Usually I sat in that impeccable sitting-room which tried so hard to be comfortable, and felt that I was visiting a museum of interior design. Now I sat back. She had nothing to threaten me with, I thought, and I was intrigued, with some of the whisky inside me, to learn why I had been summoned. I even had time to notice how she looked; a beautifully cut tweed skirt, I remember, Harrods or Burberrys (or more likely a small shop off Bond Street), a dark-blue silk blouse, her blonde hair swept back from her forehead in a smooth easy wave, a tribute to skilful hairdressing. Underneath that careful mass, her slim face could appear too sharp, as it did that evening, the make-up unable to camouflage the tightened lips (her lips, unlike Caroline's, were thin) or soften the rather narrow eyes. She smoked a lot and drank vodka.

'You know Ian's been back, of course,' she said.

I nodded, and braced myself against the sudden power of panic. Of course I did not know!

'He phoned you once or twice. Then he learnt that your mother was not well. Is she better?'

'A little.'

Marion hesitated for a moment: her manners prompted her to pause for further enquiries but the urgency of her own concern was such that she side-stepped the issue. I noted that and the panic roared up.

'He talks to you a lot.' Marion said this rather sadly, without resentment. 'I wish you had been here. He needs someone to talk to.'

She smiled, not a nervous flash of teeth for reassurance but a friendly, wry smile which declared an understanding.

'I used to resent that,' she said. 'But he needs it. Have another drink.'

She helped both of us generously and returned to sit in the armchair opposite mine in front of a log fire unnecessary in that well-heated house, even on that icy day. The arrangement was so like the hotel fireside in Bath that I laughed aloud.

'Yes,' Marion said, responding. 'I *did* resent it. I suppose that was silly.' She looked at me shrewdly. 'You could have been a useful ally over those years.'

'What's happened?' I could not bear her manoeuvring any longer.

'He's met this girl. Did you know that?'

'Yes.'

'Has he introduced you to her?'

'No.' The lie was prompt, my automatic loyalty to Ian still unimpaired.

'I'm sorry. I don't mean to cross-examine you.'

'It isn't . . .' I said, seeking refuge in an urbanity which anyone less tense than Marion would instantly have recognised as a fraud. 'It isn't . . . unusual . . . for Ian . . .' I was off-balance or I would never have trespassed so far, but she appeared not to notice.

'No,' Marion spoke without bitterness. 'I'm sure we're both aware of that.'

I might have taken another tissue here: certainly, as she began what amounted to a cross between a confession and a plea for understanding, I raked up the tissues from the box as regularly as if I were staunching tears: dabbed, crumpled and threw them on the logs, somehow dreading that I would miss my aim and sully the carefully arranged Victorian flower tiles on the hearth.

'Of course it's happened before,' Marion began, briskly. 'At one time I was almost haunted by that monologue Joyce Grenfell used to do. Do you remember it? She was being informed about her husband's faults, particularly his sleeping around – though I'm sure that Joyce Grenfell didn't say *that*. Yes, she admitted it, yes, she knew about it – but "he always

140

came back to me", she said. She said it as if it were a kind of victory but I always thought it the saddest thing. Pathetic really. I dreaded people thinking I was pathetic. So I went around a lot; I even slept around a little, but I didn't enjoy it. I wanted to. But, I suppose it's background or whatever: I'm just monogamous. So is Ian, oddly enough: but on two levels. He really loves me, you know – don't look embarrassed; I've made up my mind to spill all the beans. You don't object, do you? There's simply no one else I can talk to as openly. *Do* you mind?'

Her politeness was genuine: if I had indicated any social unease, she would have stopped, I'm sure of that. But I wanted to know what had happened. I shook my head, blew my nose and sipped the whisky.

'You see, he wants me to be there, but he simply can't love me all the time. He keeps falling in love and, being Ian, the feeling leads to action. He's very faithful to his women, I think: for a while. Then it stops – the love or whatever, I mean – just like a light clicking off. And then he moves away. It might seem odd to you, but there's a way in which I respect it. He never lies about it: I know that if I want to leave him I can: I know he would be generous in any settlement. Part of me hates it and hates him for it: another part thinks that I ought to be able to stand for myself, not depend on him. I suppose both of them come from my family. We're all proper and very English home and country, as you know. It would be silly and false of me to try to deny that. I can't bite the hand that fed me.'

I liked her resolute loyalty to her past. Like Ian, in a way, although she could appear trendy, she kept to her roots and made her moves only after she had thought through what she herself wanted to do. The rather obstinate lines which creased at the top of her nose as she declared her allegiance were more attractive to me than all the chiselled, dieted, newspaper-noted cast of her face. If one of the qualities for which you admire people is to judge them by the distance they have travelled from their inherited starting-point, without repudiating their origins, then Marion scored high on both counts: for in her

141

attitude to Ian she had moved light-years away from any understanding her parents might have had. As she went on to say.

'The thing I like most about the feminists is just that determination to stand for what you are and to avoid being stereotyped. It's a little complicated in my case, maybe it's even perverse, but to react as the wounded wife would have been just as pathetic as being the all-forgiving Joyce Grenfell doormat. I like Ian: I love him really. When our life works together it's marvellous: when it doesn't . . . well, I look around my friends and don't see very much else that's marvellous. And being with Ian has made me make my own life. There's no bullshit in him, you know. Even when he's head over heels with someone he'll follow it through, he won't be cheating, he'll spend all he has. He's made me a lot tougher than I would have been. He doesn't respect anybody who hasn't worked out their own opinions on what they're talking about. I know you think I'm part of the Brideshead hangover: my parents and all their shooting friends consider me quite left-wing.'

She smiled, this time with that irresistible inner amusement, and I remembered Ian's delightful stories about Marion's puncturing dinner-parties on the merchant-banking, landowning circuit.

'He's been very good for me. Why should I walk off?'

More whisky, more tissues: she drank along, glass for glass.

'No, there's no bullshit,' she repeated, rolling the glass between her palms, returning to what was clearly a theme. 'You see, there are things about Ian . . . he's very violent in a lot of ways . . . my father's one positive comment on him was that Ian would have made a "fine soldier". I see what he means. Ian goes out to do battle with those roles: he wants to conquer them and more than that he often wants to sack and loot and rape and pillage – the whole bit. It's as if he invents his own wars because he knows there will be no real ones worth fighting in any more. That's how I've come to see it. He wants danger – sometimes I've been rather a disappointment to him there,' she laughed, 'he pretends to be put out by my passive resistance – but that's only one of my tricks; he knows that; and he knows I can't fox him. It is war, though, for him. As if the only possible way to live life were to charge and charge again. It's the same with his feelings about women. You know how truly tolerant and egalitarian he is – in work, in the way he responds to people, whatever race or creed goes without saying nowadays I suppose – but whatever sex. There's nothing sexist in him – that's why he can bring out the feminine side of characters so wonderfully well. Yet, in one sense, there's a totally unfashionable, hair-raising side to him. We went to see the *Oresteia* a few years ago, and there are those lines which say something about the women not really counting in the birth of a child: she's just the nurse for the man's seed. Something like that in the trial scene at the end. The audience hooted, of course, but there's a sense in which Ian profoundly believes that. There was something in the programme note, a quotation from Aristotle about men being superior, women inferior, and that didn't make him blink either. Of course he laughs at himself and it isn't something he would ever admit but it's to do with this battle thing, and this no-bullshit view: he knows that in the end men can out-gun women – or he would claim that – and he acts on that conviction.'

'Whatever the consquences?'

'Yes.'

'Even though his no-bullshit view is nonsense?'

'It's hard to take, isn't it?' She spelt out the next sentence slowly. 'Power, sex, talent and money: those are the four realities according to Ian. He isn't interested in power. He pretends to be interested in money but that's a game – in fact it's rather sweet, he's still a little bemused at getting paid such a lot for doing what he enjoys. He sees his acting as an accumulation of failures or half-successes at best. But sex . . . well.'

She asked me to put a couple of logs on the fire and I took advantage of the job to poke in the scrap ends of tissues which littered the logs like artificial snow. As I was doing that, she went out for a moment. 'Sex . . . well'? It seemed to be the one profound way in which people could define themselves

143

nowadays, cut off as most people were from power of the sort enjoyed by Aristotle's friends or the money commanded by so few or the talent given to even fewer. Sex was where they could see themselves in action, in competition and in reflection. And not only the sex between lovers: the sex in any relationships, the sexual balances inside oneself, the link with darkness, the access to that acute pleasure . . .

She came back with sandwiches, salmon and beef with slices of tomato and cucumber, as ornately presented as a tea-tray at the Ritz. There was even a minute green vase with a single red rose rising up straight as a baton. It was as if she could not do anything less than well. We ate a little, saying little, Marion fielding my compliments graciously while staring into the fire.

Then she shocked me. 'I went to see her,' she said. 'I've only done that once before. Some time ago.'

'What happened then?' I wanted time to absorb this. What had driven her to go and see Caroline? What had she found? What was happening?

'He reaches people somehow,' Marion said, determined, it seemed, to prolong my frustration. 'It's the same with you, isn't it? Somehow he – I can't quite express it – he *knows* you. Maybe that's rare: certainly it is in my life. Even when he's boring and tedious – and he's often that, *you* know that – he's still *there*. Do you understand? He reaches me,' she said, softly.

I made no attempt at a reply: she was right, I knew it, but I was not going to flatter him by agreeing.

'When he fucks you,' she said, calmly, 'you know you've been fucked.' She looked at me rather sadly. 'I'm scared to talk about it, you see. That was just showing off. I want to but I don't want to: I was using the word to egg myself on. Ian says that: "egg myself on".'

She covered her face with her hands and I thought she was going to cry.

There was nothing I could think of to say or do. Marion was not the type of person who encouraged help. As if to frustrate even my second thoughts on the subject, she looked up, tearless, and continued.

144

'It was silly,' she said. 'Ian was on the phone to her in his study; the door was open and I walked in to see if he had any cigarettes. I didn't creep in. I wasn't spying . . . I heard him telling her that he had only come back to see *her*, that he had only thought about *her* . . . it was Christmas Eve. Maybe that was it. I broke all my rules. The more I pushed him the more stubborn he got until, I'm sure, he was making claims for himself and this . . . Caroline, she's called . . . far greater than he had either thought or intended before I interfered. But I couldn't stop myself. He'd only been back a few hours: we'd gone to bed: I was happier than I'd been for months. I couldn't help myself. Have you ever felt like that? Ian says you're always so organised and controlled – he admires that. So am I, usually . . . most times.'

'Why did you go to see her?'

'I didn't sleep for about five nights. Ian was with her some of the time, not all; if he saw her in the evening he would come in about one or two as he's always done. There were two days when he stayed with me – he was worried about me – but again instead of accepting his help I just went on and on about this little tart.'

The word hit my brain and lodged there. I stayed on only because my curiosity outweighed the outrage and confusion I felt. And I hoped that in her story there would be some sign for me.

'So I went to see her. Ian gave me her address. I phoned and said I'd be there in half an hour.'

And? And?

'Her flat-mate turned up unexpectedly after I'd been there a few minutes – so we went to her bedroom.' She took a deep breath. 'It was full of Ian. His photographs, photographs of them together, I could see letters from him by her bedside table. She had the grace to take down the photographs. I let her do it.'

I imagined that scene: elegant, implacable Marion; Caroline bustling about hot with embarrassment.

'I couldn't believe she was such a *girl*,' Marion said, scornfully; then she checked herself with me, as, I imagine, she checked herself with Caroline. 'But I understood it,' she went on, 'not because she was young, not even because Ian "has a terrible effect on women", but because I could see that she had been lonely. In the month or two they had together before he went off to New York he had given her everything she had ever wanted. You *are* lonely when that goes. I know.'

And now the kaleidoscope of the last few weeks twisted yet again and I saw myself not as the patient hunter but the old stand-by, the link with the great love, the sponge delegated to soak up a little of that flood of emotion.

'I can see why Ian's attracted to her. She's young, of course, that's important. But if it was the usual male menopause I would not have been as afraid when I heard him on the phone: and he wouldn't have been as obstinate. Besides, male menopause! It's another cliché. Some men act like forty when they're twenty or sixty, or eighty for all I know. And vice-versa. It's all balls – averages. She's – lovely.' Marion spoke carefully now, straining as if she were compelled by not only her own instinct for fairness but by the deeper instinct – to correctly identify the enemy. 'And there's something innocent about her – you can see it best when she smiles – and even though she's been through some sort of London life she's retained it. Just the old-fashioned quality which Ian would recognise where thousands wouldn't and cherish where thousands more would think nothing of it or sneer. She has a good figure, good hair, all that's nothing outstanding but it's there, and it counts and she dressed to suit it. There's something else though: it's something Ian said, he said it was to do with her background, the Borders, the people there – I don't believe in all that – but she *has* got an intensity . . . an intensity that isn't oppressive or earnest. There's something complex about the way she feels, I'm sure of that, something that can draw in and give out endlessly. I was right to be frightened. I wished I hadn't gone.'

She looked exhausted. There was so much I wanted to brood over that I could now scarcely wait to be gone. But she needed some reassurance. From me.

146

'I think he'll see her again when he comes over,' she said, very quietly. 'And I don't think I'll be able to bear it. I don't know why. Perhaps it was the way she looked at me as we talked: she wasn't gloating or triumphant – she was even more frightened than I was and she showed it more. But she looked so *sure*.'

'No!'

Marion's look instantly changed: gratitude softened her eyes to a threatening flow of tears. 'You think not? You think it's just another . . . you know him so well . . . before you came, when I asked you . . .' she tumbled over the words, panting after hope, 'I thought – stupidly – that if you spoke to him, the next time, you could find out – not spy . . . just, if he brought it up . . . you think it will pass. I know it will, but,' and the gratitude fell away leaving her forlorn, 'she looked so sure. And I feel . . . I don't know . . . abandoned?'

For what might have been a full minute she gazed through me while I ached to leave, to run away and hide and pore over this polluted hoard of unwanted revelations.

'You've been very good to listen to all this,' she said finally, forcing herself to that professional briskness. 'Ian goes on about you being the best listener he knows.' She reached out to touch me. I too would have had to stretch out my hand and the gesture was beyond me.

'You've run out of tissues,' she said.

And I left with the gift of one of Ian's large white handkerchiefs."

Chapter Eight

(1)

"I'm free *all* the time," Caroline said, overbrightly, "and I'd love to see it."

"I thought of going to the five o'clock performance – it won't be so crowded – maybe you'd like dinner afterwards . . . ?"

"Not dinner. It always costs too much and I'm in no position to pay you back."

"Something then . . ."

"Yes . . . something would be fine."

"Outside the Academy?" Willie wanted to sound brisk but, as ever, he felt himself impelled to draw out the conversation. And she felt strained: he wanted to fathom her mood.

"Yes."

"Good." Had he explained his ostensible reason? "I have to see it for Walesa – "

"You said. A bit creepy, really."

"Yes." Willie, who was standing at the telephone, all but brought himself to attention. "Just before five, then."

"Fine . . . Bye."

She put down the telephone. He had not said goodbye.

He had to snap out of it, and he would. They would go to see the film, he would work out a quiet place where they could eat – as it would be early he could easily find an uncrowded restaurant – and he would tell her what he felt. He had hesitated about the film but it would be easier, he felt, if they had something specific to talk about for the first half-hour or so. He did not trust his courage.

Yet it had to be done. For months now he had behaved in ways disloyal to his sense of decency. The list of excuses he had

148

discovered for himself had always troubled him: now they seemed altogether distasteful. Besides, Marion's report had left him no alternative. If he did nothing, Caroline would be lost to him without his having put up any fight at all.

He sat down at his desk and went back to the Brezhnev script. There was not enough evidence for him to work out in any spare and transmittable form the power play inside the Politburo which had led to the invasion of Afghanistan. Was Brezhnev sick? Were the more hawkish comrades taking over? Brezhnev's long series of illnesses seemed both genuine and diplomatic. In February 1980 he was filmed (deliberately?) casting his vote in the elections despite the arctic weather – and despite forgetting his identity papers! It was important to work out Brezhnev but essential to have a line on him both for himself and for the preparation Willie was now doing for Lech Walesa. That was why he wanted to see Wajda's *Man of Iron*. He had cleared the use of clips but not yet decided which he should incorporate.

Working on Walesa depressed him. There was most often the sense, when he drafted these documents, that the men and women had enjoyed a good innings: sadness broke through rarely: perhaps that was merely because he was inured to it, but not altogether. By definition, those he wrote about had made a noise, created something, caused a stir and sometimes triumphed. Walesa's life would be cut short – not that Willie believed the Jaruzelski junta or the Russians would be so crass as to get rid of him at the moment – but he had become exactly the symbol of secular counter-authority most threatening to their authoritarianism and it was not unknown for accidents to happen in the night. Walesa had caught both his imagination and his sympathies – Willie reacted in the same way as most Western liberals. Walesa had jolted the amorality of Cold War and détente alike, uncovering those basic principles which the balance of terror and the expediency of co-existence had varnished over.

Everything about the man appealed to Willie – his homeliness, his religion, his ordinary circumstances, his boldness: it

149

was worlds away from the preoccupations which had been besetting him for the past months. His own life, viewed along-side that of Walesa, seemed so self-indulgently puny as to be shameful. Yet still he could not find that focus for admirable effective action in his own society: individual acts of astounding heroism, yes; examples of fidelity and devotion, yes; but the society itself seemed subsumed or disintegrating under the pall of declining prosperity, afraid to act in case it broke the spell, able to generate no tides or movements which threw up great issues in which the face and future of a society was fired. Or was that no more than a convenient excuse? Yet what would Walesa have done in, say, Newcastle in 1982? It was a trite question but it only served to emphasise even more how far from any centre of thought or history his own country seemed to be.

He worked for another two hours and returned to a neat flat, a pleasant meal, Joanna resolutely sympathetic. She talked about her day in her new job at the publishing house. Willie felt exhausted by her determination yet he knew that he ought to nourish it.

(2)

"I know that it is hopeless (Caroline wrote), but I don't mind. If that sounds pathetic, I don't mean it to be. What I've had and have (?) with you has been like a windfall. I've always told myself that – even when it seemed that it could go on forever. I've always held onto that thread which takes me back to what I was.

Except that you've changed me a lot, I think. In some ways I'm unhappier: I know this can't work out, I know how much I want it to. On another level, being with you has made me realise how limited my own talent is. I'd hidden, up to now, in the "group". I love acting and the theatre but I can't frankly see myself being offered much exciting work. You're very sweet about my work etc. but I don't really believe you. I'm "resting", as they used to say, now: I'm doing some

150

(unpaid) work for the Spokesmen – they're rather like Jake's group but not as good – they may take me on as ASM plus possible small roles: and they may not! Your cheque was very nice and I don't want to hurt your feelings – I know it's just generosity, no more – but I tore it up. Thank you, though: honestly.

Being unhappier is OK, I think. I look back and wonder how I could have bummed around for so long. I think that the way I feel now enables me to work out what I want to do. Perhaps it's only when you're unhappy that you have to think about what you want to do. Up until now I seem to have just floated along. But I'm deciding on things now: I'm taking lessons to speed up my typing – there seem to be temp jobs available all year round in London – maybe it's a small thing but it makes me feel I can make myself more secure. I suppose wanting to be secure is what you fall back on if you daren't hope to be happy.

I'm sorry this is so gloomy, darling, but there's something I can't get out of my mind. I suppose Marion has told you – although, from what you say, very little is said between you – and if she has then I still want to say something.

She came to see me and we talked. I liked her. She's very beautiful – you've not mentioned that, really – *really*, stylishly beautiful. And it was impressive that she should ask to see me – you'll understand that. She seemed so sure of herself – and so sure of you. She didn't patronise me – or us – although she did point out that it had happened before. But she made me feel so low. Not just depressed – that followed: low. I am, after all, from one point of view splitting up a marriage. However absurdly old-fashioned that might seem to you – and to *me*, in principle – in fact it still counts for a lot when you're brought face to face with it. She just seemed to know you so well – and I could sense all those years you'd had. I don't have anything strong enough to fight against all that. There was nothing I could say but admit what I felt about you . . . I would have liked a different sort of talk – but that would have been impossible of course: silly

151

of me to think of it – but, stupidly, I would have liked to talk to her about you. I talk to no one about you – except Willie, and less and less to him. She's very *nice*, isn't she?

When she left, though, Ian, I was shaking. Literally. It was quite extraordinary. It was two days ago and even now, writing to you about it, I feel too shaky to set it down properly. I got embarrassed about your photos and letters; she had to come into my bedroom and there's only the one chair – she sat on the edge of the bed – where we had been, I wanted to – tell her? It seemed so *wrong*.

What I'm saying is that it wouldn't have seemed so wrong if I thought we were going to carry it through in some way. I've never expected that and it won't happen, will it? So it is hopeless. And as I said, I don't mind.

But I think I should mind, Ian. It's weak, isn't it, just to drift along like this? I'm dependent on you so much and yet I see you so little. You'll get bored with me or tired of me sooner or later. For the sake of my own self-preservation I should stop seeing you. I honestly can't imagine what that will be like. But I know that I ought to for my own self-respect. I'll never stop loving you – you know that. And I'll never find anybody like you. I think about you *all the time* – still: more than ever. But if I don't act for myself now, I'll never be able to live with myself: however wonderful the old moments might be, I'll always know that it will be bound to end. Even over Christmas, my love, I felt that you were straining to show you loved me – almost as if you were determined to show you could be "faithful" to what you'd said and done. I wish you hadn't said a lot of those things – but I can't blame you for anything – see how hopeless I am?

I've re-written this letter scores of times in my head and it's always been more fluent and less mournful than this. I just don't have the energy to do this as well as I would like to. You see, my love, I have to leave you.

I can't believe I'm really saying this. After meeting Marion I know that she is your fundamental commitment whatever else you might say or do. I suppose I can't bear the realisation

152

that I will never be that. I didn't feel jealous of her, though; just tired. Suddenly tired, as if I'd been hit by vertigo. I wish you were here. Isn't it funny how it all comes down to clichés? "I wish you were here," "I'll never stop loving you," "I can't go on like this." The English teacher at school used to chastise us if we used clichés.

Good luck darling: God bless, and thank you.

Love,
Caroline"

(3)

She looked so crashed out that Willie hesitated to tell her what he had decided he had to tell her. They had talked a little about the film, but even in that conversation she had seemed to tire very quickly and he found himself delivering a self-conscious monologue on recent Polish history, sweating as he ploughed on alone, scanning her mood to find a way to understand it.

He had taken her to a small Greek restaurant in North Soho. It was practically empty. As if to mark an era of thrift, they merely ordered lamb kebab with a carafe of red wine. She ate little and slowly, obviously having to force the food past her lips.

Willie was thrown. He had built up his courage to declare himself to her: he had rehearsed it so often that he had begun to find a fatalistic delight in the prospect. Now that she was sitting there, forlorn, his natural inclination to be helpful and soothing reasserted itself with a tidal inevitability. Yet he beat it back: he had to say it.

"I'm sorry to be so boring," she said, and the sad reflection of her old smile made him reach out to take her hand. It was a gesture he would never have made had her unhappiness not so transmuted that smile that he had no alternative but to reach out, as if to touch her would be to help begin restore it. She let him hold her hand. She looked at him questioningly, almost pleadingly, he thought.

He took a breath.

153

"It's Ian," she said. Willie felt despair.

"You know we've been together. Having an affair." The phrase was unnecessarily vehement and she withdrew her hand as if to underline it further. "It's all over but I feel a bit down, that's all. It'll pass."

"All over?"

"Yes." Caroline looked very steadily at him: behind the level gaze was a shakiness which yet again teased at his avuncularity. But he made no move: he could sense further: she needed to convince herself – and, just possibly, him as well – that she had her feelings in order if not altogether under control.

"I'm thinking of going back to Scotland," she said. "There's a lot going on there now. It would have been better if I'd never left it. Not because of Ian." She blushed as she rushed to explain herself. "There was a chance, once, to get into the Glasgow Citizens as an ASM. If I'd taken it I might have done something . . ." And then she was silent.

"I would miss you if you went away," Willie said, labouring against the unexpected constriction which hemmed in his lungs.

"That's nice." She took his hand and smiled more cheerfully, more friendly. "But you are very nice. Ian always said that."

"There's something I've wanted to say – "

"About Ian? Please don't. It's over, that's all."

"It's difficult . . ."

"Yes," she replied, as if he had been commenting on her condition. But something in his intense love, however masked and deeply restrained, must have touched the open wound she had striven hard to cover up. Her fingers gripped his hand fiercely. "But I have to do it. I mustn't see him again."

"This is the wrong time," Willie said, a clammy hopelessness anaesthetising his will, "but – "

"I didn't want to talk about it," Caroline said. "But you know him so well. He *has* done this before, hasn't he?"

Willie made no move.

"He has," she said and nodded to herself. "And there's no

154

reason why I should be different – and there's Marion – it isn't fair on her . . . I have to make a life of my own."

"It needn't be on your own," Willie said. And the mask fell away.

Caroline simply stared at him and slowly took her hand from his. Willie desperately wanted to deflect that stare or dodge it but he forced himself to hold it.

"The thing is, Caroline . . ."

"Don't say it – "

"But for months now – "

"Please, *please* don't say it. Just don't *say* it, that's all. Please."

The words of love and devotion, of his committed affection, of his willingness to wait, to stay or go, to want merely her knowledge, her acknowledgement of his feelings, welled against his tongue and he could not dam them up. As he blurted out his lines she hung her head. When he had finished she was silent.

Willie drank some wine: the coarse red seemed not to quench his thirst but to sharpen it. He poured himself some more.

"Why did you have to say that?" She looked at him reproachfully. "I thought you were a friend."

"I am. And if that's all you want then that's what I'll be."

"Why did you have to *say* it?"

"I mean it." He paused. "I love you: I think about you incessantly. I've never loved anyone as I love you and never will. I can't stop it. I don't want to."

"That's very nice of you."

"I wanted you to know. That's all."

"That's all." There was only dullness in her tone.

"It's a bad time. I should have waited."

"*You're* married as well," Caroline said, mildly, following her own train of thought. Then, "Does Ian know?"

"Of course not." Willie drank more. Now his dream was released he wanted to look at it and caress it. "I know I'm married," he said, "but I've never – before – and anyway if you

155

– at all, at any time – thought we might . . . or even just see each other regularly, I would leave."

"But Ian says Joanna depends on you."

"I think she used to. There's always that raft in any marriage. You depend on each other."

"I thought it was more than that. The way Ian put it, I admired how you stood by her. He did."

"It's changed." Willie wanted to sidestep this bartering talk about his marriage. He had wanted to present the fullest promise of the possibility he saw for Caroline and himself. It was all becoming too particular for his grand vision.

"Why?" she asked.

"Joanna's sorted herself out."

"So now you can leave her."

"You make it sound as if I was jumping ship."

"No." Caroline was set. "I'm just interested to know how you can contemplate leaving someone you've lived with for so long."

"Caroline. Please."

"Don't back away, Willie. I want to know. It happens every day and maybe we come across more of it than most people – in telly, and the theatre – but I still want to know how you can think of doing it."

"It would be because of you."

"Yes. But what about her?"

"She . . . we haven't loved each other for years, Caroline. I don't think I've loved anyone at all until now."

"But all that time together . . . ? Wouldn't she crack up or – I don't know." Caroline's purpose seemed to leave her. The question, though, had to be answered.

"No. She's better now. And I would always be there to help. If she needed it."

"Maybe that would be the worst thing you could do." Caroline paused. "But wouldn't the guilt of it drag you down – and the worry about her – wouldn't it?"

"I don't know."

"You haven't thought about it," she said, her double

156

pain intensifying her insights, charging them with a piercing clarity.

"Possibly not enough," Willie admitted, humbly. "I've thought about you so much."

"Yet what's that to me?" Caroline raised her voice, wildly. Willie glanced around, the automatic fear of a "scene" even at this point strong enough to trigger off the social reaction.

"It's the wrong time."

"No. If you've been thinking it I'm glad you've said it." The wildness was only marginally muted in deference to his embarrassment. "I should have guessed something or other anyway. I suppose I did."

"Did you?" Willie clutched at this small recognition.

"Ian teased me about it once or twice. We thought we saw you once, following us. Or just standing there, outside the theatre."

Willie's confidence swooped down dizzily. "It was me," he said, eventually.

"Oh God . . . I'm sorry."

"I just wanted to see you."

"Oh God." Whispered.

"It didn't matter how. I just had to see you."

"Please don't tell me any more."

"You still love Ian, don't you?"

"Willie . . ."

"You do." His brief flicker of faith was snuffed out in realism.

"That isn't the point."

"If you weren't in love with him – "

"Willie. Listen. I want us to be friends."

And nothing else? He dare not ask for fear of the answer.

"Will you?" She took one of his hands in both hers.

The overwhelming feeling he had was of a wonderful image being condensed into a small prosaic frame. If only he could really say and show how he felt; if only he could let out the depth and undoubted endlessness of his love for her; if only he could make her feel what he felt instead of that plodding

157

declaration, that unsatisfactory conflict over Joanna for which she seemed so much better prepared than he –

"Marion," he said. "You were thinking about Marion. Marion and Ian. Not me at all."

"I would like to be friends."

"You still love him. What you really want is to live with him, isn't it?"

"Yes . . . but I can't."

"There's no room for anyone else, though." Was there hope in that? That no one, no one at all could reach her until – "Until you – yet."

"I think I'd better go home."

"I'll get you a taxi. You look tired."

Untypically she let him do that. She was worn out. It had taken all her energy to absorb and stave off his declaration while yet retaining him as a friend: the friend she needed as a lifeline to Ian.

(4)

He had the taxi drop him in Notting Hill Gate and began an irresolute ramble back to his flat. There ought to have been some exhilaration or at least some relief, but all he felt was the incursion of added worries. Why was it that what had seemed so grand and even pure in him had come out as the bid of a middle-aged man to a young woman to staunch a common male menopausal crisis? Just as plain and ugly people could have the same visions of romantic glory as those enjoyed by the favoured, so stoic and careful people like himself could have dreams of a consuming, all-overturning love. But why had he not been able to express it with greater fire? He blushed to remember his declaration: no better than a catalogue, nothing to tell of the force of it.

He tried to fend off a feeling of having been diminished by what he had done, but the sense of disappointment was too strong. Even now, walking alongside the northern railings of Hyde Park and still smarting with the memory of his ineptness, he could conjure up his thoughts of her: it was as if they existed outside and untouched by the real contact they had had together. In fact, what he had said, the confession he had dreaded, had not affected that image at all. But ought it not to have done?

There was a welcome light drizzle. He turned up his face to it every now and then, enjoying the freshness. Home came too soon.

"You're very late," David said, a little censoriously.

"I walked back."

"You're soaked."

Willie nodded and tugged off his coat.

"Joanna's asleep," David announced. "She had rather a skinful."

"Really?"

"You can't be surprised."

"I am. These last few weeks she's been better."

"Perhaps she got worried about you. It's after one."

Willie felt the cut of guilt. Joanna had been trying so hard. He ought to have remembered that.

"How bad was she?"

"Bad. Look. I'll have to stay here tonight now but I want to catch the first tube and I came here to tell you something."

"I see." Willie glanced towards Joanna's bedroom.

"She's out to the world."

"I'd better get myself a scotch. Want one?"

"I brought some ale with me."

Willie shivered as he poured the scotch and took a quick gulp neat before watering down a respectable measure to his usual taste.

"Well now," he said as he sat in his usual chair. "Are you *sure* Joanna's . . .?"

"*Drunk*," David said and said it so flatly that Willie felt a shiver deeper than the tremor from the cold. What force of rejection was working inside David to make him capable of such a flat, emotionless response which seemed to deny any relationship at all? How had he allowed the young man to become like that? Or, in truth, had he set the example?

159

"We're – at the Arts Centre – looking for help," David began, fixing Willie with his new "hard" look: the "this-is-a-far-far-realler-world-than-you-have-hitherto-known" look; Humphrey Bogart speaking lines by a late convert to Trotsky. Willie tried to frown away such subversive thoughts but he was not entirely successful. He could not yet take David's new seriousness seriously.

"It wasn't my idea to come along to you."

Willie appreciated that David had not yet tried to exploit him and his momentary scepticism about the young man was deleted. But he wanted to be alone to absorb his own evening: what had happened needed all his thought to put into order. And there was Joanna, unconscious, laying up guilt. He tried hard to give his attention to David. He wanted to say: please, let it wait, not now – but he was too entrenched in obedience to his own law of being available.

David had grown a moustache. This tardy observation helped focus Willie's fragmented interest. A long gentle scimitar of a moustache, like Lech Walesa's, Willie realised, it drew a dark line across his strained thin face as if making a declaration. "What we want to do is this." David placed the beer at his feet and leaned forward to spell out his point with maximum emphasis. "Have you seen *The War Game*?"

"Yes."

"Good." David nodded, rather reluctant to put aside his prepared speech on Peter Watkins' remarkable film drama of the sixties in which the effects of a nuclear attack were portrayed with such realistic vehemence that the BBC had banned it and the CND movement had adopted it as its main propaganda weapon. "A lot of people have by now," David added a little chidingly. "What we want to do is to bring it up to date. For our own area. As a community arts project. We would get everybody involved. The kids would get involved – film turns them on, you know, more than painting or books – they have a pop-film – TV-oriented culture which exploits *them*: we could let them be the exploiters for a change. And you can imagine how the project would raise the political con-

160

sciousness of the whole area because everybody would have to be involved – the fire brigade, the hospitals, ordinary people in factories and shops and offices, kids in schools – if we could make it we could just be the first. All the other centres could make their own. The whole nuclear-free zones idea could find its real expression in the active participation of the people."

"Who would make it?"

"The community. We would be there to help but it would be a community thing."

"The point about *The War Game* is that it was one man's vision. That was its strength, I think. Not to mention the fact that the man concerned was an extraordinary film-maker."

"We're not worried about technique," David said, briskly.

"I see." Willie decided not to keep his silence. "You ought to be. A poor film would do you more harm than good." To put it as mildly as he could.

"We're not interested in good and bad in an aesthetic sense."

"You ought to be."

"That's just a reactionary hang-up," said David, and this time Willie did let it pass: it was late enough. A last word.

"Just let me say that I think that you are demonstrably and, if I can intrude the word, philosophically wrong."

"We need two things," David went on, literally regardless of what had been said: not a suspicion crossed his mind that there was a grain of truth or reason in Willie's objections. "We need equipment and we need a front – respectability, if you want to call it that." He frowned even harder as if that word had to be pumped up against his will.

"What about money?"

"We'll get a grant."

"As simple as that?" Willie's surprise was unfeigned.

"Yes. We have funding for special projects anyway and the committee knows the GLAA if not the Arts Council would be very keen to come in on this."

"I see. So what am I? Equipment or respectability?"

"Both, we thought," David replied, stonily.

161

Willie nodded and started with the easy one. There were a fair number of independent production houses springing up now and his connections were good enough for him to provide about half a dozen sensible introductions, which David copied down in block Pentel capitals. He then gave an estimate of costings for film stock, laboratory charges, the use of editing rooms, dubbing expenses and print costs. Again David put it all down in the notebook: Willie felt he was giving evidence on which he would later be cross-examined.

"Now the other thing," said David, closing the notebook and having the grace, Willie thought, to look a little uncomfortable.

"Respectability."

"What we mean by that is a way of selling ourselves. Using the establishment's methods to infiltrate the establishment."

"I thought that's what you might mean," Willie said sweetly.

"You see, to make this work, we'll need, as I said, the fire brigade, hospitals, police – police! – schools, all that bureaucratic bourgeois reactionary set-up, and they would be more likely to come if we could get you to say that you, your outfit, was taking an interest in this film – would even show it on a slot – you have them, access slots. Of course it wouldn't matter whether or not you *did* show it – in fact there were some on the committee who could see a real advantage in getting it commissioned and then getting it banned: but that would probably be expecting too much."

"Probably."

David was now sufficiently alert to spot the dryness in Willie's tone. "What's your objection?"

"Simply that I'm not involving my 'outfit' in any enterprise where it is being used in the way you so plainly intend to do. That's all."

How pompous it sounded, he thought: but there it was.

"They said you'd react like that," David answered, his crestfallen look flipping him back to that recent former self Willie had found so sympathetic: he had to beware not to give in to that remembrance. "I said you would go along with us."

162

"Sorry. All the rest, I'll help as much as I can – but not that. I wish you hadn't asked, but there we go."

"I thought you said you were going to make documentaries now."

"I hope to."

"So why don't you do something about the Bomb? The two most important forces of our time are the drive to give more power to the people, whether it's Solidarity or our own unions, and the anti-nuclear movement. And they are one and the same. It's inevitable that they succeed. Your job should be to heighten the awareness of these forces. The fundamental trouble with the so-called free Western media . . ." David went into a spiel which sounded to Willie very like the well-prepared sermons he had sat through on Sunday after Sunday in his childhood. Just as he had often found that the greater part of his mind could opt out of those sermons, so he clicked off now, after vaguely worrying at the effect of such a massive dose of dogma on the hitherto apparently open and curious mind of his stepson.

But what *was* his documentary going to be about? He had gone back to the habit of his early years in television and listed every idea which came into his head. The result was like a shopping list for a hungry village; there was a desire for everything with discrimination nowhere. It was resolving itself into the sort of documentary typified at their most successful in the Second World War by Humphrey Jennings and long out of favour. Willie wanted to give a picture of the time, not through the technique of argument or the eavesdropping method much favoured now, but by building up a series of images around a central idea: there, though, was the problem. What was the central idea? Perhaps Jennings' poetic documentaries would only work because the central idea of the war held everything together: whether it was children in a playground, women in a factory, or lovable comedians doing a broadcast, the documentary flowed on the current notion of all the country being at one, at war, necessarily coherent. Wherever he looked now there seemed to be incoherence. And yet . . . people were

163

sane, things did not fall apart, heroes, though hard to find, were
surely still being heroic: the problem was the centre. In his
wilder moments he thought of basing it – though transferring
it – around his love for Caroline. Like *Letter to Timothy* it would
be an address to a young woman of today. But what would he
bring in? The formal mourning of Brezhnev at the coffin of
Suslov? The body piles on hidden dumps in El Salvador? The
Princess of Wales in her latest lace? Choirs of schoolchildren
in the Albert Hall? He was foraging for connections which
seemed determined not to yield any pattern. Yet, doggedly, he
"saw" that a documentary which could make a connection
between a private care or passion and the public orders and dis-
orders of the time – which, after all, were so present in so many
lives now through television – such a work could express the
times we lived in directly and comprehensively yet personally.

"Do you really think there will be a nuclear war?" Willie
asked, suddenly, surprising himself.

"What do you mean?" Interrupted, David stalled.

"Just that. Do you – *you*, not the committee, not the party
workers – do *you* feel in your . . . heart, guts, whatever, that
you live with that imminent possibility?"

"Of course."

"It *can't* be 'of course', David. Please. I want to know. Do
you wake up in the middle of the night and sweat? Do you think
'This could well be the last time I do X or Y?' Do you want to
– I don't know – rush back up to Cumbria and see the Lakes
because it might be for the last time? It's important."

"Oh God," David said. "Grandma phoned. Or rather the
doctor did. I forgot. Sorry, Willie."

"What did he say?" Willie looked at his watch. It was just
after two. "When did he ring?"

David concentrated hard. "About . . . nine o'clock."

When you, Willie, were unloading your unwanted affection
for Caroline.

"Mum took it." David's guilt drove him back to a rare
familiarity with Joanna. "She was a bit upset."

164

And Joanna, upset, drank herself out of her resolution while you –

"The doctor said you could call him first thing in the morning."

"What did he say?"

"He wouldn't. He wanted to talk to you. I should've told you when you came in."

"That's all right," Willie said – and to be certain he emphasised the point. "I'm sure there's nothing I could've done until tomorrow morning anyway." He paused. "If it had been *really* urgent he would have rung back. He didn't, did he?"

"Not that I know of," David hesitated. "I went down to the pub for a sandwich."

"Joanna would've said."

"She was drunk by the time I came back." David's monotone was pitiless.

"There are worse conditions."

David looked almost startled at this unaccustomed reprimand.

"She's been trying hard recently," Willie went on. "No thanks to me. No thanks to you. Never mind."

Self-righteousness and self-pity opened the doors to recrimination, any relief from the confusions which were now sickening his brain.

"I'd better go to bed." He stood up. "Anything I can do about the equipment, just let me know."

Willie walked quickly across to the door, searching for a phrase, even a word which would somehow resolve what had passed between David and himself – to tie up one thing at least.

"Thanks," David said, meaning it.

Willie turned and smiled. David looked relieved and the furry moustache stirred in a matching acknowledgement.

"They had decided that my mother needed intensive treatment and the nearest hospital was seventy miles across the borders from Cumbria, in Newcastle. They insisted on sending an ambulance for her which she thought scandalously expensive and embarrassingly public. However, she was soon grateful for it: the road across the high uplands was forever dipping and climbing and her pain was best nursed lying flat on the little ambulance bed. In order to make it easier for me, she pretended to fall asleep soon after we hit the old Roman road, giving me the chance to continue for myself the musing with which I had clumsily tried to entertain her. She enjoyed learning and I was relieved to be able to talk – just to be able to talk to her even though it was about Agricola and Vindolanda and mile castles. But when she closed her eyes my mind did not wander further into the history of the Romans on this far frontier: I wanted to sleep too.

I could settle no order in my mind. Here was my mother, dying slowly and very painfully. It would have been unnatural for me not to have been moved and drawn into her agony: while above that natural tie, I had always admired her and enjoyed her company, loved her. All I wanted was to be able to help over these last few weeks or months: the doctor did not know how long it would take. 'The treatment could arrest the spread and stabilise her condition for several months,' he said, 'or there could be another sudden deterioration as there has been over the last week or two. And then there's the matter of will-power. It's quite amazing how some of these people hold on.' Some of these people! Still, the doctor was young and trying his best.

Joanna had been very understanding – indeed there was relief there, too: just as I was relieved to talk to my mother about a subject remote from both of us, so Joanna welcomed the simplification of our lives which this brought. For the option was clear. I must go and stay as long as necessary. Joanna could not only know where I was and approve of what I was

166

doing but also, I suspect, hope that the exercise of duty would strengthen dutiful feelings elsewhere. And, paradoxically, the approaching death of an old person whose life has not been wasted is sometimes a healing catalyst. In that end, new beginnings of established relationships are seen as possible and, on the finite scale so concretely brought home, better than other, open-ended, beguiling attractions. Yet her helpfulness could not evaporate the reservoir of guilt which had filled up over the past few months.

I had decided to give up thinking about Caroline or having anything more to do with her. My last meeting, in retrospect, seemed shameful. Clearly she had no powerful feelings for me: in fact she treated me as a kindly niece humours a rather trying uncle. It was also quite plain that she was still passionately in love with Ian. That, I had to swallow, was none of my business. I had offered to be of help. She would ask if necessary. There was an end to it. A middle-aged infatuation, a common enough occurrence, thankfully rebuffed without causing any real damage. I would make it up to Joanna.

As always, being parted from Joanna made me think more tenderly of her. Throughout most of my marriage I had envied sailors, travelling salesmen, politicians and businessmen called on irregular but frequent missions away from home. It was only the intense cohabitation with Joanna, I now thought, which had deadened perfectly serviceable feelings. The rack of marriage is the ceaseless living together. As I thought of Joanna, crushed affection, bruised love, repressed endearments, scorched tenderness – all showed signs and hopes of budding: as I thought of her from a distance of three hundred miles.

So it seemed a settled hierarchy, as neat as an early Renaissance painting which has just discovered perspective: foreground – mother; middle distance – Joanna; moving towards infinity, disappearing, giving the painting its sense of scale but far, far away – Caroline. And then a jolt of memory would upset the whole pattern: Caroline would press on my thoughts until I felt suffocated, needing to see her as I needed

167

air; Joanna would re-assume the conveniently dismissable unfair caricature into which I cast her when I wanted to ignore her; my mother's pain would retreat, become like an impenetrable mist, nothing to do with me. I distrusted myself.

As I sat in the waiting-room through those five days and pretended to read the magazines and papers, I did not know whether it need matter that I distrusted myself. Perhaps it was the force of my mother's powerfully stealing death pressing on her, pressing on me; perhaps it was the wound of my life with Caroline which might have been and, not being, caused an unseen bleeding of energy, of unfulfillable possibilities, the drowned cries of those voices of ours which we never use, never hear, never know: whatever, my own self then appeared indisputably negligible. It was so odd, this courteous attention to an inevitable death: the visiting hours, the whispered reports, the steady chat, the gossip about others 'worse off' or 'doing well' in adjacent wards. That inexorable black ultimate dark blank unknown terrifying unaccountable mouth of death was about to close on the woman who had borne me, and I sat in a waiting-room reading back copies of women's magazines. A few hundred miles away, all that I would ever have the last chance to know and feel of passionate, reckless, hurtful, vivid, dangerous life mourned for someone else and I withdrew, politely, to a waiting-room of inexplicable good manners or to a jail of ineradicable timidity. The thing I was was never so lumpily evident as then.

Perhaps I was simply numb in the face of her nobly borne pain, stricken by the daily sight of her becoming thinner, whiter, more beautiful as the will not to complain transformed itself into a stoical tranquillity. Perhaps. More truthfully, though, I felt that her approaching death called my life, which she had given, into question. What, in this last quarter of the twentieth century, with all the privileges of work, comfort, education and opportunity I enjoyed – what on earth was I doing? What subscription was I paying? Who would benefit from this life given by this woman? Where was any sense of history, of adding to the common good, of doing all those

Sunday-school simple things she believed in so totally as I had done as a boy – but which now I felt to be the inaccessible, even irrelevant reaches of life?

I had time to think. I could see her twice a day but only for half an hour a time. I think she would have preferred it had I not been there. She had to make special efforts she would otherwise have been able to avoid and besides she wanted, I knew, to be alone in the tunnel of this unconceivable pain.

I stayed at a boarding-house in Jesmond, an inner middle-class suburb, academics still leading their incongruously leisured lives, overpaid media men such as myself, bureaucrats and organisers, in short, the new fat cats of the meritocracy, the lower-ranking officer class of an England which still knew how to take good care of its privileged own. It seemed as cut off from my mother's world as she from the worlds I carried in my brief-case in carefully typed sheets. Cut off, too, from the other parts of the Newcastle I strayed through in those strange five days: the wind-blown, litter-scattered, echoing city centre which seemed to know nightlife only as a few fugitive couples scurrying along the pavements; or the Bigg Market, with its pubs and cheerful Tyneside history, which, on the Friday night I was there, seemed a bare forum with the pub doors as escape hatches, swallowing up the youths whose violent shouts had replaced the old market cries and changed the nature of the place from a locale of homely barter to an arena. Cut off, too, from the inevitable high-rise flats, the motorway-city architecture. Cut off, truthfully, in a sense I could approve of and identify with. Here, in the suburb perhaps, was liberal England's last stand. Plenty of time to think on that too, as I put in the hours wandering past the gardens full of swings and play-schooled children, trim working mums, two cars, the business of modern living and modern manners crackling through the modern marriages and deeply protected occupations. Caroline and Joanna, by comparison, seemed in another country.

As with everything else, during these days, I was entirely confused: nothing was fixed for a moment in my judgement or

169

appreciation. Only that one presence, there, in her white room, frail and smiling to conceal the hurt, subject to violent charges of radioactivity, drugged, doctored, pumped alive, looking at me with increasing abstraction, forcing me to ask the questions which for her now seemed so insubstantial, so far away, so tired she was, so thin now, so tired."

(6)

"Armstrong!"

Willie looked across the small saloon bar and identified the speaker. The use of his surname helped him identify the man.

"Armstrong. William J. Class Six. Junior School. Early forties."

"Mr Paxton?"

"The very same."

"Will you have a drink?"

"A half. Bitter. Thank you. Yes – Armstrong!"

Willie turned back to the bar to get the drinks. His mother had been back in her own house for a couple of days now and he had settled all the arrangements. He was to go back to London by sleeper that night and had slipped down to the pub to stock up on cigarettes.

"About forty years. Thank you," Mr Paxton said. "Ago. It must have been."

Willie nodded. A little fatter, redder in the face, hair possibly a little thinner, moustache grey but still thick – but so little different from Willie's memory of him as the stern teacher running the top class at the Junior School. A tough old-empire sergeant-major who had picked up some polish from the officers.

"Of course I've seen you off and on," the teacher said. "And," his voice dropped – unnecessary, as they were the only two in the bar, "how's mother?"

What to pluck out of that slow motion maelstrom that would make any sense at all?

170

"Not in great pain, I hope?"

"Sometimes. But they give her drugs."

"Some people swear by them. Cheers. Give her my best."

"I will." Willie finally extracted the cigarette packet from the cellophane. "Smoke?"

"I don't mind." Mr Paxton's large fingers eagerly picked out a cigarette and Willie thought of pensions, state poverty.

"How long have you been retired?"

"Four years now: four years and six months. I was just in my mid-twenties when I took over that top class." Mr Paxton sipped at the half he could so easily have drained. Willie began to work out how he could get the next round in without making it too obvious. And how soon he could get away.

"Do you know how I got the job?" Willie shook his head. "Mr Scott – you'll remember Mr Scott – what a man he was! I've never know such an independent-minded man; he hated school inspectors, you know, couldn't abide them; when they turned up he would go down the town to do a bit of shopping – but a clever man, he could play the piano, do woodwork, teach religion – of course he was a big churchman – but he said to me 'Mr Paxton,' he said, 'you're a local man' – I was only born at Fletchertown, you know – 'and that'll do you no use in a place like this unless you can keep order . . .'"

It was no good. Willie respected the man, and wanted to appreciate the worthiness of the life . . . but his preoccupations put up the shutters of boredom. What was he talking about? Concentrate. Caning?

"And you know what he said?" Mr Paxton paused, highly delighted with the whole story. Willie by the shake of his head bowed him through. "He said 'Correct,' he said, but 'never on the hand,' he said, 'that's cruel. Never on the bare flesh.' And, do you know, he was right. I'd just guessed, of course, but it was about four times a day. I used the cane till I retired, you know. Every day. And I'll tell you something. I never had one complaint in over forty years. Not one. And there's still grown men'll come up to me and say 'Mr Paxton, you were right, I must have been a right little pest.' That's what's missing now,

171

I'm afraid: discipline." He drained the glass. Willie moved swiftly.

"No, it's my – "

"It's not often I have a chance to see you. If your old pupils – "

"Did I ever give you the cane?"

"A few times."

"I thought you were a rather well-behaved boy, weren't you?"

"Make it a pint, please – and another scotch, thank you – was I?"

"Yes. Very neat. Weren't you?" It was clear to Willie that he hadn't a clue. "Well, cheers."

"You left the town, didn't you?"

"For twenty-five years," the teacher said. "The wonder is I've settled into it again so easily. Being a pub-man helps, you know. I've always liked a drink or two, never to excess, mind, *never*, but I wasn't afraid to admit it. Even in the older days – which were a great deal stricter, you mark my words – people respected that. And of course, as I've always said, once you have people's respect you have everything you need."

"Where was it you went?" Willie lobbed out the question dutifully.

"On the west coast. Down Maryport/Workington way, a place between them. They built the school from scratch – new – I was the first headmaster and I stopped there until I retired. I had a wonderful speech prepared for when I retired, you know," his eyes, small-pupilled, green and grey they seemed to Willie, certainly unusually coloured, sharp, infinitely cheerful eyes, beamed now in anticipation of a story against himself, "and I couldn't say a word of it! They'd given me presents – well, I totted it up later on, there was almost a thousand pounds' worth of presents. Couldn't say a word of my speech: overcome by the occasion."

Was it that he came out of a more innocent world, when lads from local villages battled their way through to unpretentious training colleges and came back home to do their bit and pay

172

off their debt? Was the lack of knowingness, the naivety, the simplicity in a way, to do with the difference in generation or with the man himself?

"What was it like down there? On the coast."

"Terrible in one way. You know. All that unemployment in the Depression, sixty and seventy per cent, left its mark. And beginning to head that way again now. People hanging around street corners, nothing to do. I go back once a week – on a Wednesday, on the bus with my old-age pensioner's ticket – just to look around the market and say hello, have a drink, see the town. Not the school. When I left I said I would never set foot in it again and I never will, it doesn't do; but all those young fellows, you see — I taught some of them, I taught some of their fathers, just wasting away – a shame really, a scandal you might say."

The old schoolmaster went on delivering his relentless confession of a decent, sociably useful life. Willie's thoughts were scattered by this well-drilled autobiography. Yet he was hypnotised by it. Such a good life: it was a territory which had closed up behind and about him over the last twenty-five years. To leave, as he desperately wanted to do, to cut himself off from this endless, honourable coherence, would seem a betrayal. But he wanted to go. Perhaps he could not bear to look on a good life.

"Books," Mr Paxton asserted, "that's what counts. I would always have books in every classroom at that school. I would beg and borrow them – not steal! – but surround them by books and you have the chance, you see, that they'll read. I would get up to all sorts of tricks to get them to read. Even the little hard cases – and believe me there were hard cases, several of them have spent a good deal of their lives since school in Her Majesty's jails, but never mind, they gave me not a minute's bother. Bring comics, I would say, read comics. And, funny thing, parents, who could hardly read themselves often enough – *they* would say at those parents' nights I had, and they would all turn up for those parents' nights, 'But Mr Paxton – comics?' Anything, I would say, that sets them off. Anything at all. You see, you have to believe in it. And that's my conviction. Get a

173

child interested in reading, interested in books, able to handle them, and you've given him the key of life. I've put it in my will. When I die. Some money set aside to buy books for that school. For every classroom." He paused and smiled knowingly. "I've been boring you," he said. "Old schoolmasters never die, they just talk other people to death. Scotch, is it?"

"No, I –"

"Have one on me . . ." He heaved himself to his considerable height. "Do you know, in the four years since I left school, my pension, with this inflation-proofing, has gone above what my salary was in my last year. Ridiculous when you think about it, isn't it?" He looked puzzled and then grinned. "Makes no sense at all, does it? Have a double . . ."

(7)

The meeting with Eric was brief.

"It's a sod," Eric said, containing himself in his seat with the same evident effort as he contained himself in the new executive suit and tie which ill became his muscular frame, "but the fact is, Willie, the fact is – the plain fact is that . . . well. As you know we're shovelling off the obit department – no reflection on your work, none at all – on the contrary, praises sung high all round. *But*. This is the point."

"The point" brought him to a full stop and he looked at Willie with desperate sadness. The flimsy camouflage of executive embarrassment which had characterised him in his earlier meetings with his old mentor was now totally stripped away. He was the man behind the desk, the man up the hierarchic tree who had to expedite the nasty decision. Willie realised what he was going to say but felt too numbed by the realisation to follow that instinct which even so and even now urged him to help Eric out. Yet, Willie observed, as the axe fell in slow motion, there was at least some genuine pain here, some "facing it". Something real even though the blow was being given, not received.

"The point is – now don't ask me how this happened because they've explained it until they're blue in the face but I still don't understand it. Anyway. To do with a new method of accounting and the altogether mind-blowing fact that despite all the expansion that's going on we seem to be having to shed people . . . they're offering redundancy payments to several people across the board – quite substantial in certain cases, especially when people have been here for a long time of course." Eric looked away now and took a deep breath. "I think they're offering you a decent enough deal."

Willie had seen it coming – but only for a moment or two. Until now he had sensed nothing of it, nothing of the movement of the company over the last two or three years and particularly over the last few months. He had been nowhere near that quick of information which could have scented out the new deployments and wangled in to secure his own tenure. He had failed to observe one of the cardinal rules of all institutions under strain: forget the job, watch the politics. He had regarded internal politics as no more than passing gossip and his redundancy was due, at least in part, to this lack of understanding. All big institutions become closed political systems; survival and advancement within them has often very little to do with the outside world or with the impact or externally considered importance of the work done – and sometimes everything to do with the old rules of court, who's up, who's down, who's in, who's out; the favourites, the grapevine, the empire-building within empire-building. Willie would never have accepted, for example, the fact that promotion can come out of failure as often as out of success and that, contrary to reason, it is by no means always the most talented or the most well-merited who rise. Those who rise are most often those who most want to rise. Those who fall, or those who, like Willie, are pushed aside, are generally those who have exposed themselves as being ready for this sort of treatment. Therefore when it suits someone's game plan to have a few victims, men or women who seem to occupy the victims' bench are fingered

175

and out. And bosses need victims in order to remind themselves and others of their power; or, in extremis, to retain it.

"Sorry," Eric said. "I fought like hell against it. At one stage I even offered my own resignation. I told them how appalling it was, how much they owed you. If only you'd come up with a whizz-bang documentary idea – but even there I argued your case . . . I'm afraid it's needs must. It's hellish, isn't it?"

"Yes," Willie said, giving no comfort. He could not yet absorb it. "Yes," he repeated. Fired.

"If there's anything I can do . . . I mean, we'll still be able to take on freelances . . . if the idea's right . . . I'm sure it will be . . . it's just the basic stuff they want to cut back on . . ."

"I see."

"I wish I'd never taken this bloody job," Eric said, bitterly.

Willie smiled a little.

"You do it very well," he said. "Don't worry."

(8)

He did not tell Joanna but took her out for a meal in Covent Garden. She drank carefully and they talked about his mother a great deal. Willie felt a roar of emptiness and fear gathering its force inside him all the evening through but he ate trout with almonds without choking on the bones and drank Chablis with moderation. The future burned away before his eyes and he was unable to focus on the present.

When Joanna had gone to bed he went to his usual chair and made some calculations. He had always been too easy-going and generous in his financial affairs. The money he would get plus what he had would keep him going for a couple of years at most. Living at this level in London was hard to sustain on much less . . . perhaps he ought to move out to the country . . . perhaps he ought to fight the redundancy . . . perhaps he ought to use the money to set up an independent production company . . . perhaps he ought to give it all to Joanna, give her all he had and leave . . . to busk a living. After all, with a degree and a bit of experience, he could . . . The whiskies went down,

176

the notes grew tinier, the calculations finer . . . Redundant, obsolete, fired. Well, well.

It was a sort of insanity that led him to phone Caroline at this time – way into the early hours of the morning – and in this state: but he did. Her muffled, baffled-from-sleep voice touched him by its very sound without her saying a word. If only that voice, that mouth, that face . . .

"It's . . . Willie. Look. I'm sorry to have woken you up. I didn't realise how late it was."

"That's all right." Such a sensual drowsiness. "It's all right. What time is it?"

"I don't know. I've . . . I've been up to see my mother."

"Oh. How is she?"

"Not well. Not really. But . . . holding on. Look. I'll ring off."

"No. I'm awake now. I'm awake. I'm sorry about your mother."

"Yes. How are you?"

"Oh, you know. I've had flu. Silly, really. I've been in bed for the last four days."

"Oh dear. Is it that bad – I should ring off, shouldn't I?"

"No. No. Just a sec. Let me get a cigarette. Hold on . . . There. That's better. So."

"Have you found a job?"

"I was supposed to go to Glasgow for an audition but the flu . . . I'll ask them to rearrange it . . . if the job hasn't gone."

"Are you still determined to go back north?"

"Well . . ." She paused and changed tack. "I thought you might get in touch."

"Oh."

"After the last time. I suppose I expected it. But your mother – how stupid of me – sorry. Everything goes with this flu."

"I thought . . ." Willie, tell the truth? "I thought it would be best if I didn't. Best if we didn't see each other again, in a way. I thought I was behaving like a silly old man – you were quite right to put me in my place, and done very nicely, too."

"You're not a 'silly old man'. Not at all."

177

"You know what I mean. Let me ask you. I know it's late but. Are you still in love with Ian?"

"Please, Willie . . ."

"Do answer. It would be such a help."

"Yes."

"And what about him?" Willie closed his eyes tight as if a hard light were being directed onto his unprotected eyeballs.

"Ian?"

"Yes. Does he say he loves you?"

Caroline paused. It was so private, so magically private, so necessary to keep secret. But Willie was a friend, of Ian, of her, of both. And to tell someone, to say, as she longed to, as she needed to, as she reached out for the letter which had just arrived from America frantically covered with stamps to hasten its first-class journey, to tell someone would be heaven.

"Yes. I think so."

"That's what he says."

"That's what he says."

"And you believe that?"

"Willie . . ." Somewhere between a prayer and an admonishment.

"You believe him?"

"I believe him."

"Good. So. Good." Willie nodded at the cup of the black plastic telephone. "Well then. That's all right."

"We could meet."

"Yes. We'll meet."

"Whenever you want."

"I'll ring."

"Any time. Even at – two-forty a.m.!" Her jollity grated against him like the screech of wire on metal.

"Goodnight, then, Caroline."

"Goodnight."

"I'm sorry I disturbed you. I'm sorry about that."

He put down the telephone quickly, not wanting her to have the last word which would charm and torment him further. He lit a match for a cigarette and spent it burning the leaves of

178

calculations he had made. He denied himself the cigarette and went to his bedroom as quickly as he could, aware of his sleeping wife. The full force of his hatred for Ian, his jealousy of the man who took so much so carelessly and left so little in return, came almost sickeningly into his mind. There was no living with it.

Chapter Nine

(1)

New York was very cold. The radio in the yellow cab ripped out statistical freezing degrees with great relish on the road from Kennedy Airport and the cab driver, a Pole, interjected with excited outbursts about the intensity of last week's frost and the prospect of tomorrow's snow. Cold and the news of the cold, the entire city's awareness and preoccupation with the cold was early and prominently established. New York liked its dramas and cold was the taste of the month. It was undoubtedly very cold in New York.

"You British?"

It was not so often these days that Willie felt his heart sink in that odd vacuum-sucking sudden swoop-dip manner, but as this question came from the front of the cab with its inevitable challenge to stand up and be counted for all the sins and virtues, true and false, of his country, to be the reluctant ambassador often for what he most disliked, yes, his heart sank.

"Yes." From the North, he might have added if the driver had given any indication of having been to England. "From the North" meant that you could disclaim some responsibility.

"I got a sister in Derby town. That's in the North." The driver had a sawing, hoarse, shouty voice, not unattractive, just lacking in variety. "You been there?"

"Not to Derby itself, no."

"Nice place, she says. No work now. Everything close. Shut!" He lifted his hands from the steering wheel and clapped them hard together. The car was travelling at 58 m.p.h., Willie noticed.

"It's pretty bad everywhere."

180

"Worse in England, huh? And worse in the North? My sister says. She writes me all the time."

"Yes?"

"So why should I go over? She says all good people movin' out. Australia. There's a place. She say all good English people going there now. Everybody goes to Australia."

Willie felt slightly challenged. "It's bad, yes. Is it bad here?"

"No." The driver took out a cigarette. "Here it's terrible. Pittsburgh is closing up."

"We always think of you as rich."

"That's the trouble."

"Tell me something," the driver went on. "Why do you give your Prince of Wales ten million English pounds a year just to wave out the windows?"

There were on the Triboro bridge: the wonderful cityscape of electric twilit New York rose above the Hudson – the great towers and blocks, the forest of skyscraper and glass – to be enjoyed and stored away, a sight to be harvested in full . . . Willie glanced at it regretfully for a moment only and then leaned forward. "Well," he began, to the smoking, friendly Pole, "it isn't quite like that . . ."

He decided not to call Joanna. He had told her he was going away for a couple of days but he had not said that he was going to New York. His office knew and should Joanna ring in he had told his secretary to give all the information. Joanna rarely rang in. She had never looked on the office as anything other than an alien and rather antagonistic world: the counterforce.

The hotel room was neat, clean, a traveller's adequate camp. By the clock on the wall it was 7.30 p.m.: in his head, London time, it was half-past midnight. He decided to stay up for two or three hours to try to make sure that he got really tired. He rang room service for a bourbon, punched on the television and unpacked the few clothes he had brought. As he went from his suitcase to the drawers, he flicked the television around the dial, from news to sport to Spanish films, early Hollywood

181

films, game shows, canned comedy and, it appeared, the new star of American television – the weatherman telling everyone how very cold it was in New York. He settled for a talk show, using the box as a comforter.

He fished three-quarters of the ice out of the bourbon, added some water and enjoyed the drink. He lay on the hard, tightly made, almost military bed – why, he wondered, had the Teutonic spirit taken over the mass tourist industry in the States? – and leafed through a magazine of the week's events as if he had come for a holiday. The usual plethora. The great flush of restaurants and bars and clubs, the hydra-headed movie houses, so many that the city had to be blocked out to describe them all, the Broadway shows, off-Broadway and off-off, and the concerts, exhibitions . . . like London, New York on the pages of an entertainment guide presented a city stuffed and pounding with earthly, shady, sensual and intellectual delights. Out of his window Willie looked down on the grey mush-frozen streets, the merest trickle of people, few cars, the lights of the shops playing to empty houses. He wished that he had ordered another bourbon.

But his calculation had the effect he wanted. By ordering just one bourbon he was prompted into a decision. Should he order a second and wait the twenty minutes for room service or should he – as he wanted to – get up and walk around town a little? It was helpful, he had found, in the soft-brained limbo of jet-lagged time, to peg your way towards obvious decisions by such apparently crass little markers. He went out.

The radio man, the taxi man and the weatherman were right: it was very cold in New York. His light English overcoat barely turned the north wind "whippin' in from Sib-eria tonight, folks!" and his sensible shoes threatened to slide on the crusted icy sludge. But Willie wanted to walk a little. There was something about dunking yourself in New York as soon as you arrived which appealed to him. Even in the cold, the sense of a European capital with a beat, the feeling of the European tribes gathered on the rock of Manhattan bringing their tales from the past and their dreams of the future, the precipitous architecture, again from Europe but here made manifest in massed ranks, the signs and delis and the bookshops and hard cracks – it was a crackling city.

Willie's route was not aimless. His hotel was near the theatre district and he arrived there, cold, getting colder by the minute, just after the shows had started and the theatre foyers gulped down their audiences. He soon found what he was looking for. There was Ian's name, six foot high, headlining reviews which bawled out his "brilliance", his "exhilarating stage presence", his "matchless timing", his "great acting", his "definitive performance". "This you must see to believe," said the biggest banner of all. The only people in the theatre street, besides Willie, were one or two late-comers and a man packing up what looked like a stall. A few taxis crunched through the hard ruts of slush. Willie looked at Ian's name intently as if it needed memorising. He shivered deeply and looked around for a bar.

The nearest was Sardi's, a convivially theatrical Broadway restaurant not to his taste and out of his range on such an expedition, but the nearest. Feeling the real numbness of cold in his skull, in his feet, in his fingers, bone becoming cold, he went in and shivered even more violently in the blast of heat. Provided he would leave the table by 10 p.m., sir, there was no problem in finding a table, none at all sir, the cloakroom is over there, would you like to go straight to your table? The all-American politeness ushered him to his table, against the wall, underneath a phalanx of caricatures of theatrical persons only a few of whom he knew and only a few of them he could recognise from the caricatures.

To eat alone in public without print disciplines thoughts wonderfully. Trapped against the wall of caricatures, Willie avoided the unseeing eyes of others by assuming an air of intense preoccupation which very soon became the thing itself. As he unfroze over Californian Beaujolais and safe steak he raked over the reasons behind this abrupt decision to fly to New York. What was revealed was a labyrinth always leading to that unknown discontented unfulfilled centre of himself which had

183

been awakened or alerted by Caroline. Since then, as much hindered as helped by Willie's discreet pursuit of his goal, this force, as if magically brought to life, had insisted on its rights, pressed its suit, pushed against all the deeply entrenched constraints in Willie's character and background and would have air, would have a voice, would have its day. Perhaps, he thought, Caroline was a catalyst: she had certainly had that effect on him; from what Marion had said, she had had that effect there; and Ian?

He knew nothing about Ian. As he thought about that hugely lit billing on Broadway, the neon monograph of an emperor, his own provinciality and poverty of achievement crowded all about him, cramming him into the anonymous audience which applauded the great figures, or at least watched them from the other side of the footlights. Ian would take what he wanted, as he always had. Perhaps for each character Ian created, someone's real character had to be absorbed or wolfed or sacrificed. It need not be such a fantastical thought. Acting such as his called on all the powers. That raising up, that invocation, could demand rare energy and release powers difficult to appease. Caroline's heightened ordinariness of beauty, her unfragile innocence, the grace, finally, of that smile: all this might have answered a need in Ian over and above the Pygmalion aspect, the "whoever I pluck shall be a rose" hubris, the sheer greed of his appetite, the . . . Willie wiped the napkin primly around pursed lips. He had to contain himself until the right moment.

It was not so very easy to make the meal spin out, without conversation, without print. Yet he wanted to stay there a while longer, until the theatres came out at least. He wanted to prepare himself properly. Coffee came on the instant, souring the wine. He took a brandy and ordered a cigar. More and more he was losing touch with himself. Was he a remorseless hunter bent on revenge preparing himself thus in some primitive ritualistic fashion – by aping and parodying the life-style of Ian, somehow entering into Ian's spiritual world in pursuit of his self-appointed task? Was

184

he a tired, once dieted, now once again self-indulgent nowhere man?

How did this stand up against the last sight he had had of his mother – in her bed, so glad to be "home", so concerned not to bother anyone, in some unchallengeable way the freeholder of a valuable life?

Willie found himself, as had begun to happen quite often recently, remembering the time of his nervous breakdown: the press of events succeeded by the aridity of nothing happening, the unexplained upsurge of panic, panic roaring from some furnace of fear or rage or need and sweeping through the defences of his mind until it burnt itself out leaving scorched senses, withered stalks of confidence, the ash of terror littered everywhere. It was so odd. For that time of his life – a year, eighteen months – there had been days when *every moment* had seemed about to split open like an atom and explode in his face; when *every moment* had sometimes to be sweated through, lips held together by the bite of teeth to send back the cries for help, for what? Why? Just for some aid as the armies of repression and infancy burst through the adult redoubt to rape and plunder and destroy. Image after image was lurid. Nothing neutral there. No final subtleties of grey, no cherished gradations of autumn, all the iconography of Old Testament fire and brimstone hailing on his brain somehow bereft of skull cover and there, raw to the outpourings of his own other self, other selves, screaming through the blank universe of his mind like comets, trying to land, trying to flee, fragments of himself, directionless, ambushing every attempt at coherence, at unity, at tranquillity.

No; he was well out of that now: way, way from that. That came into the gut of the mind, that hit the bone of the body, that stung the centre of the nerve with a bare needle. Now he was jarred, that was all: and tired; tired of all this, wanting a resolution, that was all. And here, in the cannon's mouth, seeking it. Action would answer.

He steadied himself and began to count the caricatures. The restaurant started to fill up. Hurriedly he paid the bill and left.

185

Still cold: ah, but a soothing cold now, a cold to be welcomed and snuggled against for the definition it gave, a cold to be hauled down the throat and used to rake away the fug of self-scaring memories and brandy fumes.

In a doorway, opposite the stage door, which, he had noticed, was just along from the theatre entrance, he stood and waited. Weight on one foot then another. Hands in gloves in pockets, double glazing. A cigarette.

There he was! Even at that time and in that temperature a loyal cluster of fans broke cover and ran for the autograph. Ian smiled and smiled. A large long black limousine drew up – cocktail cabinet in the back no doubt, darkened windows, chauffeur out of an advertisement – and Ian stepped inside, ushering forward his companion, a blonde, loving her bouncy new-shampooed tresses so much that she left them free to shine even in cold New York.

It was time to go.

(2)

"Just for a couple of days," Willie said. He was standing, alert, beside his disordered bed. Noon precisely. Time of call well thought-out.

"What about tonight?" Ian asked. "Would you like a ticket? A couple of tickets?"

"I don't think . . . No I can't really make it. You know, meetings, Americans, talk."

"Sure. Well, what about after lunch? Today. Come round here, I don't leave for the theatre until about five. We could talk – what about three, three-thirty?"

"OK. Yes. OK."

Willie took down the address and put down the phone without dropping it. Ian had been so friendly, open, expected, decent, unhurried, accessible. It was a shock to have to realise that of course Ian had no idea of his purpose or the extent of Willie's knowledge of Caroline's intimacy with him.

Willie put in the three hours sensibly so as not to let his

186

impatience grow up to suffocate such tentative plans as he had. He went up to the Frick and spent an hour in that most proportionate and companionable museum, almost alone in the rooms hung with Turners, Rembrandts, Whistlers, Corots, Constables . . . He was reminded of Bath, of Joanna, of that sense of order and acceptance which seems so rich and easily arrived at in the past and was to him an unslittable oyster. For lunch he found an excellent small coffee house, clean, cheerful, two eggs, ham, potatoes, coffee, yes *sir*! and more coffee yes *sir*! and inexpensive. He walked towards Ian's flat, lost his nerve, caught a cab and arrived early and circled around the block like a plane stacked high above Kennedy, waiting until its time was due.

Ian's latest apartment – he had already changed address twice – was an immense loft in SoHo, "one of the early ones", Ian explained, beautifully converted and furnished, with the added touches of a sauna, a jacuzzi and a circular bath which just missed being a swimming-pool. Ethnic rugs decorated finely honed beech floors; Village avant-garde art circa 1957–67 spaced out the white spacy walls; voluptuously comfortable furniture littered the acreage of studio space and the sound system was backed up against one of the walls like a piece of monumental modern sculpture. The girl who let Willie in was unnervingly attractive. Willie was sure he had seen her somewhere.

"Eileen Francis," Ian said and rattled off three of her recent London roles. She was over in New York playing in a Pinter revival off Broadway. "Another Brit hit," said Ian. "They'll end up hating us here, you know. Most of the actors do already."

And the blonde? Willie did not ask.

"Tea?"

"Yes please."

"Earl Grey, Lapsang, Darjeeling, Jasmine, Orange Pekoe? We take our tea seriously in America."

"Whatever's going."

"What a wonderfully British answer. Right. One moment.

187

And fear not – the pot will have its bottom properly warmed."

Willie felt shy in front of Eileen. He had anticipated finding Ian alone and his natural shyness was compounded by a feeling of annoyance with himself that he had not anticipated such a three-hander.

"Ian's told me all about you," Eileen said, her voice silkily stagy.

Willie stared at her.

"Don't worry. It was all very complimentary. And you can take it from me that isn't at all usual with Sir. Sir's a bit stroppy, not to say sarky, with the generality. You're friends from way back, aren't you? I mean really way back, school, university, all that?" She did not wait for a response from Willie: it would not have mattered much anyway. He had none to give, this re-run of his life's reflection was more than enough to cope with. How many times had Ian told "friends" of his the same tale about their "friendship"? What was it? A talisman? A proof of Ian's fundamental and indomitable integrity? A joke?

"That's one thing I envy about men," Eileen said, drawing her red satin trousered legs under her achingly tight bum on the black velvet-covered four-seater sofa. "You have these friendships that go way back and hold on through whatever you do. We can very rarely seem to do that. Maybe it'll start happening more now that we've managed to make some sort of dent in the macho consciousness, but I wonder. You're a telly man, aren't you? Ian says you're very serious about it – one of the few who are, he says – and very good."

"That's nice of him."

"Oh Christ! You probably think Ian and I live together. Not that you would disapprove and not that I would care if you did but we don't. That is we do. We *live* together. It's very convenient for both of us and rather cosy all round. But we don't – well: point made. We hunt alone – damn! Shouldn't have said that!"

"How long have you been in New York?" The question, laminated in banality, came so lamely from Willie's nervous

188

lips that Eileen paused for a second and then knifed up in laughter.

"Hello, hello, hello," Ian said, bearing a tray before him. "What have we here? What are you a doing of to my good friend, you unscrupulous tarty actressy *personage*?"

"Embarrassing him!"

"Well, belt up. He's not used to pornography in satin at tea time in New York. Have a cup of tea and a *digestive biscuit*! And then leave us men to our manly talk."

"Yes, O master."

"That's better," Ian said, delicately pouring the tea through a strainer, camping it up with such a deft slightness that Willie simply had to smile his applause. "There we are then. We men must have our rights and keep our dignity and all that wonderful nonsense my father proclaims so passionately at the Rugby Club or wherever. Milk or lemon?" Decorous knees prissily together, Ian held up the elegant teapot by its bamboo holder and let the liquid splash down into the cups, a mocking mini-cataract.

When Eileen had left after a rather protracted tea, Ian stretched out, lit an overlarge Dutch cigar, and gazed at the ceiling with the contentment of someone who had enjoyed a feast.

"What brings you here then?" he said, the common-or-garden question and tone contradicting the oriental sensuality of his pose in that disconcerting way which so beguiled Willie. "More politicians?"

Willie said nothing.

"Don't you ever feel inclined to give any of them a push? When you have your piece all nice and ready, all up to date, wouldn't you like someone just to . . . top them so that they don't do something stupid to mess up your script or just drag on forever being so boring that your great *oeuvre* ends up as a thirty-second clip?"

"Sometimes," Willie admitted. "How are you?"

"Mustn't grumble. Got on the right side of the critics for *once* – for *once*! – and the crowds come in like bees to the jam-jar, standing ovations every night, people in the launderette ask for your autograph, the barman at the place I use down the street has a cocktail called after me – it could go to your head if you let it and of course I do. What was it old Zero Mostel, RIP, said? 'If you've got it – flaunt it.'"

Willie had never seen him so buoyant and secure.

"And of course, New York's overrun with the Brits at the moment," he ran through the British plays currently on Broadway. "It's a bit too much all-change-for-the-District-Line sometimes."

"Why too much?"

"For secrecy's sake, Willie. Secrecy, the privilege of whatevers, the spice of whatsits, the diamantine gift of thingumibobs. Secrecy, being abroad; abroad *is* different, you know."

"I saw Marion recently."

"Bang on the nose! You're a tonic, Willie, you really are. After weeks of 'Have a nice day' and 'You were wonderful' and 'Would you like to consider a two-picture deal, a three-picture deal?' – along comes Willie, the incorruptible Englishman with a face like a plank of wood and no tact, no grace, nothing but the truth. So you saw t'wife, did you, Willie m'lad: well there, sithee, how went she then, sithee?"

"I'm in love with Caroline," Willie said.

Ian unsprung himself from the coiled-up camp, the slap-happy carelessness, with such a rapidity that Willie could have rubbed his eyes: another, a different, an altogether changed man was now before him: sympathetic but suspicious; alert. His voice lost all trace of parody or play.

"Caroline." Ian repeated her name, dully, as if testing a coin.

"I've been in love with her for months. Sometimes I think I've always been in love with her . . . I suppose that sounds ridiculous."

"No . . . No."

"Are you?"

"What?"

"Are you in love with her?"

"Willie . . ." There was concern, not reproach, in Ian's voice and Willie saw his friend's anxiety.

"I'm perfectly all right," he said. "A bit tired after the flight and with the strain. But I would like to know."

"Have you told her – Caroline – have you told her, your feelings?"

"Yes."

"When was that?"

"Just . . . the other week. Last week, I think – no, ten days – no, two weeks ago. I thought I would have remembered. Before Newcastle. Two weeks."

"What did she say?"

"She was very nice. She doesn't love me. I can't expect that. But then, she wasn't happy."

"What a mess. You, me, her – her, you, me." Ian squashed the cigar flat and took out a cigarette, offering one to Willie only as an afterthought. Then he put his head between his hands.

"Well?" Willie persisted, speaking lightly still, the strain and constraint locked together in some deep complicity within him, letting the merest saving breath be released. "Don't worry about me. It doesn't matter what happens to me. But I want to know – for her."

"I don't believe you." Ian's voice was unaffectedly hard. "I don't believe you got in a plane and came three thousand miles just to find out what you already know. You came here because you want her and I'm in the way and you want to see me off – one way or another, however disguised and low-profile it all is – that's what you want, isn't it? You want me off the job, don't you?"

"I want to know. I want to know so that she can be sure."

"What does it matter whether she's 'sure' about me or not? What matters to you is whether she's sure about you – you came here for two reasons, Willie: to try to edge me off and, *and*, to get me to help you."

"You must be mad."

"Oh come, Willie. I know you. Face it. I'm glad you did."

"But do you love her?"

This time, his words came so painfully slightly that Ian looked at him with pity. Willie was now almost stone-faced with tension, threatening to crack. Gently, Ian turned the question.

"Do you?"

"Oh yes." Willie nodded and seemed set to cry but a strangulated sigh blocked the show of desperate sorrow.

"More tea," Ian said and instantly went off to the kitchen where Eileen had taken the tray and washed up.

With Ian out of the room, Willie rocked back in his seat, mouth agape for air. He had not imagined it like this: it was not supposed to be like this at all. He had to make a better show than this. For every reason, he could not just cave in like this. Reaching deeply into himself he drew on all the resources he could muster, castigating the superficial nervousness, quelling the new fear of the old breakdown recurring, hauling himself onto a plane of reasonableness, of competence.

"Willie," Ian spoke quietly. "I thought you were asleep. Look. I have to go to the theatre. No," he held his hand up like a policeman, "there's nothing I can do about it. I have to be there at half five, I always am. I take it you don't want to see the show – OK. Let's meet afterwards. I have something to do later – but – I'll fix things. You know the theatre? Stage Door – right next to the main entrance. Opposite Sardi's. I'll leave a note with Frank at the door. If you don't want to come in I'll see you there about quarter to eleven. OK? There's the tea. Stay here as long as you like. Eileen's harmless. I *must* go."

He grimaced apologetically, and left.

(3)

Willie gave him time to get clear and then he too left, the tea untouched. Ian had appeared to winkle out his motives so swiftly. Was it all as simple as that? Willie felt almost slighted that what mattered to him so deeply should be so easily parried.

192

He had to fight back. WALK: DON'T WALK: WALK. He hailed a cab and with no real purpose went towards Central Park, stopping just a few blocks short of it. It could be a destination. Through the canyons of expensive apartments he walked, attentive to nothing but his own sense of feebleness. He was not breaking down. He was not going to break down. What he had experienced had been an echo, not a tremor. He needed, though, to fight back; he needed to discover why it meant so much. It was time that he acted.

Willie was ashamed to own the thought but what he would have liked to do would have been to seize and enjoy casual sex, paid for if necessary. Somehow such an untypical act would have burst the drum of some of his apprehension and taboos. He paused on the edge of the sidewalk, looking across to White Christmas Central Park. Yes. A woman. To be the hunter, to be sexually acquisitive, to walk up to a stranger in the street, to take the dice-roll from the lottery of prostitution, to tear off the faces of morality and timidity and caringness, to be at the bone of himself. To betray not only Joanna and the ideal of Caroline, but his own notion of himself. In the cold air he grew hot at the thought of the so easily available sex a couple of score streets south on 42nd Street. Squalid, hard-faced, unsentimental sex for the sake of whatever sex was for the sake of at its most peremptory. Love stripped down to action. He was surprised at the strength of this want. He despised its implications. He had never paid for sex nor been able to divorce it from genuine affection and the possibility of lasting intimacy. Now, as if out of vengeance on himself, or to prepare for his new role by trampling on the forms and assumptions of his past, he wanted to do it. It was the first way in which he could act. Perhaps the only way, now, to put your body in danger, to seek out some edge, some brush with fortune, with accident, with unknowable forces. Perhaps casual, even bought, sex was one of the few throws left for a metropolitan man fenced out of traditional masculine "virtues" by the defence works of the time.

But he let it pass. A coward soul, too steeped in his idyll for

193

Caroline? Or was it his prospective disapproval of the act that was the real damper? He caught a cab to his hotel and determined to work: waiting idly would be corrosive.

There was something of the failed scholar about Willie. Bereft of reading matter he felt socially shorn, as clumsily exposed as a man who has lost his spectacles. Those obituaries had always been over-researched; in fact the real trouble had been to pull himself away from the reading and melt down the findings into the mould of a programme. Books told no lies, made no false promises, stayed faithful and alert, were ever-reliable, held surprise but not misfortune, comforted without oppressing, were dependents but claimed no danegeld of responsibility. They were better than life if the life you had was as low-burning as his had been. He read.

(4)

"Mr Grant, sir, hel*lo*." The uplift on the final syllable was cheerfully adoring. Ian had the grace, Willie thought, to look embarrassed. He ushered Willie before him as they were led across the Pool Room of the Four Seasons and settled at a table just a few feet from the feature which gave the room its name.

"I thought you might not have been here," Ian said and grinned. "I'm trying to impress you."

A waiter alighted like a swallow onto a telegraph wire.

"Soufflé, gentlemen?"

Again, Ian looked embarrassed.

"You have to order it first even though you eat it last. Speciality. Yes? Two, please."

"Thank you, Mr Grant. Nice to see you again, sir. My sister saw you and thinks you're terrific. She's an actress out West. She said it was an honour to be in the same profession. She asked me – I said you came here – "

"Of course."

The signature fled across the menu. The waiter picked it up, looked and passed it back. "To Ninette."

194

"Ninette."

"Thank you, Mr Grant."

"Could you ask the wine waiter to bring us – champagne, Willie? – champagne. As soon as he could. The Bollinger NV. OK?"

"Right away, Mr Grant."

A look of fugitive moroseness temporarily unsettled Ian's face. "I gave up coming here months ago," he said.

Willie offered him a cigarette.

"'If you've got it, flaunt it.'" Ian bent across for a light. "Perhaps he was wrong. Do you still make notes on everything you read?"

"Not everything."

"It always impressed me." He inhaled deeply. "Other people's lives generally do." He paused. "I shouldn't have been so glib this afternoon. I suppose I was a bit shocked by what you said."

"Were you?"

"It made what *I* felt seem so superficial. You've always had that effect on me. But when it comes to Caroline . . ." He looked around, flicked a wave at three or four sets of curious and attentive eyes, "yes and no . . . I *don't* understand what you're after, that's all. I shouldn't have pretended I did. Ah! The booze."

They waited in silence while the champagne was poured out.

"Cheers?"

"Cheers."

"Low on calories. Low on alcohol." Ian drank too quickly and visibly restrained a belch.

Willie looked around the room. It was basically an office-block floor, given a certain pomp by the pool, but inescapably a Function Room, reminding him of those barn-like places above old Victorian pubs which leased themselves out for trestle-tabled weddings and funeral parties. Perhaps the food would be superb and the service superlative and the bill reassuringly big, but it was no place for confidences. Was that why Ian had chosen it? To make the gesture of intimacy in the

195

full knowledge that this particular place would spike any attempt at it? Its streamlined expensiveness seemed organised to dispel all possibilities of privacy.

"Are you especially hungry?" Willie asked.

"What's this one, Willie?"

"I'd like to settle the bill – I'll pay – and go somewhere less . . ." he looked around.

"Where we can talk?" Ian smiled. "You really are serious, aren't you?" He poured out more champagne. "OK. But waste not, want not,"

By the time the bill had been settled – Ian made no competitive moves over this – the bottle was empty. Outside, Ian's ridiculously large limousine gleamed like a getaway car.

"Let's take a cab," Willie said. "Give him the night off."

Ian nodded and made arrangements with the driver to be picked up late the next morning from an address not his own. He made no attempt to disguise this: indeed, Willie sensed a trace of bravado. He did not want to speculate on Ian's possible nervousness; it was difficult enough holding his own arguments and intentions in place.

"Somewhere ordinary," Willie said.

"The thing about this town," Ian said, as they bumped speedily south towards the Village, "is that there aren't many places which would own up to that description. On the other hand, unlike nanny England with all its closing times and orders from the telly to go to bed and remember to pull the plug out before midnight – a lot goes on late even for those who can only afford a couple of beers."

Willie looked out of the window at the snow-mantled sidewalks, content to let Ian deliver his monologue on the democratic entertainment values of New York. Unexpectedly, he thought of his flat and of Joanna: he should be with her: he should be with his mother: he should be trying to regroup his forces, help David, come out of the social coma of the last decade. Surely there was enough there.

"What *is* it about her?" Ian asked, putting the question

196

precisely as the cab drew up in front of a small restaurant bar. Willie had no time to answer. It had been meant to unsettle.

The maître d' raised his eyebrows when Ian came in, but a confidential exchange that he would like a quiet corner to discuss business — Willie by implication cast as a mediating figure — resulted in a display of discretion which nudged on ostentation but got them to a corner table further isolated by the empty tables surrounding it. Ian visibly changed his public image: in the Four Seasons he had been on parade. Here he worked at anonymity. Willie had seen these changes rung many a hundred time but he still wondered at them.

"Ordinary enough?"

There was a long, highly polished, well-stocked bar patrolled by a young man in a scarlet waistcoat; a deep, rather narrow dining-room with small tables dressed in blue-and-red-checked cloths; overlarge and very spruce potted palms to emit someone's desired atmosphere; a piano at the far end, presently bereft of its activator; on the walls several grim charcoal portraits which were for sale. About a quarter full. The constant media reiteration of the exceptionally cold conditions had deterred the night lingerers.

"It's fine." The best of American democratic decent, he thought.

The waiter came over; the meal was quickly ordered and a bottle of Californian Cabernet came "Right away, sir" flanked by two large schooners of iced water, on guard.

"Are you going to draw first?" Ian asked, squinting through his wine glass, "or are you waiting for me to say 'ready'?"

Willie refused to play: yet. Ian was already casting him as the grim plodder: this enabled him to dance away from the subject and mock it. Perhaps, he thought, he had never in his entire life spoken to Ian honestly, for it was not only that he played different roles, not even that he further controlled any conversation by casting you in complementary roles — he had, Willie realised, a desperate determination not to step out of an assumed character. Underneath every mask was a mask. And the flickering awareness of Ian's understanding of him, his use

197

of him over the years, came suddenly into focus: there was something almost psychic about Ian, some combination of insights which could "read" you like a part.

"You have to decide how to begin, Willie," Ian said, smiling now, truly as if he had monitored Willie's thoughts. "I'm happy to drink." And he yawned – *yawned*! – a genuine yawn, looked at his watch with blatant though not insulting calculation, tilted back his brightly painted wooden kitchen chair and clasped his hands together behind his neck.

Willie held onto his silence. It was his only effective opening strategy. He took out a cigarette – forty a day now? Concentrate. He had come this far: he had not even admitted to himself, until now, how far he had come, how much of himself he had risked and betrayed, how much there was to confront, how essential it was to put the finest blade on the most painful spot and cut deep: and do it now. The moment would not come again.

"I knew we went in for understatement," Ian said, "but this is ridiculous."

Now Ian was to be the down-to-earth realist, Willie the inarticulate figure in a coarse comedy. Yet the silence had become more than a tactic – if indeed it had ever been that in the first place. He could not and would not speak into this eddying mirror of a man he ought to know so well. The waters had to settle. He absorbed the accusation and smoked the sweet drug America had provided for the world.

The steaks came and Ian fell to with conspicuous gusto. Willie was not hungry.

"It's good," Ian said. He pronged a big chunk and held it out. "Want a taste? It'll build you up."

The exasperation, Willie thought, was at least a beginning.

"Look," Ian said, continuing to spear the chunks of red meat and feed himself with a finely judged display of undisturbed healthiness which banished to irrelevance and morbidity what he now made appear to be the portentous silence of Willie. "I know what you want to say. OK. Say it. Throw it up. Then maybe we can forget it." He reached out for the bottle and

198

added "And maybe not." No smile. Who was this? Ah yes – the "hard man", the "no-bullshit baby", the "don't waste my time", quite close to the "who the hell do you think you are?" Willie did not relax: there was a long way to go.

Then the pianist sat down, and his first song was "As Time Goes By". As the lines on "love and glory" floated sadly down the long room, Willie felt himself panicked by the coincidence. Perhaps it *was* merely portentous, this quest? By what token did a comfortably off middle-aged acceptance man of the fat 'n' easy Western world look to words and notions as bold as those?

"The favourite song of armchair heroes," Ian said, calmly slicing through Willie's thoughts. "Don't you think?"

"Could be."

Ian raised his glass and grinned. "It can talk."

In the instant, Ian slithered back to his amused and hovering detachment, saying "this is a small matter, old pal, a squib, a squiggle, no more than a slight graze on the body of our friendship – remember it? Me and you? All those years – all of that?" Willie shook his head to be rid of the train of thought which he picked up from Ian like a contagion: he felt himself yet again absorbed into the other man's mind, bewitched by him. As, he now realised, he had so often, perhaps always, been. In the labyrinths of Ian's postures he would be lost: unless he held onto his single thread doggedly, accepting mockery, ignoring ridicule, however blindly, clasping the one line. It was time to declare it.

"I want you to know," Willie said, with difficulty, holding himself together by holding Ian's look, "that I think you're destructive," he hesitated, swallowed, his throat was dry, "wrong and no good."

"Is that all?" Ian's response was immediate.

Willie paused: the accusation had been hard to deliver.

"You mean you came three thousand miles to tell me that?"

The pianist played on. Willie had hoped for a charge of energy after his words; instead he felt indescribably tired. But he had to go on.

199

"You could have put it on a postcard."

And at that moment of acute tension for Willie, Ian found the time and space to look around, catch the waiter's eye and indicate he wanted the plates cleared and another bottle of wine brought.

"Do you think I don't know that?" Ian said.

But Willie was prepared for the feigned submission. "I think you glory in it."

"You're mad." Ian took a drink and put on a character which Willie did not quite recognise; a character, then, he concluded, which might be somewhere nearer the truth of him than he had ever been before. "You never fucked Caroline, did you?"

Willie was startled.

"*Did* you?" Ian looked on him with open sexual superiority. "Of course you didn't."

So the accusation had gone home, Willie thought: Oh God, he found himself saying inside his mind, please God let me make him understand that I mean it. Please God let me hurt him. Please God let me damage him. Into some sort of awareness? If possible. If not – just the hurt.

"You know sod-all about her," Ian said, only angry-seeming, though, Willie estimated: not yet, not really skewered. "Do you know what bath-foam she likes? Do you know her mother had a mild attack of angina and refused to admit it? Do you know she likes to break out of that lowland Scottish murderous sobriety and behave as you would prissily think like a slut? Do you know what books she's read? Do you know what size dress she takes? Do you know which teeth have been filled? Do you know that she's transferred all that childhood puritanism to feminism and do you know that she could understand that what I wanted didn't violate that? To you she's the madonna of the Borders. Crap!"

"It wasn't only Caroline," Willie said, keeping tight, cards close, summoning up from the dregs of fatigue all the emphasis he could muster.

"I don't believe you. Everybody's packaged into an obituary for you. Always has been. For you and millions like you who

200

don't want contradictions or dirt or inconsequence. I've seen the stuff you do: very good, but fuck-all to do with life. Madame Tussaud's on celluloid, which is what most people want: harmless wax easy to melt down. That's how you see everybody because you haven't the guts to look hard enough. It isn't like that, Willie. Caroline knows that. Why do you think I went for her? Why do you think I *still* – even though I'm here, I'm seeing another woman tonight – would *go* for her? Come on, answer. Come on!"

"She's . . ." Willie stopped: why *should* he answer? Why should he become party to this pseudo-realpolitik? Ian was not genuinely trying to get at the truth: he was not yet even crossing swords. This was sabre-rattling. "She's in love with you," Willie said.

"So?"

"She is."

"So?"

"You encouraged her."

"I did?"

"Now you've abandoned her."

"Have I?"

"You've hurt her."

"Ah." Ian took more wine and observed that Willie was drinking sparingly. "I loved her. Correction. I love her," Ian said, quietly. Was this real? Willie tensed himself against the seduction of the confession. "It was the smile at first. You must have noticed. What a stupid thing in a way but it *was* that. What did it say to you, Willie? That smile?"

Tranquillity, mystery, a source of pure life – clichés all, but most faithfully made manifest in that smile. Ian nodded, once more at ease in Willie's unspoken thoughts.

"Exactly. All that. And if I want to bitch myself – which I generally do – I could say that her apparent ordinariness was refreshing, her little talent, her seeming lack of demand: all on the surface, Willie. She isn't ordinary – I've never met a woman who was. She could be a good actress. She made big demands – she made me know how much she wanted me and what seems

201

to you a passing screw *could* have been the big drop." He rubbed his neck. "I can still feel the noose."

You still love her? Willie wanted to ask if that were really true and if so what it meant: he was being beguiled, he knew that. Ian was lulling him into understanding. He did not want Ian's version of understanding. He had his own. He must stick to it. Yet he longed to dwell on Caroline, to talk about her with Ian, to slake his parched love in a cataract of details and celebrations. Oh, Ian knew. He knew the intense connection between those who love the same person. And he was exploiting it.

"It wasn't only Caroline," Willie reiterated. "When I told you what I think of you I wasn't only referring to Caroline."

"What was it?" Ian's confession had restored his balance. He ticked the words off on his fingers. "Wrong, destructive and no good."

"I saw Marion."

"You *have* been busy." Ian's riposte was vicious. Nearer, Willie thought, that bit nearer.

"She's in a bad way."

"Marion can cope."

"I'm not so sure."

"How the hell do you know?" Nearer.

"I know when I see someone near breaking point."

"Ah yes. Special knowledge."

Ian first looked embarrassed at this jibe and then – Willie followed the change of expression accurately – he thought, he dug in, cast the care aside. One more mask gone. The mask of a long-serviced and residual loyalty.

"Marion knows what I'm like," Ian said. "She's known for years. She chose to stay."

"And that answers it?"

"Willie," Ian said, hunching forward across the table and riveting his eyes on him, "there are approximately five thousand things you ought to know about. And that's just about sex." He offered a grin, designed for apology for the jibe, for the reference to Willie's breakdown. Willie

202

rejected it. He felt very cold and sipped a little wine. The pianist played on.

"I like it," Ian went on without breaking rhythm, as if the peace offering had not been made, "very much. There aren't many of us left."

"That won't do," Willie said, firmly. "Talk seriously."

"You . . ." Real anger this time. Unmasked?

"You were going to tell me that Don Juan has had a bad press," Willie said. "We were about to have the standard line on contemporary hedonism. How our hero was born and raised in times of unnatural and unjust constraint. How he discovers the hypocrisies of Victorianism and, seeking true liberty, casts off the chains of public and private conformity. How he swims down the adolescent river of unnecessarily frustrated lust into the permissive ocean of the sixties where he finds his true self. How everything goes. How the only reality now is to find yourself. How this new licence overthrows responsibility and decency. How sex becomes the only measure of the real man in a pagan world poised between two holocausts. How predictable."

"That was pretty good," Ian said.

Willie checked himself. He had allowed Ian to regroup. He ought to have maintained his reticence. Now he was confronted once more with a face composed to play in any number of keys. He had lost the advantage.

"And it could be right," Ian added. "Can I pinch a fag?"

Ian was one of those rare people who could smoke now and then, go for months without, get through a pack in an evening, stop for a year.

"The place is getting empty," Ian said, looking around. "Don't you like the thought of the big city at night out there covered in snow? Don't you want to get out and find a riot of a time somewhere?" He glanced at his watch. "I'm late."

Willie ignored all that. "Marion," Willie said.

"It hasn't worked for years . . . as you know." Ian was a little ratty: he was not used to being brought to order. "I found out

203

I didn't like marriage, I didn't like children and I didn't much like Marion. Quite early on. What am I supposed to do? Hurl myself up on the cross of family life? *That's* the alternative you offer, Willie, and don't duck it. You say: *your* hero sticks by his folks and his faults and his inherited principles – which might be a face-saving word for fears – and just puts up with it. I'm not taking that bloodless bondage, Willie. I think it's shit."

"So that's all right?"

"No. *Not* all right. But I'm not going to accept your world which says that the only real way to judge a man is by an assessment of his behaviour as a family man. That's a dictatorship of a particular and stinking little morality, Willie, which has derailed more lives than all my hedonism. I admire guys who find satisfaction in marriage. You see? I'm still enough of a victim of my own past – *our* own past – to admit that I actually *admire* them. Why admire? It's what they find good for them. But I do. Finding all the emotional variation you want in a wife and kids sometimes strikes me as a wonderful thing. But not for me: maybe – alas. Maybe – thank God."

"And Caroline can grieve and Marion can . . . cope. You hide away in generalisations."

"What do you want?"

"It wasn't only Caroline and Marion I meant when I said what I did. I meant to yourself as well. Self-destructive; no good to yourself; wrong about yourself."

"Do you fancy me then?"

Willie refused even to register a reaction to the question but Ian persisted: the lateness of the hour, the lag effect of the evening performance, the drink, the truth? "I'm serious. Not now. Not tonight. But ever. Come on – think about it. Think about it!"

"Sometimes I've wondered," Willie said, eventually, making a stiff attempt at utter veracity.

"I thought you might have." Ian relaxed: another reprieve had been granted. "I've always fancied the idea of fancying

204

blokes but never actually met one I've fancied. True confessions time, eh, Willie?''

The trap had been well set and well sprung. Willie felt his energy ebb and forced himself to continue the attack, knowing that he had lost face, the initiative and authority. Before he could recharge himself, however, Ian spoke again.

"You see, if I believe in anything – I mean private things, not democracy or socialism or Oxfam or any of that, I'm just the usual mindless liberal on all of that – then it's this. We're freaks – all of us well-oiled Westerners at this time. People like you who slog through the obstacle course and get nice clean jobs with nice interesting wages . . . If you look around the planet – that's freaky enough. People like me who are paid to indulge our fantasy and entertain yours are even further out. We're soft, fat and cocooned. The only thing, the only real thing we actors can still get is a sense of danger. Because we are super-fluous, we can be ignored, despised and eliminated – the thumbs-down. And what we get from *that* is the chance to play for some bastard descendants of what your man was just singing about: love and glory. But love, to me, is nothing to do with duty or suffering or idealism of any sort. It's passion, experienced constantly. And glory is nothing to do with the mad gang-show put on by the political puppets, even the political rebels, even the solitary heroes you read about every day in the papers. It's getting an audience, two or three thousand of your own kind, to follow you into a character and his adventures, to teach them to remember revenge and honour, cruelty and deceit, or what they really are. They're part of the same thing. 'A lonely impulse of delight.' I'm sure you remember. I have my own rules: I look for the heat every day I can: when I find it I make for it: when it cools I leave it. Your philosophy says that's adolescent, grow up: to grow up like you and your kind is, to me, to give in. I want to see the spark, Willie, when the flint hits the stone. And I want to be the flint.''

How near was that to Ian's truth? He was clearly concerned

to be believed. But he had come to dislodge Ian, not to be appeased by him. If he left Ian as he had found him then he would have failed. That crude thought was still his guide. What was the point in opening the waters if you did not walk through them? What would have been achieved if he and Ian parted friends?

"You are saying that you have the right to be totally selfish all the time and claiming merit from it."

"If that's all you see." Ian shrugged, grimacing a little, disappointed that his credo had not met with the big Amen.

"When I look at the harm you do to others and to yourself, that's what I see."

"What harm to myself?" Ian was genuinely curious.

"Oh of course: the worse you behave, the more danger, therefore the greater self-righteousness."

"I thought you would understand."

"I do. But I also disapprove. No – no." Willie put up a hand to quell Ian's incipient interruption. "Because where does it stop? What do you do? You betray people, you betray yourself: do you begin to betray the law, do you commit crimes? That's the real thing, isn't it? And if not, why not?"

"I do not accept that I betray people, Willie. I do not accept that I betray myself. Nobody gets told any lies. That look of logic in your little lawyer's prattle is bullshit. We should get the bill. My turn."

The hovering waiter swooped to the table like a bat on a mouse. They were the last customers. The pianist had gone, unnoticed, Willie realised sadly, and unapplauded.

Out in the street it was so cold it hurt your head.

"I'm coming with you," Willie said as Ian hailed a taxi. "I'm not finished yet."

"You can go off people, you know," Ian said, shivering into a wolfish grin. "Come on then."

Inside the cab he said, "Adam Clayton Junior Boulevard. 78th Street West, I think, somewhere around 10th."

"That's Harlem," the driver said. "That's what they call 'deepest Harlem'."

"That's right," Ian said. "Lock the doors, put your foot down, and sling us another of your cancer sticks, Willie. Past three o'clock, eh, and all's well!"

Central Park registered its coldest night for almost a century.

Chapter Ten

(1)

"Jingle Bells," Ian said. "Magic."

Central Park was fairyland. The steeps of thick snow, trees encrusted with polished hard flakes glinting under the lights, the silence of night and nature encircled by the sleeping piles of New York. As they swung into the wide avenues of Harlem, Ian adopted the manner of a courier.

"The snow makes it look as grand as it used to be, doesn't it?" Ian peered out of the window. "Everybody used to come up here in the twenties and thirties – the Black Renaissance, the Jazz Age, all the clubs and the bands, the new dances. Now it's one of the dustbins of New York. They say it's coming up." To the driver, "What do you think?"

The driver indicated no interest. The pocked road surface, the ice and crests of frozen slush, appeared to take most of his concentration: what was left scanned the sidewalks where still, in this weather and at this hour, groups of young blacks fidgeted on the shoplit corners, as if on night patrol.

"A friend of mine came to live up here," Ian went on. "You might meet him tonight. A painter. I'd known him in London. He came over here, broke, loved New York, didn't like the arty-flash of SoHo or the Village – couldn't afford it anyway – came up here, near where we're going, and got a small apartment. It was like a cowboy pitching camp in the middle of Apache country. For all the macho in this city, there aren't many white men who would walk around these streets let alone live in them. He was dumped on twice in the first week but he put up with that. He's an extraordinary man, one of those homosexuals who seem truly fearless in a quiet, uncamp,

208

unshowy way. Then they opened up his apartment, tore up his sketches, splattered the walls, and stole his paints and canvases. He went down to the bar around the block – not the one we're headed for, this is the last of the great thirties bars and they've kept it nice, you'll see – he went to the bar on the corner where he knew the . . . culprits? . . . would be likely to hang out. He walked in, perhaps the only white guy who'd been in there for years without a police uniform and a gun, and he asked the barman if he knew who had done it. Just asked in his English voice if he knew the people who'd wrecked his place. It was about six-thirty. The place was packed. They all laughed. Then he turned and, as he told me, he saw the gang all around one table and knew it was them. Speaking directly to them he said he wanted his paints and canvases back. He couldn't afford any more. Without them he couldn't work. He had to have them back. They ignored him, of course: why bother to crush an empty eggshell?

"He went across to the piano. It had once been a piano bar but the pianist hadn't turned up for two or three years. And he started to play. He's very good. This disarming campy Englishman suddenly thundered across the keys – the old Dixie jazz, new numbers, he's a touch player, never had a lesson, always loved the piano. They were yelling after two minutes: after ten minutes the roof was coming off. In the middle of the hottest piece he could play he stopped, stood up, closed the piano lid. 'If I don't get those tubes of paint and those canvases I won't be able to work," he said. 'I'll have to leave Harlem. I don't want to. I like it. I'm going for a walk down to the Park.' And he just went out.

"When he came back the door to his apartment was open. The canvases and paints had been thrown inside. Three of them were waiting for him – would he come back and play the piano? No, he said, he wanted to tidy up the room. But he would come the next night. Which he did. He's painting their portraits now – they are sensational. They queue up. He still plays the piano now and then."

Willie passed no comment. None was required. Ian had

plainly said let's forget it, put it behind us, this can't affect us, really, can it? Not the long-embedded friendship we have. There was hope there, Willie thought. He had one card left to play.

As the car bumped cautiously forward, Willie became intensely aware of Ian and himself. Ian out for sport, for edge, for some sort of kill, visibly expanding into the night, reassembling himself from the intimate, guarded, watchful person he had been in the restaurant. Willie himself, drawn-faced, eyes prickly against the lenses with tiredness and the smoke, grubby, almost lost, holding on to a mission which no one had asked him to undertake. Two bodies, though, he was most aware of, in the back of the battered cab, two people who had watched each other, perhaps in a way watched over each other for all those years – the forties frozen in war then lavished with promise, the fifties perceptibly shifting to change, out of the cocoon of Empire into the thaw of optimism and change, the operatic extravaganza of the sixties, the retribution of the seventies – and in the cab he could "see" Ian throughout that time as in so many snapshots. In character, in newspapers, in period costume, in interviews, in his room, in pubs and studios: yes, he did know him well. In one way he carried more of Ian's history and life in him than anyone else – perhaps even including Ian himself, whose art of remembering was matched by a talent for forgetting.

It could depend on how much Ian valued that knowledge of himself.

"Here we are." Ian turned and winked at Willie. "You didn't believe that story I just told you, did you?"

Willie was thrown: he took cover in silence.

The neon name was boldly scripted in copperplate. Ian gave the driver an over-large tip. Willie could feel him pumping himself up, getting into yet another character. It was remarkable. In those few moments, by a hand-shuffle of his hair, a few tugs at his clothes, but, more essentially, some deep instruction to himself, his looks changed. He was the Actor now, the Famous Actor. Success could be useful protection in a place like this, Willie realised, as they hastened the few frozen yards across the empty sidewalk. That would be one reason for Ian's change.

The other he saw the moment he walked into the unexpectedly elegant warm bar: she was called Julie, tall, beautifully shaped, wasp-waisted, high-breasted, long slim-shanked, electric hair, at the lighter end of the dozens of shades of black in the room. Her smile was quite magnificent.

(2)

"This is Willie," Ian said, and added, with no apparent colouring in his voice, "my oldest friend. Willie – Julie."

Ian then left Willie and Julie to go on a mini-walkabout in the elegant bar: the flesh was pressed, the big "Hi" cannoned around the room: you pseud, Willie thought.

"He's very popular," Julie said, arranging her amazing figure beside him. "Some of the guys act and sing, you know, and Ian's already helped two of them." Pseud? The waiter appeared, lean, polite and unsmiling, a bottle-green waistcoat with brass-type buttons, a red bow tie, snow-white shirt. "Ian always has Eddie's Special. Eddie runs the bar."

"Beer," Willie said, over-firmly. "Michelob please."

"One Michelob, one Special – more orange juice?"

Julie shook her ornate head of hair.

In the few minutes Ian spent table-hopping, Willie learnt that Julie was a model, that she was studying acting, singing, dancing and accountancy, that she had never known such a nice place as this could exist in Harlem, she came from Queens herself which was a little tacky but had some very nice people there, really very nice. Now she had this apartment up on the West side around Columbus which was the new "it" place – really – he ought to come down there, there was no trouble, people said it was like the Village in the old days. He looked hot; perhaps he ought to take off his coat. She helped him: he felt like a pensioner.

Willie was glad of her conversational generosity. He seemed not so much to have boxed himself into a corner as raced out onto the prairies with no detachable cover. Julie's courteous garrulity, the bar's unprivate and crowded formality (it's the only really nice place in the neighbourhood and they want somewhere nice, you know, the people who run the neighbourhood, they keep it nice, Julie explained) and his own fatigue all threatened to smother his purpose.

Marion, Caroline, Julie: what they had in common, Willie thought, was the feminine gender; little else that he could see. Of course, they might all be sensational in bed or peculiarly skilled in massaging Ian's ego or privy to a common art of intelligence: he was not to know. But to judge by appearances and this first impression only, Ian was here engaged in a quite different adventure from that which still bound him to his wife and that which had drawn him to Caroline. Yet, when Ian returned to attack Eddie's Special, he did not seem all that different: he teased Julie's pretensions in a sly, affectionate way. His eyes and occasionally his hands brushed across her with a palpable and returned excitement: Willie felt increasingly spare.

Perhaps it was the nervousness induced by this which caused him to knock over his Michelob when he stood up to go to the Rest Room. Julie was very nice about it: it wasn't her best dress; if she could only have a clean cloth and some cold water? But it was rather a large stain: look, she would go powder her nose and work on it.

"You always were a clumsy bugger," Ian said, tenderly.

Willie fought down the absurd sense of gratitude which raced up to meet this assuaging of his embarrassment. He went to the Men's Room and returned as quickly as he could. It was the last chance to have Ian on his own.

Ian was in earnest conclave with the only other white man in the place. Willie guessed he could be the artist-hero of the – invented? – story.

The table had been restored. A new beer stood on a new table mat. Willie endured yet another introduction. The decibel level

212

increased, not dramatically but sufficient to strain any tired mind. The chance was slipping away. Ian and Chris were talking about a poker school which had been going in the neighbourhood for the last three or four months: Ian wanted to try his luck. Willie sipped the light frozen beer. The place began to go out of focus.

When Julie came back she was wrapped around in a coat which would have become Anna Karenina. Ian smirked, unattractively, Willie thought, and slid his hand into her coat after she had sat down: she opened her large leather handbag and showed him the crumpled dress. Chris accepted an over-enthusiastic kiss. Willie wanted to go. But he would now play his last card.

He stood up with care. As he anticipated, Ian insisted on coming to the door with him, his protector, his friend. No taxi in view the length of the boulevard.

"I'll walk," Willie said, sucking in the bitterly cold air.

"No bravado," Ian admonished, still gentle, still tender.

"No taxi," Willie replied. "Anyway, I feel like a walk."

Ian, coatless, shivered violently. "I'll leave you then," he said. "You should be all right at this time. 'The pure in heart . . .'"

Willie summoned up his resources. He felt very foolish. But fear of seeming a fool, even being a fool, ought not, he thought, to stop you doing what you thought was right.

"You've explained away how you behaved to Marion and Caroline and yourself," Willie said, his face solidifying with the cold. "You've explained it in your own terms. I think you ducked it. Never mind. But what about me? Not what you've done to me with regard to Caroline but what you've done to what I think of you. Caroline has highlighted it, that's all. I ought to have shaken you off years ago." Ian subdued his shivering and listened hard. Willie went on, steadily. "*I* think you're no good – *and* wrong, and destructive. I don't like you. I don't want to see you again. I've been like those people in the bar, putting up with you for the wrong reasons. You've played on me. You play on this place. Harlem isn't your playground.

213

It's depressed and painful. You're simply spoilt, immoral and bad."

He turned into the empty street and walked away, not staying for an answer. Empty.

(3)

"That should have been the end of it (Willie wrote). It was not the resolution I had hoped for – but I could not imagine what that might have been; I just wanted to *feel* better, to *feel* – justified? I guess I expected some sort of immediate reward for holding onto a decision. Pathetic. Nothing that I have done, of any importance, for better or for worse, has been altogether free of doubts. Yet there was a feeling of relief as I walked away from the bar. The force of the Arctic blast could be seen as a celebration of a cleansing. I enjoyed thinking it might be.

A taxi came soon enough. What I wanted to do now was to live as well as I could, as truly as I could, within my own lights. 4.30 a.m. in New York meant 9.30 p.m. in London. I telephoned Joanna to ask about her and about my mother.

'I think she wants to see you,' Joanna said, careful. Careful not to sound drunk or careful not to seem to be putting on pressure? It did not matter: I was ashamed of the quibble.

'I'll go up there as soon as I get back.'

I hesitated. The fact was that Joanna's distant, subdued, undemanding voice quite suddenly brought her into mind and, more important, into my heart. As if the telephone were Aladdin's lamp and out of it the Genie of love completely forgotten rose up, speeding across the icy Atlantic. Perhaps this was the reward. 'How are you?'

'Fine.' The automatic reflex was no more than I deserved but still I was disappointed. 'Where are you?' she asked.

'New York.' I waited for the echo to clear. 'I'm coming back tonight. I'll be there the morning after next, your time. Did you find out exactly how Mother was?'

'They're not holding out much hope.' The deadness in her voice slapped me in the face. I had behaved badly to her. There

214

was time, though, wasn't there? I would have to live with the memory of Caroline – but I could subordinate it, couldn't I? Joanna, alone in that dreary flat, needing help; so much lost for her.

'It'll be lovely to see you again.'

'Caroline telephoned.'

There is no cure for whatever it is that I have. The mere sound of her name melted my resolution, shivered what I had thought to be my firm structure of intention. All I wanted that instant was to know what Caroline had said. She had phoned! She had turned to me! However pathetic my celebration of that paltry act of recognition might seem to you, I have to confess its effect on me. There would be no way I would ever be free of my feeling for her.

'I suppose Caroline's the woman you've been seeing.'

'Yes.' But . . . But I didn't make love to her? What did that matter? How is it that even such hopeless selfish ties of personal affection can upset a balance of decisions apparently far more important and far-reaching? 'What did she say?'

'She wanted to get in touch with Ian but she hadn't been able to contact him.'

Once again, I *had* to be free of it. The blow I felt was insane: the murderous urge towards Ian, truly dangerous – and bad. I wished to destroy, to do wrong, to do him no good: all that I had so confidently accused him of. It had not been cut out: all the talk amounted to nothing. Nothing at all.

'She's a friend of Marion apparently,' Joanna went on, registering the pause as no more than the expectation of more information. 'Marion took an overdose yesterday. Her cleaner found her and she seems all right now. She didn't want Ian to know but . . . Caroline seemed to think he ought to. She sounded very upset: almost hysterical.' Joanna paused. 'Perhaps you could tell him – if you think he ought to know. Caroline said that Marion had been insistent not to tell him. She sounded frightened. What do you think?'

'It's terrible.' I could not organise my reactions at all.

'Will you be able to tell him?'

215

'I don't know.'

There was a measurable silence. Joanna's 'presence' had disappeared as suddenly as it had arrived: and it was as if she knew.

'I'll see you soon then.'

'Yes.'

'Goodbye then.'

Abstracted, I took time before acknowledging her and she put the phone down. I imagined her as she sat there in London. Placed the phone quietly on the receiver. Turned back into that gloomy room. Took up a drink? Turned on the radio? Fled once more to the old unknown – to me – life of – what had it been? The bars of big hotels, I guessed, cocktail lounges, foyers, old flames still spluttering a little illicit desire? Nothing that had nourished her: nothing that had made her strong or happy. Pity is supposed to be avoided. My self-pity for her stirred me out of self-pity. For years I had recognised our mutual lameness. I hoped I had years to find a remedy.

Marion. Overdose. *Marion!*

I phoned Caroline. 'Where is he?' she asked after the barest preamble.

Whose sake was I going to lie for this time? His, hers, my own? It had to stop. 'I left him in a club in Harlem.'

'Did he say when he would be back in his flat?'

'No.' Even that single syllable, delivered, believe me, in a neutral, non-committal tone, carried enough of a charge to her alert ears. Those in love have more than six senses: perhaps its power has been underestimated, even by the poets, for in immediate response to my sober 'no', Caroline said, 'He's with someone, isn't he? Going back to her place?'

'I think so.'

'Thanks for telling me.'

Her unjust sarcasm was unapologetic.

'If Marion wants it kept from him . . .' I began.

'She tried to kill herself, for God's sake!'

'How did you know?'

'She sent me a letter.' Caroline's voice choked into a terrible

216

grieving sob. Through the convulsive misery, she repeated, 'She . . . sent . . . me . . . a . . . letter.'

'Oh God, I'm sorry.' I waited, wrenched by that wounded, penitent sound.

'It's her . . .' Caroline heaved in breath, steadied herself. 'She's the one you should be sorry for.'

If she sent Caroline a note – would she then not have sent a note to others; to Ian?

'She rang. I went to see her,' Caroline said. 'And' – once more the convulsion threatened, but she forced it back – 'And she apologised – to *me* – for the note. She said it had been vindictive. She didn't know what had come over her. She's never done it before. She's desperate that Ian shouldn't know.'

'But you want to tell him.'

'Yes.' I could sense, almost see her pulling herself together. 'She must have wanted it known or, or she wouldn't have written to me,' Caroline said, speaking steadily, a steadiness so willed it moved me even more than her sobbing had done. 'She must have known I would tell Ian. That was part of it. That's why she kept saying she was ashamed, I think, although I'm the one who should feel ashamed.' She paused. 'And I do. But – the point is – she might try again, mightn't she? Ian *has* to know she needs him there.'

'Would you like me to tell him?'

'Would you? You've known him so long. He always relied on you in some way.' As if to make restitution for what now seemed an unjustified earlier harshness, Caroline added, with chillingly cajoling levity, 'I used to get a bit jealous of you sometimes.'

'I'll get in touch with him.'

'Thank you. And . . .'

'I'll tell him he can phone you if he wants to.'

'Thank you. You're . . .'

'If I ring right away I might still catch him at that club.'

'Oh – yes. Of course. Well. Goodbye.'

This time I made no attempt to echo the farewell but sat on

217

the edge of my bed in the plain overheated hotel room, holding the phone, listening to the purr.

I found the club's number. Ian was not there. I asked for Chris. 'This is Willie,' I said.

'Oh. Ian's friend.'

'I need to find him urgently.'

'He left. Some time ago. Right after you. He seemed a bit uptight.'

'He's gone to – Julie's, I think. Do you know where she lives?'

'Sorry.'

'Does anybody?'

'Wait a minute.'

The buzz of the club came through the earpiece. I strained to pick out Chris's voice. 'No luck,' he said. 'They don't really know her here. It was Ian found the place. Are you in trouble?'

'No. Thanks anyway.'

'Sorry I couldn't be more helpful.'

I remembered Ian ordering his car for midday. Presumably it would deliver him to his apartment.

I slept as if drugged and woke with a fierce headache.

I was outside his apartment at 11.30. For an hour and a half I stood there – suitcase in one hand, briefcase in the other, fearing only that Eileen would appear. It was weak of me, but I could not face the hurdle of her inevitable hospitality and curiosity.

At one o'clock, taking some almost weird satisfaction from being deeply, painfully cold, I went for a snack in the nearest coffee house. I phoned twice: no reply. I was back in place just after two.

The next three hours were strange. I seemed to drain away and become part of a slow-motion metropolitan flotsam. To keep warm, I walked up and down, but only occasionally and always looking back at the entrance. There were two men – alcoholics? in despair? in a chosen world? – in adjacent doorways, huddled from the cold. As time went by they began to nod to me. No one else took any notice. A young black sold

218

me a welcome woollen hat and mittens. The snow-ploughs scraped at the deeply frozen mud. There were no patterns I could see, only an endless interrupted procession of New Yorkers, muffled against the cold, hurrying along the sidewalks.

It the being in that one place which was strange: being and waiting, taut with waiting, hating him for it, for her, for all this: and I had put faith in him. Loved him? At times, yes. Oh, he was remarkable. I had done enough work among the great dead to know something of the sacrifices, strengths, abominations and forces needed to claw that last long distance separating the many who were good from the few who were really great: and in his hard profession he was undoubtedly great. But I was no longer prepared to pardon the blight as the acceptable price. I was dazed. Thoughts of Marion: I saw her in that highly wrought room, splayed on the large sofa, her white throat somehow thrust forward, bare, offered up, head tilted back, neck longing for the cut. Of Caroline, wreathed now in ageing knowledge, cut off from youth, cut again. Joanna, cut off from a normal life; my mother about to leave life. And Ian buoyantly, brilliantly, effortlessly uncovering his craft through the years, hiding the scars and the penalties under a display of ease which disguised the strength of his talent even from some of his most acute admirers. In the street, images of them all pressed onto my mind as the cold fed into the blood. I bordered on a kind of madness towards the end of that vigil, in some drowsy way enjoying the cold which cramped me, in some sickly way calling up loved memories, tormenting myself, mocking the insanely compulsive meditation on so small a circle of life while the planet roared through a universe of struggle.

Before going to the theatre I drank several cups of coffee as hot as I could bear. The doorman only let me in after he had delivered a note to Ian, who was making up, stripped to the waist.

'You look buggered,' he said, addressing me through the bulb-boundaried mirror, 'There's some brandy over there.'

219

I took a glass, without even saying hello. Ian's full attention was on his face. I did not know how to begin. Ian, your wife has tried to kill herself? Ian, you bastard, you shit, Marion took a bottle of hard white lethal tablets, swallowed them, sucked them down, wanted them, wanted oblivion. Ian, can you not take care? Is care impossible? Is it true that to capture and harness and aim that mysterious energy you have to live on some visceral instinct? I can't follow you – do I want to slash off your wings because I envy your flight? You are becoming someone else, yet again, every second further away from such of yourself as I know. Maybe you are no more unknowable than anyone else, only more accentuated in the mystery of yourself. I will never know your Caroline, your Marion, even your Joanna. You had *her* too, didn't you? Had to. And me. Your dependence has balanced me. I loved to help you. But you came to be helped. You were the seeker. You wanted. You *want*. Your wanting is your power. You have to feed it, haven't you? Fuel, need, hunger, conqueror, blight, vulture: and out of it . . . what? Oh – pleasure, yes: admit that.

'If you came to tell me about Marion,' Ian said, without turning round, 'and I suspect there can be no other reason, then I know already. My agent phoned from London. I've been talking to Marion all afternoon. And if you want to know why I'm not rushing back to London to beg forgiveness and fulfil all your Christian hopes, then I'll tell you why. She had every right to do what she did and no right to think she could crush me or anybody else with guilt and ruin. And,' he turned flame-faced, wigged, brown-chested, cold, 'if you want to know what I *did* for her – I told her she was stupid, *stupid*, OK? And I said that if she wanted to get herself on a plane over here I would be glad to see her. She'll be here tomorrow morning.' He paused and then concluded, deliberately, 'Which will give me one more glorious night with Julie.'

I left, not having said a word."

220

Chapter Eleven

(1)

Marion chainsmoked: she had become very thin. To deflect comment she dressed with particular and elegant cunning. She registered, in Caroline's first glance, that the disguise was inadequate.

"It's very good of you to come again. Please . . ." She indicated the bounty of comfortable chairs. Caroline moved across right away. There was something more than brisk, almost military, in Marion's speech and gestures. The strain stared out like a ripe bruise.

"Drink?"

"Gin and tonic," Caroline replied, quickly, knowing it would be available, easy, no fuss.

As the drink was poured she chanced a look around the room: the sort of room her mother would dream of her possessing, she thought. But for herself? Too studied, too much of a setting. For Ian? A perfect front.

"I hope that's all right." Marion held out the chunky crystal glass, the ice cubes and slice of lemon still bubbling. She waited while Caroline sipped.

"It's fine." It was too strong. Marion chose an armchair facing her guest and inhaled deeply.

"I thought I ought to see you. Last time was . . . I behaved very badly. I wanted to tell you that . . . face to face as it were."

"There's no – "

"It was *very* silly. One simply shouldn't behave like that."

Marion wanted neither sympathy nor understanding. Caroline was here to be instructed on the exact terms of her

221

feelings and actions. Marion stubbed out a half-cigarette and pulled out another.

"Did you tell anyone, as a matter of interest?"

"I tried to tell Ian but I couldn't get hold of him." Marion's slight nod indicated gratitude for the keeping of a trust. Blushing, Caroline continued, "So I got in touch with Willie."

"Did you?" The flame leapt up from the lighter.

"He was in New York. I'm sorry. But," Caroline struggled on, pinned though she was by Marion's gaze, "I thought Ian ought to know."

"And of course by telling him yourself you'd be giving him one in the eye." Marion opened her lips, showing teeth.

"I suppose so." Recognition of the truth of the comment caught Caroline's throat like a wire.

"We all need revenge." Marion drank a draught of her vodka. "Don't we?"

Caroline's lack of response did not disconcert her. Her own world enclosed her.

"Another?" She held up her glass. Caroline shook her head. With marked steadiness, Marion went across and poured herself another stiff measure. She stood and looked down at Caroline with undisguised dislike.

"I can't see why you should be the one who did it. The straw breaking the camel's back, I suppose. Cheers. I'm going to divorce him."

Caroline waited until Marion sat down.

"Does he know?"

"Not yet," Marion revealed, carelessly. "I want to get it right. If you were about to ask me why I've waited so long I can only say I must have been mad. So the field's yours," she added, and raised her glass, mocking the younger woman. "*Bonne chance.*"

"I'd decided," Caroline hesitated, but the force of Marion's aggression compelled her to say what she would otherwise have kept buried, "to – not to see him again."

"Bravo! I decided on that a thousand times, my dear. Like giving up smoking. Much the same sort of thing."

222

"Look, Marion . . ." Caroline struggled to repress her sense of guilt and disadvantage, to put her point.

"No. *You* look." Another cigarette stubbed the rare china ashtray. Another lit. "I'm not doing it because he's a shit. So many of them are, don't you agree? And he has things to offer . . ." again the lips drew back. The discordant rasp of innuendo unsettled Caroline further. "No, it isn't that. Just that I'm bored with it all. His ego, his lies, his women, his successes, his stories, even his seriousness – even all that I respect about him – and," she was stern now, the cigarette an extended forefinger, pointed at the heart, "he is *marvellous*, don't forget that – *marvellous*." She stopped, drew on the cigarette and sank back into the ornate dumpling cushion. "I'm bored. Somebody else can do it. Why not you?"

"I don't want to."

"Oh?" Marion shook her head. "I don't believe you. You think I'm a little bit off my head and need appeasing. I *am* a little bit off my head, but sometimes that helps you see clearly, don't you agree? You'll change your mind when it sinks in that I mean it."

"I'm going back to Scotland. To Glasgow."

"*Glasgow?* Don't be absurd."

The simple snobbery made Caroline laugh with relief: laugh genuinely, laugh unaffectedly. Marion peered at her for a moment and then she too began to giggle, the first warm sound which had come from her since Caroline had come into the room. "How stupid," Marion said, attempting to stop, "just because I said, I said . . . Glasgow!"

The word was scarcely out when both of them ricocheted into another burst of easing laughter.

"That was good," Marion said, her voice softer, her eyes sparkling from the brush of tears. "You see, it'll be all right."

"Are *you*?" Caroline asked, riding on the new wave of friendliness.

"Bit shaky. Correction, *very* shaky. But under control. I'll miss the bastard."

"Are you just . . . leaving him? Just like that?"

223

"Why not?" Marion's reply was foolproofed in its tone of good faith. "People do it all the time. People I know. Maybe there's another England where it doesn't happen. Perhaps London's a foreign country. But yes, why not? I've had enough, Caroline. There's no more to be said. It's so simple I can scarcely believe it. It's over."

Marion reached for her handbag and drew out an envelope. "This is for you. Don't read it now. I'd rather you didn't. And," the smile, this time, was accompanied by its usual disarming intention, "please don't bother to telephone me. I'm going down to Norfolk to spend a week or two with my sister."

Caroline took the letter. It signified the end of the encounter. For form's sake the two women chatted for a few more minutes. Caroline admired the plants, Marion complimented her on her hair. Caroline asked about the material on the cushions, Marion pointed out the flaws in the decoration; the offer of another drink was refused.

Caroline walked onto a bitterly cold London pavement, clutching the envelope.

(2)

"David wants you to see his girlfriend."

"Oh no. Please." Willie needed no please, Joanna thought; he looked utterly exhausted.

"I think you'd better," she said, gently. "It'll hurt him if you don't."

Willie was so tired he failed to notice the new tone of concern for her son in his wife's voice. "All I want to do is sleep."

"I'll get them up. It'll only take a minute."

Rather coquettishly, Willie registered, mistily, Joanna came across, kissed him on the cheek and then swirled across the room in her old bold Yellow Book dressing-gown.

Willie stood. To sit would be to sleep. He had come off a sleepless night flight, taken a morning train north to see his mother, spent another sleepless night unable to recover from jet-lag, unable to reach Caroline, whose phone was out of order,

224

and unable to fully digest the timetable and deadline given him for his mother's remaining life. In order to spend as much time as possible with her he had caught the sleeper back to London, ignoring all his previous experience of sleeplessness in the stuffy jolting cellular cabins. Before him were mountainous decisions. It was 8 a.m. And he was instructed to meet David's girlfriend!

"The coffee's just made," Joanna said, conspiratorially, holding out the coffee-pot like a bribe. "They were up. They'll be through in a minute. Sit down."

He was too tired to disobey. He had not yet taken off his coat.

When David and the girl came in, he stood up and smiled. She was stunning.

"This is Marilyn," David said, with unmitigated pride. "This is Willie – my father."

"How do you do?"

Marilyn beamed and nodded vigorously. David looked from one to the other most carefully as if he were a referee about to give the last instructions to a pair of boxers. "I met Marilyn at the Centre," he said. "She's a dancer."

"Part time," Marilyn qualified the description cheerfully.

"She works in Woolworth's," David said, again appraising Willie's reaction most minutely.

"'The Wonder of Woollies'," Marilyn chanted. "It's not so bad."

"It's quite near the Centre," David said. "We can meet for lunch."

"I'm supposed to be slimmin'," Marilyn said, pinching her waist severely. The South London accent, which had been suppressed, came out strongly on this serious subject.

"She's totally non-political," David said, with awe, with pleasure.

"I don't like any of them," Marilyn confirmed, happily accepting Joanna's offer of a mug of coffee.

Willie felt a little superfluous. Clearly they expected him to contribute nothing at all.

"Oh," David swallowed what he made appear a lump of

225

coffee, "thanks for all those contacts, Dad. The film's shaping up really well, really well. Thanks."

"I wan' him to make a real film," Marilyn said. "He *could* with actors."

David glowed as if a cloud of compliments had burst over his head. "We'll have to go now," he said.

"Mrs Benson gives us hell if we're late."

"The Northern Line," David explained, "takes us there."

"I hate that tube," Marilyn said. "It's like bein' in a sewer. Gives me the creeps."

"We'll come back at the weekend," David promised. "Marilyn wants to go up to Hampstead."

"I fancy Hampstead," she said. "Better than the dump we live in." She looked around the room contentedly. "This is a *nice* place." She nodded. "Books," she added, mysteriously.

Clucking a little, David ushered her to the door. "See you then," he added.

"Yes. See you," Marilyn echoed or answered. One more beam and she was gone.

Willie turned his rather numbed gaze from them to discover Joanna smiling more happily than he remembered for years.

"He's crazy about her," she announced, unnecessarily.

"Yes?"

"They were terribly noisy in bed." Joanna poured herself another coffee as if awarding herself a prize.

"Were they?"

"God. It's a relief!"

"Why?"

"I thought he never would. I've thought he was queer for years. I wouldn't have minded. I wouldn't have minded anything if he had just done *some*thing. I couldn't stand his . . . constipation!" She lit a cigarette. "Marilyn will sort him out."

You've discovered that you love your son again, Willie thought, and his tiredness was alleviated by the pressure of pleasure. "I didn't ever realise how worried you were."

"It wasn't worry so much. I just couldn't stand him. All that loner, soulful, self-righteous, celibate nonsense. I hated it. That was all."

"I see." Willie took care to phrase his next words carefully and to empty his tone of all inflammable potential. "Do you think one of us ought to allude to the fact that she is black?"

"Oh, Willie!" Joanna rumbled with a belly-laugh so mischievous and infectious that Willie had to wave at her to stop: he was too stiff and sore to laugh.

"Perhaps it is ducking the issue *not* to mention it."

"My God. Even when you have a clear conscience you feel guilty. Not that you ever have anything else."

Joanna looked at him lovingly. "I know that you don't – go to bed – with that girl. And anyway, who am I to judge you?"

She came across and embraced him, heavily. Moved as Willie was, he was also quite weak and he tottered, a little unbalanced.

"I'll run you a bath," Joanna said, "and then you can sleep all day."

"Are you out?"

"Women of the world, me and Marilyn, and I have my own Mrs Benson who gives me hell."

The phone rang.

"Sorry it's so early," Eric said, "but Joanna told me you were coming back on the sleeper and I wanted to be sure to catch you. Can you come in this morning?"

"Could it be this afternoon?"

"Tied up with bloody meetings. I wouldn't press, Willie, but there's something you ought to know."

"I'm a bit bushed."

"What about twelve, then? Just after twelve? And a lunch."

"It can't wait?"

"Not really." Eric chafed a little. "You've been out of the office all week, Willie."

"Twelve."

"Thanks. See you."

227

"Willie," Eric proclaimed as he came into the Office. "You look great."

Willie stared at him and then shook his head: there was no real harm in the man.

"I should have asked about your mother," Eric said, chomping on his bottom lip as he walked around his desk to plant himself in the armchair splendidly co-equal to Willie's.

"It's just a matter of time now," Willie said, steadily. The incipient realisation of his mother's certain early death was gathering to a head the force of sorrow which had been building up over the months.

"I'm sorry." Eric jerked around for comfort in his comfortable seat and resolved his plight by slinging both legs over one of the arms. He looked out of the window for a few moments. "The thing is – I think I have a job for you."

The innocently patronising sentence touched the older man.

"We would have to make you redundant, of course," Eric went on, cheerfully, "but then we could do a deal. It's the new pattern." He took a deep breath and Willie feared a dissertation on Channel Four, the new opportunities for independent producers, the impact of cable and satellite and video – "I understand," Willie said, lightly.

Eric looked relieved. "There's this idea." Eric scowled as if the idea were a particularly large and knobbly bone he could not easily fit into his jaws. "Quite simple really. And right up your street. It's not very complicated – it's not complicated at all – but to get it across in a few words without making it seem naff, that's the problem. It's about what people believe in. Well, it needn't be. It could be just about their lives – straight biography if you see what I mean. Or it could be what they think about somebody else – that might be a way in. Anyway, it's about them. What they have to say. Famous people. Artists, scientists, academics, we could include sportsmen. Politicians are a bit tricky, they'll talk to everybody, you would have to be careful about the politicians. It would depend what level you came in on. If you could start with say Brandt, and what'sisname D'Estaing and say Carter, the word might get

228

around. The security would have to be guaranteed: totally guaranteed. And the exclusivity – that wouldn't be so hard, I think, we could make it very worthwhile, they could have a royalty going to their estate, they all start to worry about their estate, don't they, towards the end? What it needs, though, is setting up. That's where you come in."

Willie nodded: the code was not too difficult to crack. "So you want me to interview eminent people now on the understanding that the material will not be shown until after their death. This would give them the opportunity to speak with as much freedom as they wanted. You could build up a bank of profiles or autobiographies which could be marketed not only on television but on video, through colleges, libraries and so on."

"As I said," Eric agreed. "Now this wasn't my own idea," he confessed, a little reluctantly but loyal to the truth. "What I would like to do is have it done outside and be on first refusal for the UK rights. You could be the connection. And it would still give you time to make one, maybe two, documentaries a year. The working title," he confided, "is *Testaments*."

"It *could* work."

"That's where you're a key figure. As I told them. The Americans, they want to put up the money. This came up when we were discussing the sale of a pile of our material to cable. You've been in the obit game longer than anybody, you know your way around the – the sort of people they have in mind. Anyway, they're willing to put a lot into a development scheme – three years – I've said if they'll take you on board our interest would be secure. They want to meet you for lunch: they're leaving tonight, otherwise I wouldn't have phoned you this morning." Eric looked so pleased with his scheme that Willie had to applaud.

"It *could* work," he repeated. That was not enough: Eric deserved more. "Thanks." Brief but well felt.

Eric nodded happily. "And I can wangle a better redundancy if we play our cards right."

"I don't know whether I'm up to lunch with your Americans."

229

"You'll be fine," Eric assured him. "They're mad on the idea – thought your Brezhnev was a classic."

During the first hour of expensive mastication at Overton's, the three Americans reiterated in detail just how mad they were on the idea. Willie fortified himself with food and drink and dimly understood something of the attraction it had for them. "Long-term investment" . . . "tying up the field" . . . "multiple usage" . . . "corner the market" . . . "great historical value" . . . "cassette rights" . . . "print spin-offs" . . . "Library of Congress" . . . "cost write-off potential" . . . He had dealt with American television executives on several occasions and always been impressed by their earnest thoroughness, their enthusiasm and their final reluctance to deliver on any project which did not hit an available slot smack in the centre. He was also aware of their habit of contractual prevarication which came perilously close to unfair dealing: oddly enough, for all the courtesy and honourable talk, there appeared to be no notion in America of the gentleman's agreement. Until the contract was finally signed it was mere talk. But they were hooked, there was little doubt of that; even through his haze of tiredness he could tell they were hungry to start. Fame by association? The opportunity to characterise their new cable operation? A sniff of real loot? Some combination of all three, most likely: but here they were brandishing start dates, asking if he would come over to New York to meet the office, enquiring for the name of his agent, nodding deeply as a genuinely delighted Eric dropped in the names of the Great Dead whose lives Willie had rendered into celluloid. Willie's virtual silence impressed them.

When he did begin to talk, his senses and his scruples directed him to attack the project. He enumerated the difficulties, pointed out the certain possibility of overlapping projects already under way, detailed the amount of research required, raised the problem of interviewers and the obstacles of reticence, spelt out the unreliable turnover and, if they were aiming for the most important or newsworthy people, the uncertainty of securing that uninhibited scoop element which

230

had to distinguish the series. He could not have done better. Each objection met with satisfied approval: this was exactly the sort of careful and defensive editorial hand they needed.

Did they have a deal? Even his slighter queries were met with an open door: he would find it difficult, he said, to work out of New York. Perfect, they said. They wanted to set up an independent company in London, work with British crews, centre the operation here. And budgets? It could prove unexpectedly expensive – in the case of a painter, for example, if his work was scattered about the world in museums reluctant to agree copyright. We want the best possible product, they said: if the money could be accounted for, it would be provided. Make no mistake, Willie (the instantly confidential use of his Christian name made him wince with a distaste he did not respect in himself), we are one hundred and ten per cent behind this project. Eric here has told us you are the man. Eric is willing to come aboard only on condition you come aboard. We want you in with us, Willie; this could be a very, very important venture.

He waited on the pavement with Eric: a weak wintry sun made the snow and sludge glister. The Americans had decided to walk to their next appointment.

"What do you think?"

"Fog." Willie pointed to his head. "I'll let you know when it lifts. But thanks again."

"And I haven't forgotten the documentaries."

Willie nodded. "I think I'll walk," he said as Eric flagged down a cab. "I need some air."

"By the end of the week," Eric encouraged him. "Let's sew it up by the end of the week."

For some reason he thrust out his hand: Willie shook it. As if they were strangers newly introduced.

(3)

He turned up St James's and waded forward. The fatigue was now like an ocean all about him, the current pushing into him.

231

While he was still awake there was one last thing he wanted to do, to settle his mind. After that, sleep could have him for as long as it wanted.

He found a phone in a cinema foyer and rang Mandy.

"A voice from the grave!" she said and Willie smiled at the affectionate energy so readily generous. That could have been a life.

"There's something I want to talk to you about."

"Don't tell me. Broke a leg? No – palpitations, I can feel them – palpitations and a disfiguring rash in the groin."

"Could we meet?"

"I thought you'd never ask. Mind you, I have a fella now. Not butch, not exactly your lorry-driving Sartre figure, more an asthmatic teetotaller. But he's got a sense of humour. He needs one. You'll understand when you meet him. And he's an *accountant*, Willie. I'm home at last."

"What about tea?"

"Tea! I'd forgotten tea. Tea I'd thought went with the Empire. OK."

"This afternoon?"

"You sure know how to court a girl, Willie, I'll give you that. I always gave you that. You never wanted it – that was the problem. OK. Tea this afternoon. I have to be back for my cripples at five o'clock. Are your corpses OK? You know, I've often thought we should get together – professionally. I see them off, you write them up."

"At the Ritz?"

"The Ritz already! What is it, Willie? Has the President died and left you the exclusive? I wouldn't know. I only read the newspapers."

"I'm next door to it."

"I see. Convenience foods again. All right, don't extend yourself, I'll struggle into something indecent and see you among the cakestands. How are you anyway? Don't answer that. I'll never get to the Ritz."

Willie was early enough to have a choice of tables in the grandiose foyer. He looked with rather dazed curiosity at the busy

232

preparations in the voluminous hotel. So much effort to give such an expensive and insubstantial snack to a clientèle one of whose common traits would be that they were dieting. While half the world . . . the Sunday-school precepts rose like stern ghosts . . . how far he had travelled since the days that a plain Christian purse had held all the currency for a good life. And who would not agree that it had been downhill all the way?

"Having a nice zizz? Don't let me disturb you. Think of me as the night nurse."

"Mandy." Willie stood up and leaned forward to kiss her.

"Watch the table, Romeo. Breakages are extra."

She sat down. Willie felt charged with the friendliness that came from her.

"Thanks for coming," he said.

"For tea at the Ritz I'm anybody's," she said and looked around at the crowd moving towards the small tables. "Some of my patients could do with some of this. Always goes to the wrong people, doesn't it? Contact lenses, almost a stone lighter, and shock, jet-lag or flu. Am I right or am I right?"

The waiter came.

"The works," Mandy said. "Cream buns, cucumber sandwiches – surprise us."

"Indian or China, Madam?"

"They put you in your place, don't they? Indian. Willie? Two Indians – no feathers – forget it."

"You look even better," Willie said. "I've done you a favour."

Mandy leaned forward, touched his arm and, without a hint of bathos, let drop the jokiness.

"You don't look well."

"I'm just a bit tired. That's all."

Mandy pursed her lips disbelievingly. "What is it then?"

"Let's gossip first. I haven't gossipped for months. Let's catch up."

The tea came, elaborately arranged, dinkily displayed – "Do we photograph it or ask for a doggie bag?" – and they chatted about what they had done, Willie carefully avoiding all that was

233

important, Mandy carelessly indiscreet. They talked about the headlines, the new shows and films, they reminisced a little, they flirted a little: Willie bathed in her normality.

"So why did you want to see me?" Mandy's question drifted across unaggressively, even, apparently, idle.

"My mother's dying," Willie said, uncomfortably discovering that his voice quavered at the words. "There are a couple of things I want your advice on."

Mandy listened closely as he outlined the progress of his mother's cancer. He had taken careful note of the stages and had been at pains to remember the details of treatment and the exact descriptions of the illness.

"They haven't told her she's dying," he said. "I'm sure she's realised it, but she hasn't enquired and she hasn't been told. They've said the decision's up to me."

"How long did they give her?"

"A week or two."

"That's what I would have said. She won't be in much pain now."

"No. She's very thin and very weak. She still mentions going 'home' – 'when I'm better'. I don't quite know how she wants me to take it. I wouldn't be surprised if she were protecting me."

"Don't underestimate how much protection you'll need. Very few things as important as this will happen to you in your life. You'll need time to grieve. In fact," Mandy spoke with considered seriousness, "looking at you, I would guess that you've begun grieving already. A lot of people do. Prepare themselves against the shock. Should you tell her? Up to you – but I wouldn't. Not unless she asks. By not asking she's made her decision. Respect that."

"That's what I thought," Willie said.

"Do be careful about *yourself*, though, won't you? I'll send you some tablets. You're having some sort of trauma, whether or not you allow yourself to recognise it. It will happen despite you."

"I'll take care. Thank you. The other thing is – should I bring her home?"

234

"What do they say?"

"They say it wouldn't matter. She could take the pills. They would arrange for a nurse to be there."

"What do you think?"

"I think she would like it."

"Only if you can be there. All the time. Can you?"

"I think I could arrange things, yes."

"Do it, then. Do it." She repeated the injunction gently.

"I will." Willie breathed a sigh which, Mandy noticed, released as much tension as tiredness.

"I suspect, Willie," she said, "without wanting to embroil us both in amateur analysis, that you've been worried about your mother for a long time. Perfectly natural. It's more likely to have affected you than most."

"Why?"

"You love her very much. You really care for her. It was one of the things I admired about you. Still do."

"It seems a bit indecent. Someone in their late forties."

"Only because of the way we pigeonhole things. Most people who lose touch with their parents lose real touch with all the important roots in themselves. It can occasionally liberate them. But it can – and from my experience it more often does – diminish them. But it means you'll have to go through it. As I say, I think you've already begun."

"Would it be silly to take her out? Just a short trip. She keeps talking about seeing the Lakes again."

"If she has the strength."

"Well then . . . thank you."

Mandy looked at her watch and affected an attitude of panic. "I'll send you those tablets," she said. "I have your mother's address. And call me . . . afterwards. If you want to. Any time." She smiled and stood up. "It doesn't have to be the Ritz. How's David?"

"In love, I think."

"There seems no way to stamp it out. Bye, love. Take care."

The bill took rather longer to negotiate than the tea.

235

"Joanna? You're back. Good. I'm still in town. At the Ritz! I was just ringing to tell you it's going to be all right. We are. Us. I've – sorry, it's a bad line – it's a booth – I'd rather not shout – no – I've not been very good to you – I want to change all that – I know – but I wanted to tell you right away – yes: I'll catch a cab as soon as I put down the phone – but, Joanna – it isn't too late for us to try . . . well, to be kind to each other, that would be a start – I know we are – but there isn't much time left – not the – the phone, anyway I've three more tens – for us, I meant. I'm not being morbid – we have such a lot, haven't we? – but I want to tell you now – if I waited it might slip away – of course I'm sober – even if I weren't – I suppose it is ridiculous – but, Joanna – I'm getting some money – I'm leaving work, it's OK. There's an offer I want to take up – it's OK, believe me – I think we should get another flat – or a little house, with a garden – my father was good at gardening – *in* London, yes, *in* London – or a cottage. Keep the flat – but somewhere *else* – don't you think? Don't laugh, please – yes – I want you to agree *now* – I don't *know* why – we *could* love each other again, couldn't we? Joanna? Who? Caroline? What did she want? Did she sound . . . ? . . . I'll phone her – but – " The pips began their busy tattoo. "Wait a minute – hold on – *there* – yes – if she has to see me – but just for an hour – I want to see you – I'm going up to Mother's tomorrow – Joanna? – Yes: all right: talk later."

He arranged to meet Caroline over the road in Brown's. She said it would take her about twenty minutes on the tube to Green Park. He drank scotch, drowned in Malvern Water, and read the *Standard*. His cheeks burned even with the light infusion of yet more alcohol. The bar was only half full: gobbets of conversation buzzed about his ears lulling him into the warm plush affluence of the place.

There was a swing to Caroline's walk. It could be seen even in that short distance from the door to his table. Willie remembered that very first time he had almost subliminally noticed her, stepping out from the barrier at the station, scattering her golden good spirits like guineas.

"I'm sorry to insist but I'm leaving tomorrow," she said.

"Oh?"

"Home," she announced. "A glass of white wine, please," to the waiter. Willie indicated another scotch. "That job in Glasgow looks – fingers crossed – on. In about a month. I just want to get out of London."

"I'm going north tomorrow." Willie cringed at this weakness.

"I've booked a ticket on the bus," Caroline said, promptly. "Sorry. I didn't mean it to sound like it did."

"That's fine. I don't know when I'll be starting. Well." He raised his glass. "Good luck."

He could not tell whether Caroline's buoyancy was a reversal to a former state or an act of will. Whatever its source, her energy threw into relief his own spent resources.

"So I wanted to say cheerio," she added. "I didn't want you to think I'd just sneak off."

"I appreciate it."

The drinks came.

"How was New York?"

"Very cold." He was too tired for fencing. "I saw Ian two or three times. He's doing very well."

"I got through to his flat this morning," Caroline said. "Or rather, this afternoon – this morning. A woman answered."

"Yes. That would be Eileen. They . . . flat-share or whatever it's called."

"I see. But he has another woman there, of course. Hasn't he?"

Willie's silence ought to have been a rebuke but Caroline's brisk determination was not to be checked by obedience to good manners.

"You needn't say it. Your face says it for you. I would be amazed if he hadn't." She took the merest sip of her wine. "Do you think he's a bastard or are the rest of us just half-alive?"

"I think he's a bastard," Willie said, carefully.

"He said you'd had some sort of row."

"So you managed to speak to him?"

"Oh yes."

"It was more than a row," Willie said, "but less than I wanted."

"What did you want?"

"I was never clear enough about that." Willie closed his eyes to ease the itching of the lenses, but in that shuttered dark he met such a swoop of nervous drunkenness that he opened them again instantly. To deflect sympathy he went on, "The best I could think of was something absurdly melodramatic." He smiled. "Like challenging him to a duel, or doing him some harm, I'm afraid."

"Not because of me."

"Yes."

"That's just silly." Caroline frowned. "I don't want to be your idealised woman or daughter or lady in the tower, Willie, any more than I want to be Ian's part-time sexual fantasy."

"Will you go back to him?"

"Not as before."

"But you may? Go back to him?"

In reply, Caroline handed over the envelope given her by Marion. Inside it were two neatly folded sheets of expressive blank paper and Marion's unused air ticket to New York re-ascribed in Caroline's name.

"When are you going over?"

"I don't know when. I don't yet know whether."

She might wait until after Marion had declared her intention of divorcing Ian – no: she would go immediately. Do it.

"It has eleven months and three weeks to run," Willie observed, handing the ticket back.

"Is it impossible for us to meet as friends? Without all the drama?"

"I think so," Willie said, paying attention to his words: they sounded slurred to his own ears. He took his time. It would be the last time. He spoke slowly and very sadly. "What you

238

describe as an idealisation could also be something else, something I don't understand, something I don't want talked about, perhaps I don't want to understand, but something that could have completed my life. Now that I've known the possibility of it, I'll never lose it. I'll lose you – not that I ever possessed you – but I'll lose touch with you. I'll lose sight of you. I'll make a life for myself without that terrible hope, without that crucifying possibility that there just might be a life with you. But I'll never lose the feeling I have for you, Caroline. It's the deepest feeling I've ever had. I could see what they meant when they talked about the power of it, the wholeness of it, the transfiguration. Even that. That won't change. I hope to remember that for the rest of my time."

Caroline looked at him, touched, moved – but bare of any saving response.

He was terribly tired. That true declaration had been made possible by the exhaustion. Caroline saw before her a hunched, grey-faced, ageing man, worn out.

"I'll get them to call you a taxi," she said and left him on that ostensible purpose, using the small retreat to collect her feelings.

239

Chapter Twelve

(1)

"I shouldn't have come," Caroline said. "It was just some kind of feeling that I had to face you with things as I saw them."

"And there was the ticket," Ian replied, his voice already slurring. "Marion's little time bomb. A very clever parting gift. Very clever is my wife – pardon, about-to-be-ex-wife."

Caroline looked at him anxiously. He looked ill. It was not only the drink, although he had drunk steadily at dinner and fairly heavily since they had come into the nondescript piano bar. The pianist played softly, filling in his agreed time, Caroline thought, concerned to give pleasure to no one, perhaps least of all himself.

"I'm sorry," Caroline said.

"Don't be sorry. Don't be sorry about anything you do. Everybody wastes time being sorry. Life, as the man said, is too short. You're here. Enjoy it."

For a few hours when she had arrived a couple of days ago, she had thought she might. She had not rung Ian from London, but at Kennedy Airport her nerve had failed her and, to give him time, she had invented a cousin with whom she "had" to spend the first night. She had gone to the small hotel which had been recommended and spent the afternoon and the evening just drifting about Manhattan, intoxicated by the reality of a place so well known through films. Even though the cold weather continued, the streets were busy, delis open, large-windowed bars inviting, the street life seductive. It was to be the best part of her time in New York.

Ian declared himself pleased to see her and put himself at her disposal but it was embarrassingly clear to Caroline that he wished she had not come. She was impressed by the effort he made, the plans he drew up for what she should see and what they should do, the care he had taken to think what she might like. But it was such a visible effort, and he was unable to conceal an inner preoccupation which absorbed all but his most superficial energy. Eileen was good enough to tell Caroline that his performance had begun to suffer over the past few days and that his agent was meeting the management to discuss the chance of a reprieve on the contract and an earlier release.

At first, Caroline had thought that his strained attitude towards her was a result of having to reorganise his private life. After lunch at a restaurant which he had insisted she ought to see because it was so trendy (and which she had disliked for that reason) she challenged him directly.

"Yes," he said, quite calmly. "I had to sort things out. But it didn't matter. I would tell you if it did."

Caroline was silenced by his chilling truthfulness.

"Anything else you want to know?"

He went to the theatre at his usual time and she packed her bags, wrote a note, settled her hotel bill and booked herself on a morning flight. But it seemed cowardly. He had told her that there would be a ticket at the box-office.

She could see little signs of falling-off in his performance. He came on to applause and held the audience like a mirror. His voice, unmiked, reached to the furthest seats in the vast auditorium; when he whispered, they craned forward, when he let the bass notes roll they seemed pinned back on their seats. Perhaps it was because she had been immersed in American accents, but she had never as fully appreciated the power and variety of his voice. And when he spoke confidentially, long-ingly, the tone was so exactly like the tone he used when talking to her: a glance at her neighbours showed that they too were as personally addressed. Bewitched, all of them.

He was boisterous in his dressing-room and Caroline tried to drive out the thought that his plump, over-fussy dresser was eyeing her critically as "another one". They had dinner at

241

Sardi's, for her sake. His good humour had been sustained by the constant booster of recognitions, nods, autograph requests, compliments. He managed all that very easily. She was introduced as "from London" – as if it were a title – but Ian knew what he was doing: the description always succeeded in working her into those brief and fractured conversations. There was even a moment when he looked directly at her and said, "I'm glad you're here: it's a bit of a hassle at the moment, but I'm glad you've come," and she felt that she had betrayed him, her luggage in the hotel bedroom, her reservation in the computer.

In the bar, though, he had rapidly become morose. She had never seen him in this state. It was ugly. His mood was so impenetrably dark and volatile. Nothing she could possibly say would not be twisted or turned against her.

"So what did you want to face me about?" he asked.

They were sitting opposite each other. As he spoke he jutted his lean face forward: there was no trace of affection in his question.

Caroline had prepared for this but now the words fled. She wanted to stroke his face and persuade him to leave the drink and to rest. He was like a ship which had been sailing all sheets to the wind, gloriously free, and then, unexpectedly, capriciously even, found itself grounded.

"I think you should go home," she said. He poured another large glass of wine, very slowly, holding up the bottle so that the wine fell like a waterfall.

"So do I. So do I, Caroline. But where is it?" He smiled. "Don't look so *worried*. I'm only playing at self-pity. Other people enjoy it, why shouldn't I? It's got possibilities, as a matter of fact. You feel very significant when you let yourself drown in the old self-pity. Everything seems very . . . metaphysical. So what else did Willie say?"

"He just said you'd had a quarrel."

"Did he say he wanted to kill me?"

"No!"

"He did, you know. It was written all over him. In other

242

times he would have pulled out the rapier or the two-handed axe or whatever. He came here for revenge – but he couldn't handle it. Are you going to do any better, do you think?"

"Have you spoken to him? He's with his mother now."

"No." He did not mention the unreturned calls, the recent time he had got through and Willie had simply put down the phone. "Willie's ditched me."

"*Ditched* you?"

"Clever girl. Yes. It was some sort of an affair, you know. A very long one. Maybe my strongest. I'll tell you something, Caroline. Those who saw me and Willie together always thought he was the hanger-on: not true: I hung on to him. And he knew it. Don't you think he's a bit of a bastard just walking out on me like that?" He was serious: yet . . .

He switched so fast between vehemence and jokiness, wildness and plaintiveness; Caroline felt that he was scything her down, scything down everything in front of him.

"I'm going back tomorrow morning," she said.

"What a waste! Stay here. You don't have to stay with me. Enjoy New York. It's a wonderful city – especially for attractive young women who want to forget other cities. What did you want to say to me?"

"I wanted," Caroline braced herself, "I wanted to say I would live with you, if you wanted. But only if we lived together all the time. Only if you were serious."

"Thank you." Ian nodded, without mockery. "Thank you for offering that."

He finished the glass and poured in the rest of the bottle. "More?"

"No thanks."

"I'll just be on the safe side." He ordered another bottle.

"We could try," he said. "But I'd rather not. I would just mess it up. Besides, what we had is over, really, isn't it? The *real* thing we had. That only ever lasts a few months. All the rest is coming to an accommodation. I'm not much good at that. Willie was my only successful accommodation, and even

243

he turfed me out. When somebody you've known that well and that long just goes – half your life disappears."

"It won't for me," Caroline said.

"Marion said that. I was terrible to Marion. The fact that I told her how terrible I was and kept offering to push off makes no difference in the end. I'd given her to understand I was committed. And so I was. But only for those few months. Like a new star, Caroline, burning brilliantly at the start, the rest of its life spent getting cooler and older! When that sets in I feel death coming on. That's when I run away. I always have. I will again until I'm too old to run. So: no."

"In that case," Caroline spoke slowly, "I would rather not see you ever again."

"I understand that. Cut me out." He slashed the air, his open palm a sword blade. "Clean. Con . . . clusive."

"I think I'll go now."

"OK." Ian nodded. "I won't stop you." She looked ill, he thought, and he wanted to comfort her: hell, he wanted to go to bed with her. That would sort out both of them.

She stood up. He pulled out the table to let her pass. She hesitated . . . perhaps wanting a last gesture. He opened his arms and smiled. "Let me, at least, come out with you and get you a cab." Even his innocent generosity was corrupting.

Caroline did not trust herself enough to let him do that. She was shaking. It was hard to leave. It was very hard.

"Thanks," she said, "I'm sure the barman will help," and she walked away.

He watched her to the door. The barman did indeed help, casting a reproachful glance at Ian. She stood with her back to him and did not turn around even though the barman took an uncomfortable time in whistling up a cab on the street. The piano played on. Ian thought of the pleasures and even the happiness they had enjoyed. In his alcoholic saturation, he was moved to pitying them both. It could have been possible. The pianist crooned another sentimental love song. Responding to a wave from the street, Caroline disappeared. The heavy glass door closed. Too slowly, Ian thought.

He sipped his way through the bottle, floating in the pain-killing liquor, vaguely wondering what the city had in store for him, where he would end up. As always at such rare times of sentimental weakness he began to fantasise: he had done so since childhood. Then, his fantasies had seemed essential and inevitable, like dreams. Now he only sparingly allowed himself that occasional luxury, fearing them in some inexplicable way. Now they led him into areas of darkness: punishment, exposure, retribution.

He closed his eyes tightly so as not to imagine any more: his head roared with the suck and flood of exhaustion and loss and booze. He blinked, several times, hard, to recover himself.

The bottle was empty now. The barman was polishing the glasses, stacking the shelves for the next day. The piano-player had gone.

Ian stood up and took a deep breath. He needed air.

"Want a cab?"

Ian paused and shook his head.

"It's real cold out there," the barman said, "and nasty."

Ian was unaffectedly grateful for the warning. "Thanks. But I'd rather walk."

"Take care."

Ian nodded, and went out into the city.

(2)

"The sun shone (Willie wrote). I had taken the train up to the hospital in Newcastle – not trusting myself to drive after a night of desperately uneven sleep. Someone with whom I'd been very friendly at school had kindly agreed to open up the house and to warm it through. In Newcastle I hired a Rover, wanting as much comfort as possible in the back seat where she would be sitting. A nurse would travel with me in the front. The weather was the only worry. Too cold and she would have been forbidden to make the journey. A setback could have ruined everything; she was so frail it could have persuaded her against the whole enterprise. But the sun shone. On that day, with snow still on the hills and hard sludge in the streets, the sun shone and with a little warmth. Swaddled in blankets, supported by pillows, supervised by her doctor, she was settled in the car and we began the journey westwards.

I drove slowly towards the Roman road, careful of the patches of ice, of the sudden dips, careful of anything which might jolt or startle. For the first few miles, as we cleared the city, she was subdued. In the mirror I could see her white, wasted face on which she had permitted only a modicum of make-up to be applied by the nurse. The nurse chattered away and I wished she wouldn't, nor did I like her talking about my mother as if she were not there; nor did I like her relentless cheery-be. I forced myself to suppress this reaction. She was a good-hearted young woman without whom my mother would not have been allowed to leave the hospital. By concentrating hard I managed to dissolve the irritation. It had not to become important.

The old Roman road was glorious. Snow on the hills and the fields, white puff clouds in the blue sky, the great wall itself and its forts. Mile castles appearing and reappearing, the irresponsible feeling that we were on the ancient high boundary of Britain, a glance away from the furthest fling of an extinct Empire. My mother gazed out of the car window and smiled with happiness at this bold natural panorama. It was the first unforced smile I had seen on her face for months. It is what I think I will finally remember her by. A smile of purest pleasure, and a smile of reckoning: her thin face, the skin almost translucent now, gathered in that smile all the gentleness, openness to beauty, and calm sense of passing life of which she was capable. She knew.

'Thank you,' she murmured.

Her entranced state gave way to a more lively condition and, without telling the nurse that it would take us about thirty miles out of our way, I swung across to Penrith so that I would be able to pass by one of the lakes. The odds were against her having the strength to get into a car again; and the weather might never be as kind for weeks.

246

As we entered Cumbria, she began an intermittent recitation of holidays, friends, small incidents, the unheroic events of her quiet life. Despite the nurse's repeated warning that she must not tire herself, my mother – a little mischievously I guessed – indulged herself. 'Your father used to . . .' 'I had a cousin lived near here . . .' 'We drove here in our first car, your father and I, thinking we'd reached the end of the world, wondering how on earth we would get back . . .' 'We brought you here for Easter once, a Mrs Smallwood let rooms in her farm – you loved it – I've never seen so many snowdrops as she had in her garth . . .' 'This was where your father's people originally came from, they were farming people, of a sort, poor land, you wonder how the sheep get a decent meal off it . . .' And then she sank back again as I made for Keswick and decided, as a final lap, to drive around the west side of Derwentwater.

We drove into Borrowdale along the shores of the lake. I swung carefully over the double-span bridge into Grange and then turned North. The road under Catbells was all but deserted. As we went up the side of the hills, the lake appeared below us, wider and wider, edged with snow, deeply tranquil, an unfathomable cobalt blue, the massive, round-backed, Skiddaw range standing beyond. The peace and beauty of the view and the mood it stirred were, to me, profoundly, even mystically, moving.

She was crying; silently.

I carried her into the house. She was so light I could scarcely believe it. The nurse shoved me away while she settled her. A bed had been brought down. The nurse asked that another be made up on the ground floor. On that first afternoon I was the nurse's attendant.

I find it difficult to describe the next few days. At times it seemed all activity: injections, changes of bed, shopping, tidying, going to the launderette, dealing with my mother's friends, reading to her. There were other times when the house was dug into silence. The nurse would be asleep, my mother would be dozing in the half-asleep, half-awake state which was so much of her days and nights. I would look in on her, stay to be there when she opened her eyes, just to be there. She never complained and never sentimentalised; in her clear times she would talk as sensibly as always and be happiest when I fed her gossip of the town or drew up memories of us all from my childhood. These latter mundane stories were her greatest pleasure. We put together the stories – her memory far stronger than mine, her details always richer and more exact. Yes: that was the life we lived; and re-lived.

It seemed disloyal to do anything else at all – but those times of activity were intermingled with periods when nothing happened at all. There was some business to be dealt with at the office – but my one-third of a secretary was very good. Eric was understanding. The American business would not run away: they had written me a letter offering terms. Joanna wanted to come up, as did David. I arranged for him to stay in the little hotel in the middle of the town. There was simply not room for both of them in the house.

He came, stayed a couple of days, and then left. My mother's condition seemed to have stabilised again. It was as if she slid away and then held on again, held on beyond her strength before the next descent. She was very pleased to see him.

'What's happened to him?' she asked me: and answered her own question. 'Is she nice?'

'She's lovely.'

'It'll be good for him. He threatened to become very lonely.'

Joanna's tact was exemplary. She knew my mother's opinion of her. She had the wisdom, though, to understand that the older woman would have fretted for me had she not been there. After a day or so, my mother showed her gratitude by relying on Joanna for some of her small needs.

I wanted the outside world to be shut out entirely. This was quite unreasonable and over-sentimental. I wanted this last drift of her time to take place in a cocoon of intimacy, attentions and care. It was impossible. The business of the nurse alone pricked that insulated dream. And the world poured in through news, through old friends of my mother stopping me in the street to ask about her and staying to recount another chapter of the past. Even my own recent past would not lie quiet. Ian had phoned the office a couple of times – having failed, the message was, to get through to me at my home. I asked my secretary not to give him my mother's number.

To give myself a project, I began to put together some notes for David, with whose cause I was becoming increasingly exasperated. His film on the War Game seemed to have extended to a multi-media enterprise which appeared to me to be deeply impractical; the saving element lay in its undoubted value as a project which attracted local involvement. To listen to David, scarcely any local pressure group or ethnic group, religious group or social group was left out. What he asked me to do was to give him some information on what he called 'the relationship between writing and war'. This would be plundered, it seemed, by various pamphleteers, organisers, and the whole instant army of film makers. It was a task which appealed to me. The library supplied the books I needed. The cutting of quotations and researching for material was steadying: at the very least it worked as a lightning-conductor for the restlessness, the feeling of usefulness between the instances of being helpful.

After Joanna's arrival, then, the last week settled into a pattern. I would sleep in the same room as my mother and turn her over when she needed it. The bed-sores must have been constantly painful. Both of us remained shy of this. She would turn her face away. I would try not to let her feel my eyes on her wasting body. I would get her a hot drink and she would sip a little, obediently. If we talked at all during the night, it would be in whispers, she urging me back to bed, me trying to discover if there was anything more I could do to help. I slept as lightly as she: sometimes I thought that both of us lay awake listening, equally, to the other's breath, wanting to make sure.

During the daytime, the nurse and to a discreet extent Joanna took charge and I was encouraged to go down into the

249

town, fetch and carry outside the house or spend a few hours working for David.

I still have the original notes:

1. Most early writers were propagandists for war. Literally half of Homer is concerned with killing. According to Pope no two men were killed in the same way. The idea of the hero of fiction – the man of quality and the warrior – the man who kills the enemy – was early and firmly established. Most heroes of ancient history are warrior-kings: most writers advertised the virtues fired in war and exemplified by the kings seeking glory.

2. Christ in New Testament is the most effective counter-force in Western History. His precepts would have been thought the charter of a coward by Homer. In that sense he was subversive. Subsequent Christian History, though, seems more attached to the Old Testament – Revenge, the Sword of Wrath and Righteousness. David of the battles and the psalms is much more dynamic a figure than any New Testament anti-hero.

3. Shakespeare: although Falstaff mocks the idea of Honour and, therefore, the source of warrior virtue, Shakespeare's best lines are in praise of war and its heroes and the ennobling character it can display and forge.

So it went on, gathering examples from Machiavelli, Burke, Defoe, Tolstoy, Tennyson, Wordsworth, even Jane Austen – building up the case. The idea of a hero, in life and art, comes directly or at a discernible remove from war. I used the First War as a laboratory, showing how writers had entered it with all the apparel of the past – glory, honour, country, sacrifice – and come out of it in rags unable to refer to those epic words without horror or despair. It was that First War which set the tone for the century: the Holocaust horrifically re-emphasised that mindless mechanical waste, the Bomb provided a potential end to the story. But the traditional idea died in that Great War.

What I was doing for David and the fate of my mother were related. The notes showed the enormous gap between the decent life she had lived and the lives celebrated in poetry and song. If I had been called on to write her story it would have left no trace on the public records: there would have been nothing with which to illustrate it. No footage. Yet she had lived her life seriously and well, firm to ideas of right and wrong which stood resolutely in the face of the dead old glories.

One of the poems I found was by Thomas Hardy: written in the middle of the Great War and describing how the Moon had gone searching on the heath to find the spot where a father had drowned himself out of grief for his son 'Who is slain in brutal battle, though he has injured none.' Finally the Moon now looks down on the poet and says:

> 'And now I am curious to look
> Into the blinkered mind
> Of one who wants to write a book
> In a world of such a kind.'

A world she had had no part in making: her life had been the story of passive acceptance in such a world. I felt that it was up to me now, to do what I could, and to live as well as she had.

It is not unusual, I think, at times like that, for the living to gain a perspective from the dying. Nor is it unusual for thoughts and reflections usually banished because they seem too large to hold and too massive to grapple with, to come into a reckoning. It did not seem incongruous to be reading Hardy, thinking about his bleak credo and, within the hour, to be helping the nurse to wash my mother. It mattered, at a time like this, as perhaps it always ought to matter, to let everything in, to try to comprehend everything despite the barricades of exclusive expertise and the fatally easy feelings of inadequacy. The weaker she grew and the more sensitive I became to her wishes, the louder and stronger the insistence that I too should face larger questions. They should not be left to others who were better qualified.

If the world was facing very possible extinction: why should I – or anybody else who had a mind to – not square up to that, painful as it was to live with the fear that such a massive concern

251

was pretentious? It was not pretentious to die. Though I disagreed with David, he forced me to consider it. The second greatest force on earth was happening daily, before my eyes. Her frailty was almost ethereal; her stillness deeply attentive, to sounds of life? Of death? Whatever it was, she was engaged upon it with all her last strength which saw nothing trivial in the smallest things, nothing daunting in the profoundest questions. She would wonder aloud about what was unknown: with her next breath she would remind me that the curtains on the upstairs landing needed to be dry-cleaned. This last stage of the journey unshackled her from any remaining inhibitions, from that terrible invisible mesh of accumulated knots and fears which binds us and constricts us with so many private and public proofs and excuses against living fully: all of life was to be savoured.

I went into the church, one afternoon, to see what I would find. I had up to then almost always managed to evoke or remember that holy silence which as a boy I felt I could brush from the walls with my bare hands. The church was much the same. Being a weekday afternoon it was empty; it was cold; it didn't work. All that had been there, all the dedication, the certainties, the aspirations and prayers were no longer there. But it would hold my mother's funeral and I would feel no hypocrisy.

It was very early in the morning. Her breath had been so low during the night that I had got out of bed and sat in the armchair next to her. The small even sound of the air barely passing her lips, passing, faintly returning to the world. She half-opened her eyes. I took her thin small hand and held it. And held it."